The Current Fantasy

CHARLIE HAAS

BECK AND BRANCH PUBLISHERS

ADVANCE ACCLAIM FOR *THE CURRENT FANTASY*

"I was immediately drawn in. What a wonderful novel about an unusual group of California pioneers—sly, knowing, and deeply human."
> Marilyn Johnson, author of *The Dead Beat, This Book Is Overdue,* and *Lives in Ruins*

"The history of Utopian communities is a consistently melancholy one, and the aspirations of the founders of such communities are all too easy to mock. But Charlie Haas resists this facile temptation, and instead extends deep human sympathy to a group of German expatriates attempting to create a natural paradise in Southern California in the early years of the last century. Comprehensively researched, vivid both sensuously and emotionally, *The Current Fantasy* is an original and wonderfully entertaining piece of work."
> Erik Tarloff, author of *All Our Yesterdays*

"A masterful set of insights into the era and its political and social transformations... the sentiments, hopes, and incarnation of a utopian, counterculture lifestyle 'back in the day' come to life under Haas's pen."
> D. Donovan, Senior Reviewer, *Midwest Book Review*

"*The Current Fantasy* is a rich, original novel whose prose often lifted me off the page with its jolts of revelation."
> John Thorndike, author of *The World Against Her Skin*

"*The Current Fantasy* explodes on the retina like a tintype brought to life… It has heart, soul, art, and the promise of Giant Vegetables, equally charming and alarming as it tells what is perhaps the last great untold chapter of the California Story."
> Don Wallace, author of *The French House* and *One Great Game,* editor of *The Hawaii Review of Books*

Copyright © 2024 Charlie Haas
ISBN 9798325178207

Beck and Branch Publishers
New York, NY 10024 | beckandbranch.com

Cover designed by AgencyAxis
Cover image: California Spring Landscape by Elmer Wachtel. Smithsonian American Art Museum, Bequest of Mrs. James S. Harlan (Adeline M. Noble Collection). Creative Commons
Frontispiece photo: Stephen H. Willard, William Pester in front of his cabin in Palm Canyon. Palm Springs, California, 1917.

For B. K.

Bill Pester
Palm Canyon, California
1917

Berlin, 1914

One

Look at that, Anna thinks—after all this time, a little hope. Only a flicker, but in the current climate you'll warm your hands around anything.

She stands behind a counter at Aschinger's Cafeteria, ladling pea soup like always, but the letter in her pocket's been brushing against her thigh all afternoon. She's read it three times and can't wait to again, for the relief. If it wasn't for this dress she could exhale for once.

She picks up a bowl, fills it with four ladles exactly, wipes it for drips, puts it on a customer's tray and looks at the afternoon crowd under Aschinger's fake half-timbers. At a table by the fireplace there's an old lady in a black dress and marionette rouge. She steps on the back of one ruined shoe with the toe of the other, eases her heel out, looks across the room to make herself invisible, and slips a pasteboard beer coaster into the shoe. A moment later, a man sitting near her pushes his plate away as if he can't eat his last, untouched sausage, and slides it toward her as he stands up to leave.

Good, Anna thinks, take care of each other, because Germany's otherwise busy. A newspaper on a nearby table cheerfully predicts war. Some days the fear makes Anna's hands shake so she spills soup onto a saucer and has to start over, while a customer glares at her for those lost twenty seconds. People expect better from Aschinger's, each of whose locations offers the same greasy food served by men dressed like butlers and women in strangling dirndls that push their upper breasts out for review and comment.

The war can blow me up, she thinks, but I'm not sacrificing Lilli or Benji. That's been the law since the moment they first looked up at me, when they had no idea what they were but somehow knew they were safe as long as this thing looked back at them and said *Shh, yes it's all right.* And then one day you have to prove it.

Four phony antique clocks strike five. Anna puts her ladle in the rinse, rubs her cramped arms and goes to see a friend in the veal department who gives her a bag of cutlets too odd-shaped to sell. At the lockers in back she unlaces the dirndl, breathes as if she swam here underwater, puts on her own mercifully shapeless dress, moves the letter to its pocket and goes outside.

The sidewalks are crowded and the sunset's red with factory smoke. Anna squeezes onto a streetcar full of soldiers, all shouting at one another through her head. Maybe the war started while I was at work, she thinks. God knows they all seem happy enough.

She gets off at Leipziger Platz and goes to the music store, where she told Lilli to wait for her after school. That music smell, wood and rosin, gathers her inside, welcoming and scolding all at once.

Lilli's standing with her back to Anna and her head down in the horn of a gramophone, her pink and blonde reflection in the lacquer looking like a grown woman's. Anna goes behind a grand piano whose raised lid almost hides her from view. A clerk puts a record on the gramophone, and Brahms' violin concerto begins.

Anna looks around the room—a gleaming case of reeds, a poster promising *Every Parlor a Happy One*, a rack of sheet music like a sane cousin of the newsstand across the street. The clerk comes near her but she shakes her head and nods toward Lilli. He smiles and goes to get the next record.

Anna used to play this in audition, almost well enough to be called back, and she knows the story in it whether Brahms did or not. For ninety measures the orchestra paces the floor, waiting up late. When the violin comes in you see what they're worried about: she's a teenaged mess, anguished from her first notes.

"I love beauty but it hurts me worse than anything," the violin says. "I want to know nature and bodies, I want to meet the dispossessed, I want to run naked in the woods and let the rain paste petals to my skin. I want runes on my back and Chinese letters on my bathtub, I want to try morphine and—"

"You want *church*!" the orchestra shouts. "So much church!"

"I'm a *violin*," the violin says. "Next time give birth to a glockenspiel."

The orchestra gives orders. The violin makes scenes. It's a wonder they get through the movement without killing each other.

The soloist on the record plays it perfectly, stringing the double and triple stops together till Anna's arms cramp all over again. As the clerk changes records, Lilli looks more serious than Anna can remember seeing her.

A few discs later the second movement starts. Woodwinds, mediating like aunts and uncles, introduce the violin to a nice French horn. Nothing comes of it, but then, out of nowhere: the oboe.

He pulls the violin into a duet, his deep breaths and her long bowings. The orchestra stops storming and mumbles behind them, barely a chaperone. Anna was thirteen the first time she heard this. They'd had her playing Bach. That was the joy but this was the desiring.

Lilli listens with her mouth open and eyes wide. The third movement starts, that Hungarian tune that makes everything suddenly happy. Anna's never trusted it. Neither does the violin, with a minor passage like a drowning person's last shout: "That's it? One dance around a wedding hall and life is settled?"

"Exactly!" the orchestra says. "Champagne! Stay in touch!" That's why they're so happy: she's someone else's problem now.

But Lilli's still staring into the music. She's eleven, Anna thinks, too old to start but who cares? We'd get her a child-sized violin, and she and I can play together. Wherever we need to go, we'll have that.

The needle clicks on the record's last spiral. Anna waits till the clerk takes it away, then goes over to Lilli, puts a hand on her shoulder, leans down and says, "Do you think you'd like a violin?"

Lilli looks at her as if she's crazy. "A *gramophone*," she says.

಼

As if we had time for music anyway, Anna thinks as they get on the streetcar. You keep forgetting you live in an emergency, because every morning you open your eyes and you're needed over there and back here. One day you'll wake up to the walls of your building smashing in, you'll run to the children's beds but they'll be crushed by a fallen beam, and then under it you'll see—

Stop. "Would you like to see a letter I got?" she asks Lilli, and takes out the envelope, handmade of oatmeal paper.

"Who's it from?" Lilli says.

"Some people in the country," Anna says. "People who live a different way."

"Like in my book?" Lilli means her favorite picture

book, about a town where the dogs walk the people and everyone wears flowerpots on their heads.

"Better than that," Anna says, and unfolds the over-sized page.

When Anna was nineteen she used to sit with her friends in an Aschinger's Cafeteria, where they could stay for hours over twenty-five-pfennig bowls of pea soup. Everyone made fun of the place but Karl Schulz, their one real artist, who said, "No, Aschinger's is *fabulous*" in his wan voice and sketched the serving women, detailing the itchy stray locks of hair on their faces and the steam burns on their arms. For its sympathetic treatment of labor, his exhibit *Dirndl Women and Other Workers* was condemned by the censors and declared off limits to military officers, the one review he valued.

Then people got married and drifted away, and Anna became a dirndl woman herself, occasionally striking a pose from a Karl Schulz painting as if someone would get the reference. For a while she and her friends wrote one another elaborate letters, with cartoons and clippings pasted in, and a few of the words, usually the dirty ones, in Gothic script or alphabet noodles.

This one's like those. Lilli takes it from Anna and turns it all the way around to study the hand-drawn border of drunk angels, smiling fish, Adam, Eve, Falstaff and Punchinello, all made of loose ovals. The words are in an artist's handwriting, darting and looping in India ink. You could draw five lines behind that writing and sing it.

Dear Anna,

Thank you for writing to ask about Sunland. Yes, what in God's name is going on up here?

Sunland is not a city, church, school, hotel, mystic order or mixed chorus. It's only a mountainside, and yet people keep coming here, seeking a sort of nature cure for their Berlin fatigue, Munich dropsy, gallery tremor, audition ague, and conscription nerves.

A certain Dr. Richard Weiss, who takes the blame for most of us being here, says we are the future. He's got some nerve. But IMAGINE that we are!

The word *IMAGINE* is in big letters drawn to look three-dimensional, with *that we are!* in cursive climbing up the *E*. Lilli traces it with her finger. "I could write like that," she says. "You just give yourself room."

Richard Weiss is the kind of hope you want to be careful around, Anna thinks. She's been hearing his name for years, a red thread running through underground Berlin. *A* has a poem in Weiss's magazine; *B* has a picture in Weiss's gallery; *C* went to the place everyone calls Café Megalomania and the entertainment was Weiss psychoanalyzing people at their tables. "Hypnosis is old news," *C* said. "Just like that."

But then there are rumors—that money disappears around Weiss, that there have been morals charges, that hypnosis is not so different from what he practices after all.

"They never proved a thing," *D* said.

If he's right, the letter says, *then the future belongs to the surly in the morning, the rumored missing, and the underdressed for the climate. Immodesty is practiced.*

"Does that mean they brag?" Lilli says.

"It means they don't always have clothes on," Anna says.

"What!"

"You've seen what boys and girls have."

"Not on purpose," Lilli says. She reads the next line: *Sleeping arrangements are not subject to jealousy.* "What's that mean?"

This time Anna pauses before she answers. "It's about not being jealous if someone gets a better place to sleep than you," she says. Lilli seems to believe her.

They read down to the signature, which is elaborate and indecipherable, a joke at the expense of names themselves. Along the way there's an invitation to visit.

Gerhard won't go, Anna thinks. For Gerhard the answer is to stay in Berlin, where Communism will fall from the sky and save us all. I love him still, but he should think twice before he calls people impractical.

Is it safe, where this letter comes from? Is it on some army's way to Berlin, or surrounded by farms they'd want to burn? Are these people any more the future than we are, if there even is one? I have no way to know, Anna thinks. But not finding out is vicious.

Two

Gerhard connects a wire on a switchboard and for a second the blob of solder is a mirror, a convex image with his nose as a mountain and the factory around him a miniature dungeon. At the edge of the picture, a boy pushes a parts cart that squeaks under its load. When the solder cools the boy vanishes. Gerhard turns and sees him struggling with his cart before he disappears again, in a fog of smoke and iron filings.

A moment later something falls off the cart, glass smashing and something round rolling away with a mocking rattle. Gerhard jumps up and runs after the boy, who's chasing his cart and yelling, "Sorry! Sorry!" He almost catches up with it but trips against an open forging oven. His pants, filthy with oil, catch fire, and he falls on the floor screaming.

Gerhard reaches him and rolls him over. Someone throws a bucketful of sand, damping the flames but blinding Gerhard so his arm gets burned. The pain shoots up his nerves to his neck and he shouts as the boy starts to cry, but the fire's almost out. Someone asks the boy if he can stand up. He clutches his leg and says "Sorry" again, softly.

Two men pick him up and walk him outside as Hoch the foreman comes over. "All right, good, thank you all," he says. "Let's do some work now."

Gerhard goes to a sink, runs water on his burns, catches up to Hoch and says, "The carts are too heavy and the oven's open. I know you like to keep after these things."

Hoch stops walking and looks at him. "Do you want to tell us how to do it?"

"Yes," Gerhard says. "When do I start?"

"I think you should take a week off instead."

"With pay?"

Hoch smiles. Gerhard looks at him another second, almost says something but goes to his bench, drops his gloves, walks out and blinks in the sunlight. It's a warm day, but chilly compared to the factory. At the side of the building, under the DREHER TELEPHONE sign, the boy shakes in his underwear as some men put him into a black company car.

Gerhard sets off down the factory street. That was expensive, he thinks, but the boy was Benji's age, and even looked a little like him.

He's just getting used to the quiet when two noises reach him at once, a crowd cheering nearby and an airplane banking overhead, with two fat army crosses on its upper wing. Right, Gerhard thinks. It's Saturday.

In a few minutes he's at the edge of the rally. The crowd's so big it spills out of the parade grounds into the yards of houses, cheering for the planes and marching soldiers. A man near Gerhard holds up a sign saying PARIS FOR LUNCH, SUPPER IN ST. PETERSBURG, which is probably as much war planning as the Kaiser himself has done.

The middle of the crowd is packed tight, but at the edge there are picnics. To Gerhard's left a boy about eleven hops from foot to foot, pulls on his chubby fingers and shouts his critique of the English and Russian monarchs: "George's navy's full of fairies! Rasputin shows everyone his peepee and tells Nicholas what to do!" The adults around him laugh and clap.

A man who shares the boy's ruddy skin stands watching him and beaming. I'm about to do something stupid, Gerhard thinks, but if we've ever believed in anything it's time to take chances. He walks up beside the man and says, "Is that your son?"

"Yes," the man says, his eyes still on the boy's performance.

"That's wonderful," Gerhard says. "To be so young and so up on things."

"And *right*," the man says.

"Think of the future he'll have," Gerhard says. He lowers his voice. "Unless the war—"

The man turns and looks at him. "The war is a blessing," he says.

"Perhaps," Gerhard says. "Except—"

"Except what? That it's better if Germany lies down?"

"No, no, not lie down, but—"

It's no good, Gerhard thinks. It's as if this proud father can see through my pocket, to the leaflet from last night's meeting—

INTO THE STREETS TO STOP THE WAR!
FREEDOM FOR ROSA LUXEMBURG!
GENERAL STRIKE!

"You should listen to the boy," the man says. "He's smarter than you are."

His friends look up from their picnic. The boy says, "Father, who's *that?*" and imitates Gerhard's expression. A few women laugh, but the men stand up.

The father walks up close to Gerhard. When Gerhard doesn't back up the man pushes his chest. Just a tap, really, but there are four men coming up behind him.

"Let me explain my thought," Gerhard says, and as they

wait for him to finish he turns and runs. There's laughter behind him. Better than footsteps, though never rule out both. After ten paces he looks back and sees a few men going back to their blanket and a few still scowling at him.

He keeps going to the street, dodges through traffic and gets on a streetcar full of people coming from the rally. They're flush-faced, eating ginger cookies and imitating biplanes to make their families laugh.

It's dusk when he gets to his building, a six-story block of brick with a dying yard in front. He climbs five flights in the yellow stairwell, a drain for all the shouts and smells of ninety families.

The apartment is one and a half cramped rooms. The whole one has a dining table, Gerhard and Anna's bed and an assemblage of tools, books, clothes, toys, dishes and toiletries so densely packed that some things can never be removed from it again. The half is an alcove for the children's beds and the stove.

The children are at the table. Benji's head is down in three schoolbooks at once. At twelve he's handsome, the real German thing, with a small nose, bow mouth and fair skin, like an infiltrator from a better family. He believes in electricity, progress and Werner Siemens. Seeing his father come home dead every night from the telephone factory gives him no pause at all. He'll invent, he'll own, he'll create something even more wondrous than the telephone and more exhausting to make.

Lilli, writing in her notebook, elbows Benji's elbow aside. She's different from her brother in every way— good-looking but darker, with dirty blonde hair, sandy skin, and eyes complacent toward everything but the next pleasure. I can't afford her, Gerhard thinks. I have to hope the big mercantile world can.

He looks over her shoulder and sees her writing *IMAGINE that we are!* in barely decipherable letters.

"What's that?" he says. "Is that from school?"

Lilli shakes her head. "It's—"

Anna comes from the stove with tonight's veal. "It's from me," she says.

"Ah," Gerhard says, because Anna treads the air and things like *IMAGINE* stick to her along the way.

An hour later he lies in bed, reading the letter she's handed him, while she stands in her nightgown brushing her hair. *Machines are absent and life is audible*, the letter says. *The birds alone make the wildest racket. Look at this one.* There's a drawing of a blackbird pecking the ground, with soft highlights on its feathers, over a scroll reading *In a minute, I'm writing to a lady in Berlin.*

Children are welcome, the letter continues, *though we regret we are unable to terrorize them.* "I'd like to see you try," Gerhard says out loud. *If you decide to come, please let us know and someone will meet your train.*

"How'd you come to write to them?" he says.

"I was curious," Anna says, and pauses. "It might be a place to go."

And with just your kind of people, Gerhard thinks. Anna's oval face has gotten fuller since she started at the cafeteria. It makes her hopeful expression pull at him even more.

For once today he doesn't start an argument; for once this year he doesn't disagree with her about their taking the children someplace she thinks will be safe from war. I've done enough these past six hours, he thinks, losing a week's pay and provoking a small mob.

"We could visit there," he says.

She stops brushing. "Really?"

He shrugs. "I have a week off. A switchboard for Italy fell through." As good as the truth.

He puts the letter down on the bed, stands up and goes to the children's alcove. Anna follows him.

"Suppose there is a war," Benji's saying. "They'll need boys to monitor for radio signals."

"Stop *talking* about it," Lilli says. The children bicker all the time, till Benji sees the slightest threat to Lilli. Then he jumps to defend her, if only because driving her crazy is his job alone.

"We're going to the country for a few days," Gerhard says.

"We are?" Benji says.

Gerhard nods. "To visit some people your mother's heard from."

"The ones who live a different way?" Lilli says.

"It appears," Gerhard says.

"May I stay here, please?" Benji says.

"No," Gerhard says. "I think you should see this. Pack your bags."

He turns back toward bed and Anna follows him. Why not, he thinks. A few days of fresh air. Even a sensible person's nerves can get worn. I can win points for giving Anna something she wants while we let the children see the kind of landscape I fled, where if you want something more than dirt to look at, you just sit and IMAGINE it till madness ensues.

Three

The train ride to Langenhain takes six hours, with not much out the window but farms and woods. Anna and the family step down from the train to a closed depot, three blocks of houses and two church steeples, silent in flat March sun. They're putting their bags down when a mother and daughter in worn farm dresses walk up. Anna smiles at them. The mother starts to smile back, then sees two women in their twenties coming from the other direction. Her expression turns stiff and she hurries her daughter away.

"Anna?" one of the young women says, smiling straight past the farm woman's evil eye. "I'm Tilda. This is Patrice."

Tilda's squat and strong-looking in canvas clothes, a man's haircut and sandals that lace up her muddy ankles. Patrice is slight and pretty, with long blonde hair, a shiny saffron dress and blue silk slippers trimmed in scarlet.

Anna shakes their hands and introduces the family. Patrice grins at Lilli, who smiles back like she's meeting a princess.

"How was your trip?" Tilda says.

"We were the only ones in our whole car at the end," Lilli says. "It's farther than I've ever been."

"Oh *nice*," Patrice says, lightly picking up the two biggest suitcases. Tilda and Gerhard take the others, and they follow a path into birch woods. Lilli walks in front between her two new friends while Benji hangs back, glancing nervously at manly Tilda. Stop it, Anna thinks. There are all kinds of people in the world, including a few right in our building if you'd look around some time.

At the end of the woods an arch overhead is inscribed *"LIT BY THE MORROW, WE ARE THE PROMISED ILLUMINED ONES."—E. W. LOTZ* and, in smaller letters, *WATCH YOUR HEAD*. Just past it, a patchy lawn rises toward a long one-story building with flaking green paint and a sagging porch.

Forty or so people sit on the lawn, some in work clothes like Tilda's, others in fanciful costumes like Patrice's or formal outfits thirty years out of date. Some are talking and laughing, tearing at the grass for emphasis, while others nurse babies, pass cigarettes, or doze with their head on someone's thigh. Three toddlers run from group to group while a teenaged girl leads bigger children in a clapping game. Next to them a young couple sit cross-legged, staring at distant hills. A man in a threadbare velvet suit keeps starting a song on a concertina, stopping to kiss the woman next to him and starting the song again, making people laugh. Past the lawn there's a farm field where people are leaning on hoes and talking, and a lake stretching away to snow-topped mountains.

"That's the dining hall," Tilda says, nodding at the green building. "Let's show you where you're staying."

They walk around the building, past cats and compost piles, onto a rough wagon trail up the hill. A hundred meters up, two tall canvas banners hang from trees. A woman's painting pictures on them, her paintbrush and cigarette hands moving in counterpoint, and a man's coloring them in. The pictures show people in togas dancing with their arms flung out and feet flapping on the ground, playing flutes and lyres and eating grapes, their sweat flying and clothes falling off, eyes rolling in ecstasy. The style's like a cartoon, making fun of the sybarites and celebrating them all at once. A woman runs after the dancers with a load of tomatoes in her skirt while another woman pulls a man on top of her against a haystack. Everything's made of ovals, which the woman paints in fast swooshes like Japanese moons—the same ovals as the pictures on the letter Anna got.

The woman painter turns around. She's black-eyed and beautiful, around thirty, with full lips and nose and springy red hair that spreads out behind her from a silver ring. Jewish, Anna thinks. The man turns around too. He's about the same age, with stubble, sleepy eyes, and a scowl at being interrupted.

"Hello?" the woman says.

"Guests," Tilda says.

"I'm Anna. From Berlin."

"Hello," the woman says again, and goes back to work. She doesn't remember writing to me, Anna thinks. That's all right. People like that don't make friends right away.

The group continues up the hill, past an A-framed hut with half its roof missing, then a lean-to made of two doors and a boulder, with yellowed laundry hanging in a tree. The more run-down things are the happier Gerhard looks.

Tilda stops at a cabin whose white walls are turning brown and its roof losing shingles. She puts a suitcase down by the door and opens it for them. Inside there are stains like jellyfish on the ceiling and nails weeping rust in the walls, but the floor's been swept and there's a clean sheet on the bed.

"We'll let you get settled," Patrice says, then pauses. "It's better not to go into town. We're not well understood there."

"We'd have no reason," Anna says.

"Supper's in a little while," Tilda says. "You'll hear the gong."

When they're gone Benji looks around the cabin and says, "May I sleep outside, please?"

"All right," Gerhard says, "but I think we've gotten the best room on the property. You should be flattered."

"Thank you," Benji says. He picks up his suitcase, opens the door and almost walks into a man whose hand is raised to knock on it. He's in his forties, wearing a black suit with a matching cape and a critical expression.

"Hello," Gerhard says, walking up to him as Benji steps aside.

"I'm Josef," the man says.

"A pleasure," Gerhard says. "I'm Gerhard. This is Anna, Lilli, and Benji."

"I was planning to stay here tonight."

"We were led here," Gerhard says. "We're easily led, it seems."

Anna gives him a look but he ignores her. Josef's suit and cape are old but not antique. The people on the lawn in balding suits and washed-out ball gowns are wearing them satirically, Anna thinks, but Josef seems serious in every way.

"It's only two nights," she says. "I'm sorry for the confusion."

"Where are you from?" Josef says.

"Berlin."

"Is this the fashion now? To come and look at the bohemians?"

"Oh yes," Gerhard says. "Among our pampered class." He holds up his hand, full of welts, burns, imbedded wire ends and two fingers running crooked.

"Please leave things the same," Josef says, and walks away.

"I thought there was no jealousy about where you

sleep," Lilli says when he's gone.

Gerhard almost laughs but keeps it to a smile. "You're right," he says. "That man is a rule-breaker."

Funny, Anna thinks, and good work picking a fight thirty minutes after we arrive. Always challenging people, like this man in the cape, who might figure into decisions here. You made him walk away. See if you can do that to me and the children.

Four

Gerhard leads the family down the hill to supper. Near the A-frame house, someone's tried to build a retaining wall but lost heart. A little farther down, a baby carriage decomposes beside a foundation full of algae-covered water. In every small town in Germany, he thinks, there's a family whose property looks like this. Here they've gathered enough of them to put a stop to human purpose once and for all.

I wouldn't mind having my telescope here, though. That town with the depot doesn't use much electric light, and these nature men of Anna's don't use any. You can already see at dusk how black the sky will be behind the stars.

People are filing into the building by the lawn. Inside it's a faded dining hall with a vaulted ceiling, long tables, drafts blowing through tar-papered walls and candles guttering in rusty chandeliers.

A table of tureens and dishes sits by the kitchen doors. Benji picks up a plate inscribed *LANGENHAIN RE-SORT* and rubs the chipped gold rim to see if more will come off. Anna's is the same, while Gerhard's has a prayer to St. Agnes.

Lilli reaches for the next one in the stack, which has a feudal Japanese painting of a man and woman screwing sitting down. Gerhard grabs it, hands her his St. Agnes one, and covers the Japanese couple with stew. I'm not trying to shelter her, he thinks. It's that she'd see the nice picture and want service for eight.

The stew's gray and runny, with bits of wheat, cheese and cabbage overwhelmed by green squash, the kind that grows uncontrollably. Benji runs a fork through his and says, "This is just the vegetables."

Anna looks around at the tables, half-full at most, and says, "There are seats over there." As they sit down a man, a woman and a girl Lilli's age sit next to them.

"Hello," the man says. "I'm Jorgen." He and his wife could be sixty, Gerhard thinks, or forty but left out in the sun too long. They look as if they've been sleeping on roadsides for years but somehow come out of it strong, their eyes, teeth and muscles fierce with health. Jorgen's dressed like an unreliable Bible prophet, with long hair in a twine headband, a gauzy shirt hanging to his knees, and a long beard shot through with holes. His wife wears a frayed jumper, ruined espadrilles, and a stage play's worth of glass jewelry.

"I'm Astrid, and this is Trudy," she says. "Linda's ours too." She nods across the room at a girl of fifteen who's going around hugging people and eating off their plates with her fingers.

Little Trudy grasps Lilli's sleeve. "Are you coming to live, or visiting?" she says.

"Visiting," Benji says quickly. "We live in Berlin."

"What do you have?" Trudy asks him.

"Have?"

"Of your own."

"I don't know," Benji says. "A chessboard."

"With men?"

"Of course."

"Do you have dolls?" she asks Lilli.

"Yes, but I've almost outgrown them."

"Can I see them?"

"I don't have them here."

"No, can I see them in Berlin?"

"That's a long walk," Astrid says.

Jorgen shrugs. "It's the same country. I'd go with you but I get beaten up there."

Gerhard looks at Lilli and Benji. Children, he thinks, consider a life in the arts. It's work you can never be sure you're doing, but when you find yourself around people like these you're probably on your way.

He sees Anna looking across the room at the woman who was painting the banners. She's in a group listening to a handsome man about forty, with a comedian's doleful expression, a clean white shirt, and brown hair falling on his forehead. He says something that makes them all laugh, but the painter, exhaling cigarette smoke, looks at him sidelong as if she knows him under the joke.

"I'm baking in the morning," Astrid says to Anna. "Would you like to help?"

"Oh. Yes," Anna says.

"Good," Astrid says. "We mix the dough before the sun is up. Then we will it to rise."

"You *will* the dough?" Gerhard says.

"No, the sun," Astrid says, as if Gerhard's dense. "The dough has yeast in it." She turns to Anna. "Five-thirty in the kitchen?"

"Yes," Anna says, as Astrid and the others get up to go.

Gerhard and his family wash their dishes in a tub by the serving table and go to the exit, where candle lanterns are lined up on the floor. He finds one with some glass left in it, picks it up and starts to light it when the pretty woman who paints the banners comes over to them.

"Hello," she says to Anna. "I saw you talking to them. That was nice of you."

"Oh," Anna says. "We just—"

"I liked your letter."

"Thank you," Anna says. "I liked yours too." She pauses. "I'm baking with her tomorrow."

"So am I. I'm Rose," the painter says, and turns to Lilli. "Do you bake?"

"Yes," Lilli says.

"At five-thirty? So early?"

Lilli nods. "All right," Rose says. "What's your name?"

"Lilli."

"Hello, Lilli."

They smile at each other, and Lilli looks even more enchanted than she was by Patrice. This Rose has a charm to hand out, Gerhard thinks, a sensuous grace like the people on her banners. Those people are fleshy but her own figure's subtle, in a white blouse and loden skirt. She's got freckles on her collarbone and the bridge of her nose, and that red hair springing out behind her.

She turns toward Gerhard, who holds the lantern out to her. "Oh, thank you," she says, "but I live right there."

She smiles and points down the hall, indicating her door so precisely he'd swear she was teasing him. When she walks away he remembers the lantern in his hand, fumbles a match out to light it, and leads his family outside. I was right, he thinks. The stars are fantastic.

Five

Lilli and her mother sleep in their clothes, slip out of bed at five in the morning and walk down the hill in the dark, shivering. "Isn't it relaxing to get out of the city?" Mother says, but she hurries as if she's late for a streetcar and Lilli trips over branches trying to keep up with her.

When they get to the bottom there's smoke coming from the big building's chimney, gray against the black sky. Inside, the toilets in the vestibule have paintings on their doors like Rose's banners, showing happy people in togas walking to little outdoor sheds with books in their hands. Lilli and Mother use the ladies', walk across the empty dining room and knock on the kitchen door.

Rose opens it. She's wearing a yellow blouse with flowers embroidered on it, a blue skirt and bare feet. "Five-thirty!" she says. "Our reputations are made. We'll never have to do anything again. Come in."

She waves them into the kitchen. It looks like another picture book of Lilli's, the one where ducks and squirrels go around in aprons. There are black ovens, an old sink with a pump handle, and a dozen bushels of green squash lined up by the wall.

Rose gives Lilli and Mother wooden spoons and bowls of batter. "You don't really stir it," she says, "you fold it over. Do you know how that is sometimes?"

"Yes," Lilli says, and shows her. A bubble pops in the sticky batter and blows a puff of yeast in her face.

"Virtuoso," Rose says, and pours oil on the batter.

Astrid, the frizzy lady with the jewelry, comes in with her daughter Trudy. "Good morning," Mother says.

"Not yet," Astrid says. "Still this night. It's like iron."

"Try raisins," Rose says. Astrid eats a handful of them, looks up and down like she's deciding whether they help, then starts sifting flour while Trudy breaks walnuts into a bowl.

"*This* is like iron," Rose says, adding so much oats and flour to Lilli's batter that it must be against the recipe. Lilli has to hold onto the bowl and push with her whole body just to turn the spoon. Then Rose adds things it's crazy to put in bread, like squash and bird seed.

"What kind of bread is this?" Lilli says.

"People working on the farm bread," Rose says. "We're going to take it to them. What's your brother like? He seems serious."

"He is," Lilli says, talking in gasps from turning the batter. "They let him have eighth and ninth year books. He says even those aren't hard enough."

"But he's nice to you?" Rose says, putting her hands over Mother's ears.

"Not that much," Lilli says.

"That must be tenth year," Rose says. She lets go of Mother's ears and takes Lilli's bowl from her. "Perfect."

Astrid looks outside. "It's time," she tells Mother and Lilli. "You can come if you like."

"Where?" Lilli says.

"To make the sun rise," Trudy says. She looks serious. So does Astrid, and she's the mother, even if she seems like a strange aunt at the most.

"May I?" Lilli asks.

"Yes," Mother says. She'd let me do anything, Lilli

thinks, as long as someone from here asked.

Lilli follows Astrid and Trudy outside. The sky's starting to lighten, and branches shake in the breeze.

The girl who was eating off people's plates last night joins them as they walk up the hill. "I'm Linda," she tells Lilli. "Trudy's sister." She's fifteen or so, in a dress that lets her body bob around.

"I'm Lilli. Trudy said we're making the sun rise."

"We are," Linda says. "It's the true religion, you know."

"Oh," Lilli says.

"It used to be the only one there was," Linda says. "It was all about the sun getting born at the end of December and then getting killed in the winter and born again in the spring. Then some people said no, it's not really the sun, it's Jesus, and you killed him by touching yourself and so on, but if you come to church and give us money we'll make it all right. That's how they wrecked it. But the real part is the sun."

Lilli feels her eyes get wide. No one's religious at her house but you still don't want to take a chance on going to Hell.

Astrid's husband Jorgen and six other people are waiting under a blue-black sky at the top of the hill, standing around a wooden cabinet as tall as Lilli. Its door is painted with a naked man and lady, holding hands and looking up at a giant sun.

Josef, the strict-acting man in the cape, opens the cabinet door and takes out a shiny blue bottle with gold suns on it. The other people make cups with their hands and he pours something into them. Lilli holds hers out too. It's water.

Astrid says a few words and the other people say them after her, in a language Lilli's never heard. They drink water from their hands and repeat after Astrid again. Then Josef takes a doll out of the cabinet, a man in a long gold shirt and a blue headdress. "That's the sun," Trudy whispers.

Everyone kneels. Josef takes the doll's shirt off and a lady hands him a new one. He dresses the doll, puts it back in the cabinet and lays another doll on the ground.

"They're giving him a woman to sleep with so he'll get up again tomorrow," Linda says. "Just like in life."

The sky turns orange on the horizon. Lilli looks at it for as long as she can. When the glow clears from her eyes, color's filling the landscape as if it's been waiting inside things all along. Astrid dips her head and talks fast to herself, like she's praying or not in her senses. Lilli shivers even though it's not cold now.

People put things on the ground in front of the cabinet—an apple, a pipe, a little flask. Linda leaves a cigarette. "You can bring an offering tomorrow," she tells Lilli.

Josef closes the cabinet and everyone walks down the hill. Maybe it's true, Lilli thinks. Maybe they do make it come up. At least I wouldn't want to be the one who tells them to stop.

Back in the kitchen, they spread flour on the counters and knead the dough, which is even harder than stirring it. Rose comes up behind Lilli and reaches around her to help.

Rose doesn't do those tiring things people are always doing with children, Lilli thinks—talking like you're both grown up or both little, and isn't that hilarious. She just talks like she's known you forever, and now she's leaning her front on my back so her cigarette smoke goes floating around me. I just breathed a little of it in and didn't cough.

They cut apples for kuchen while the dough rises. When it's ready Rose, Mother and Astrid make loaves, and Lilli and Trudy make pictures on the tops with nuts and raisins.

While they're baking Rose asks Lilli, "Want to see where

I live?" and takes her to the back of the building. Her room is small but it has a million colors of glass, paint, fabric, paper and pottery, as if she lives in a kaleidoscope. There are clothes hanging on a plumbing pipe, a plain iron bed with a fancy wooden headboard, and canvas paintings leaning on the wall with their backs facing out. Rose draws and smokes while Lilli looks through scrapbooks full of picture postcards, things torn from magazines, and drawings of the people they've been meeting here. Everyone looks sweet in the drawings, even Josef.

"How was making the sun rise?" Rose says.

"Oh—I liked it," Lilli says.

Rose nods. "It's lovely. I've gone a few times. You have to be careful about choosing a religion, though. People like you and me might stick with one all the way to age sixteen."

In a while they go back to the kitchen to make up trays of bread and coffee for the people on the farm. All the time they're doing it, Lilli keeps hearing Rose say *people like you and me*. I'm a person like her, she thinks. If we hadn't come here, I'd have gone forever not knowing.

Six

Benji walks down the hill just before daylight, when the sky looks bruised and the trees point sickly branches at him. This is nature, he thinks. I can't see why everyone's so in love with it. His back hurts from sleeping under a tree and he's still brushing pieces of the scenery off his clothes.

Once in a long while, he thinks, Father gives me a half-smile or a discreet eye-roll over Mother's enthusiasms. It makes me happy when he does that, disproportionately so. It seems likely I'll get one of those in the course of this trip, but there's no reason we couldn't have done it staying home.

He goes into the dining hall, hoping for breakfast, but the tables are empty. Back outside, a big bearded man in work clothes is walking by. "Sir, excuse me," Benji says. "Is there breakfast here?"

"Oh yes," the man says. "In fact they bring it to you." He puts his hand out. "Rolf."

"Benji."

The man's hands are enormous and covered with scars like Father's, but his handshake's gentle. His boots look like they've been through four wars, and his arms like they could tear trees out of the ground.

"This way," he says, and leads Benji to the farm fields.

It's light enough now to see the soil, dry and chunky in some places and muddy in others. The crops are struggling, except for that green squash from last night's stew. There are no trucks or tractors in sight, just people chopping at the dirt with old tools.

A few hoes lean on the wall of a teetering shed. Rolf picks one up, waves it like a wand and says, "This is a magical instrument. You move it around and in a while breakfast appears."

He cuts into a ragged furrow with it. Benji's reaching for one of the other hoes when he hears his name called.

It's his father, in the next field over, with his sleeves rolled up and his suspenders hanging loose. One hand's on a plow hitched to a horse, the other waving at Benji to join him.

Benji walks over, his ankles twisting in the dirt. When he gets there Father's moving again, leaning into the plow and holding its rusty handles with the horse's reins wrapped around his fingers. He pulls them and the horse stops.

"This is Rudy," he says, unwrapping the reins from his hands and giving them to Benji. "Just do what I was doing."

The old horse looks back at them, as doubtful as Benji feels, then faces forward again. You could fit three of Rudy into one police horse.

Benji gathers a length of the reins to wrap around his fingers. Rudy takes this as a tug and starts walking again, making the reins go tight. Benji's chest hits the handles and he falls in between them till Father pulls him upright.

"Give me those," Father says. "Just hold the handles. Put your heels down first. Your head up. Look straight from the plow to his tail."

They start again but every bump in the soil makes the plow strike a new course, toward the woods or the mountains but never straight ahead. Sweat pours into Benji's eyes.

"Start to turn," Father says. "More, more. There. Now a wide one, ten paces. They were plowing too deep for wheat. I raised the disks, you see? They plow in straight lines here but the spiral holds the rain better."

As if I'll ever need to know this, Benji thinks. Thirty meters away, a heavy woman in overalls is digging a trench. She undoes the top of her clothing and her breasts fall out in the open.

Benji loses his grip on the handles, the plow lurches forward and his face burns. There they are, the most exciting objects anyone at school can talk about, but in person they're alarming, hanging and swaying as the woman digs. Benji's furious at Father for all of this, the breasts most of all, but when they start walking again he stares so hard at the horse's rear that he makes no mistakes for the next four turns.

The gong sounds. In the other field, big Rolf puts his hoe down and nods at Benji.

Father stops Rudy and drops the reins. Benji lets go of the handles, stumbles, waves Father's hand away and rights himself. He follows the others toward the tool shed, his back hurting twice as much as before.

A woman wheels a cart down a path from the big building, stopping near the shed just as Father and Benji get there. It's Rose, the one who paints the banners. Her cart's loaded with bread, butter, honey, teapots, mugs and glasses. People surround her, tearing off bread and pouring tea and coffee.

Benji's stomach gurgles so hard he feels the liquid jet through it. Rose holds a loaf of bread out to him. He tears a piece off and takes a bite. It's the densest bread he's ever tasted, a silo squeezed into a loaf, with oil squirting from the nuts and seeds. He puts butter and honey on the next piece, his arms shaking. Rolf nods toward a low stone wall and says, "It's all right to sit down."

Benji does, and hurts in new places. When he goes back for coffee, Rose is talking to Father and pointing at the spiral of newly plowed furrows. Father shakes his head modestly but looks pleased.

"Here's what's remarkable, though," Rose says, lifting a loaf of bread with a spiral of raisins on it and holding it up next to the field. "Lilli did this," she says. "I think she's really yours."

Father blinks, then says, "Do you? There was a man always hanging around by the spiral staircase."

"Ah," Rose says. "It's an open question, then."

"She may have meant to illustrate your hair," Father says.

"My hair," Rose says, shaking her head so it bounces behind her. "In times of humidity it forms its own government." She tears a small piece of bread from the loaf. Her fingertip follows it into her mouth.

Father looks at the field as if to share her regard for it. Last year he got into a fight with a man in their apartment house and said, "He's an idiot, that one. He's a farmer," even though the man works in a store. I wish I could remind him of that now, Benji thinks.

A man comes over to Father. He's thin and tan, in overalls and a felt hat, with a long braid of graying hair hanging down his back. "I'm Manfred," he says. "I help manage the farm. Thank you for that field. Instructive."

"You might leave it rough now," Father says. "Till first rain."

Benji walks away, still aching all over. He comes to the woods they walked through yesterday, sits under a tree and closes his eyes. He sees orange light, plow discs, coffee, Rudy's thin tail and the big lady's breasts. He's almost asleep when he sees something else: Father, a few minutes ago, his shirt soaked in sweat, suspenders down and shit on his shoes, joking with that Rose as if he was a young man in a clean suit in Berlin. Imagine, the one time you see him look proud of himself, and it's for following a horse's bony ass around a field.

Seven

Gerhard finishes the plowing by himself at four o'clock, hands Rudy the horse over to Tilda and sets out walking. Rudy should be living on a pension of oats, in a workers' social circle with some anarchist cows. The plow needs you, Rudy. You don't need the plow.

At the edge of the field, the man who helped Rose paint her banners yesterday is framing the roof of a cottage-sized building. All right, Gerhard thinks, they're attempting a decent house for once, but why is it up on pilings? Does it flood here?

He looks at a drawing nailed to one of the uprights. It shows a handsome white house with green shutters, a meter up in the air, with a ramp leading to a half-sized doorway and chickens pecking at the dirt.

Of course. Moldering hovels for the people and gracious living for the hens. This whole place is a study.

He walks over a hill and looks down at the lake, where people are lounging and swimming naked. Years ago he went on socialist outings that included natural bathing, so he's had practice at the glance that says, "Me, no, I'm not finding this terrific at all, why?" It's been a while, though.

He walks down to the water, takes his clothes off and lays them on the ground. A nice-looking nude woman walks by, looks him over closely enough to sew him a suit, smiles and puts her own body forward for equal scrutiny before moving on. No wonder their buildings are falling down, Gerhard thinks.

He wades into the water to the cringing point, swims out past the others and floats on his back, letting the cold ease his aches. What did that Rose mean, he thinks, joking about Lilli being mine as if we're both men and we've known each other forever? The local fashion for frankness, like that woman looking at me just now? Or something more?

In a while he swims back to shore, lets the air almost dry him, gets dressed, walks up to the dining hall and sits under a tree to wait for supper. He's just closing his eyes when a shadow falls over him.

"Good afternoon. Richard Weiss. May I join you?"

Gerhard opens his eyes and sees the man who was talking at Rose's dinner table last night. He wears a white shirt with no collar, gray trousers and walking shoes, the cleanest and least theatrical clothes on the property. His laundering might be half their budget.

"Please," Gerhard says.

They shake hands. Richard sits down, keeping his back straight despite the tree trunk right behind him. "I saw your plowing," he says. "Everyone said I should."

"I don't understand the fuss," Gerhard says. "My father could do that."

Richard holds his cigar case out to Gerhard, who shakes his head. "How long are you visiting?"

"We leave tomorrow."

"So soon?"

"I work."

"May I ask what you do?"

"I make telephone switchboards."

"Ah," Richard says. "With all that wiring?" Gerhard nods. "Is it like a brain?"

"Just the hair," Gerhard says.

Richard smiles. "But you grew up on a farm?"

"Yes." People are coming to the lawn and sitting where they sat yesterday, but instead of talking they face Richard and Gerhard, listening.

"Do you miss farming?" Richard says.

"God no. My father made me do it."

"Did you like it today?"

"Yes. I made my son join me." He looks around and spots Benji at the edge of the crowd, still dirty from plowing. "Have you thought of getting a tractor here?"

Richard lights his cigar. "No, we gave up machinery. *Too much civilization, too much industry, too much commerce.*" Marx. One point for that, Gerhard thinks. "Did you have tractors on your farm?" Richard says.

"No," Gerhard says. "A salesman tried to sell us one once. Steam. When he started the engine my uncle jumped back two meters. He thought there were demons in it."

"If there were demons we'd be interested," Richard says. "Get it out here and see what it can do." People laugh.

"It would save work," Gerhard says.

"With this crowd?" Richard shakes his head. "They'd be painting Hindu deities on it. They'd be worrying about the horse's feelings. They'd be making love in the seat with the engine going."

"Just what my father said," Gerhard says, and gets a bigger laugh than Richard did.

"All that electricity and coal and so on," Richard says. "Those things are clever but they're putting the earth where the sky should be. We barely have time to change the world before they wreck it altogether."

Anna, Rose and Lilli walk up at the back of the crowd and sit down. Rose puts her knees up for Lilli to lean on.

"You're changing the world?" Gerhard says.

"It's that or die, Gerhard. This war is just the beginning."

Rose leans forward to pick up her cigarettes. Her shirt gapes open at the top and Gerhard loses the thread of the conversation. "The—the war," he says. "It might not start."

"It will, Gerhard. Europe's going to bleed out this time. It's going to be refugees, amputees, widows, orphans, whole kindergartens blind and wounded. Germany lives for this kind of thing."

"Some of us have hopes for a general strike," Gerhard says.

"Rosa Luxemburg?" Richard says. "She's a nice person, but no." Three points off, Gerhard thinks.

"Rosa has a *system*," Richard says. "But the people coming along now have this odd idea that they can run their own lives. Your Rosa trembles at that just as much as the Kaiser does. Even the psychoanalysts, now that they've gone over to the fathers—they tremble too. They're not going to stick you with their ordinary unhappiness if that's going on. These new people—right now they're sitting around on a lawn in Langenhain, but they'll be coming back ten meters tall."

People on the lawn smile at being mentioned. That's how you do it, Gerhard thinks—make them the heroes.

"I don't know why people are so skeptical about changing the world," Richard says, and blows a line of smoke. "Do you know what you do? You have people living in a state of obscene decency. Instead of manufacturing you have singing. Instead of money you have good looks. In place of the army you have conversation under the trees. In a while people come to see it. Some of them stay around.

"It can be done, Gerhard. It's been done with fewer troops than this. What you need most are artists." He waves a hand at the crowd. "Artists tear everything up and start over all the time. They can't help it. We have a lot of them but we can always use more. Do you know any?"

"My wife," Gerhard says, and closes his eyes for a second. Those words weigh a ton, he thinks. They could fall out of this tree like an anvil and pin me to the spot. It would be for the best.

"Is she here?" Richard says.

"Yes," Gerhard says, nodding toward Anna.

"Ah," Richard says, "she's met Rose," and everyone turns to look.

Eight

Everyone turns to look at Anna and she feels herself blush. "She's lovely," Richard says. "And that's your daughter?"

"Lilli," Gerhard says. Rose tilts her head down and smiles on Lilli like a spotlight. The man who colors in the banners walks up behind them, sits down and takes Rose's hand. He's got languid eyes in a face full of stubble.

"What's Anna's work?" Richard asks.

"She plays the violin," Gerhard says.

"That's wonderful," Richard says. "We have a quartet here. They're going to play in a while. We should get down there." He and Gerhard shake hands. "If that strike doesn't work out, think of us."

Anna's heart catches. *Think of us*—practically an invitation, and it's Gerhard's own doing. He has to like that.

Richard stands up in one motion, stronger than he looks. Gerhard gets up too, and Rose waves him over. "It's not bad enough that we make you plow," she says.

"I'm Gerhard," he says, offering his hand to Rose's friend.

"Frederick," the sleepy-eyed man says as they shake.

"I saw you working on the henhouse," Gerhard says. "A nice design."

"It's hers," Frederick says, putting a hand on Rose's shoulder.

"They're high-born ladies, those hens," Rose says. "Anything less would shock the conscience."

"May we go home, please?"

Anna turns and sees Benji, so dirty and beat-looking she thinks he must have been in an accident. "What happened?" she says.

"Nothing," Benji says, "but I'm German. I don't want to be where people spread lies about Germany."

"Don't upset yourself," Frederick says. "Germany's dying."

"Sir, excuse me. I think it's infamous to say that," Benji says. "I want to take care where I show myself. I'm planning to go to university."

"I think that's what they do at university," Gerhard says, nodding at where he and Richard sat. "Gas on like that."

"Please don't worry," Rose tells Benji. "Really no one knows anyone's here. It's like dropping off the earth."

"You've been indoctrinated, my friend," Frederick says. "You've been inculcated."

"No, he thinks all that on his own," Gerhard says.

Richard walks up behind him and says, "Thinks all of what?"

"About Germany, sir," Benji says. "About my home."

Shut up shut *up*, Anna thinks. My smart stupid son. "Benji—" she says.

"Ben," Richard says, offering his hand. Benji hesitates, then shakes it. "Come to supper with us," Richard says. "We'll talk it over."

"I have to wash," Benji says, and starts toward the lake.

"Later, then," Richard says.

They start down the hill as a man with his hair in a braid comes over to them. "Anna, yes? I'm Manfred." He turns to Gerhard. "I didn't know you were leaving so soon. I was hoping to discuss the soil."

"I'm sure you know more than I do," Gerhard says. "Alfalfa…"

Rose lets go of Frederick and makes Anna hang back with her. "Don't worry about Richard," she says. "He doesn't get told off nearly enough."

I like her too much, Anna thinks. She's like those ovals she paints, all nerve and motion and on to the next.

They go down into the woods, to a clearing where scattered sunset light falls on pine needles and powdery leaves. Rose's banners hang from trees, the two she painted yesterday and a third one Anna doesn't see at first because it's a trompe l'oeil of the trees and mountains behind it. The painted sky's a shade darker than the real one, with a gold compass floating in it like a star.

Food is warming on a grate laid across a fire. People fill their plates with squash and the rolls from this morning, then sit on logs to eat.

An old man, two women and Josef in his cape are putting chairs and music stands in the middle of the clearing. Richard walks up in front of them and people stop talking.

"A brief announcement," he says. "We may have found some suitable land in California."

An "Oh!" goes through the crowd. "It's in the San Bernardino County," Richard says. "Near the town of Driscoll."

"California?" Anna says to Rose.

"The current fantasy," Rose says. Frederick taps her on the arm. She opens her tin of cigarettes and gives him one.

"There are several things to recommend it," Richard says. "It's said to be quiet, with water for farming. And California's the world capital of being left alone. They call it the America of America. In the valley we're thinking of, there are several groups already—Bible revisers, psychic healers, mucusless dieters. No one asks them to explain themselves."

"I should think not," Rose says quietly, and Gerhard smiles. Like two smart alecks at the back of the class, Anna thinks. This news cuts straight through me, though. Look at my family. We're not the kind of people who turn their lives upside down and move around the world. We're fakes just for being here.

"We'll never have that kind of leeway in Germany," Richard says. "I give my own treatment as a small example. Falsely accused of all kinds of things. Worse, correctly accused of things that should be met with light applause.

"We'd call the place Sunland again, but this time we can back it up. I've been to the area, a few years ago. That's a sun you can worship, for those who like that.

"We might have enough money if we sell this place. It's not certain. There's the cost of the land, passage to America, food till we grow it—"

"There's gunplay in the parliament and a cactus that makes you delusional," Astrid's husband Jorgen says. "We can't *not* go."

"To the point, as always," Richard says. "Hands?" The whole crowd raises them. He nods and says, "It might be quite a trick. We could save our lives and still go to paradise. We'll see."

The musicians finish setting up as Richard sits down. The old man and a woman in overalls are the violins, the woman who was kissing the concertina player is the cello, and Josef's the viola. They play Haydn's D-Major *Sun* Quartet, the one that starts with a sigh. It's about happiness, Anna thinks, but with those funny C-sharps warning you it can get away any time. To California, for instance.

In the adagio the cello sounds the depths of a green lake, making the people in the glade tilt their heads and smile. Just this, Anna thinks—how is this too much to ask? Safety for the children and a plain life with people like these. How do you live and die and never have that?

Haydn's finale spirals up into sun, while here the light fades till it matches Rose's banner and the fabric vanishes. The quartet's playing is full of mistakes. The old man's sharp several times, the cello comes in late, the woman in overalls misses her accents, and none of it matters. It's fine as it is, the perfect music in these woods at this hour, among these people who've worked all week.

"Are they good?" Rose whispers.

Anna shakes her head. "They're like I was," she whispers back, and Rose puts an arm around her and a kiss behind her eye.

Nine

On his third day back in Berlin Gerhard leaves for work with a sheet of writing paper and a stamped envelope in his pocket. He writes his letter on the streetcar:

Dear Rose,

I hope this finds you well. Anna, the children, and I enjoyed our visit and are grateful for the hospitality shown us.

I write to suggest that you consider a more thorough system of bracing for the roof of your henhouse. The work I saw gave me some concern for the stability of the rafters. The enclosed drawing may be helpful, particularly the use of 40-cm. centers. I don't mean to cast aspersions on another worker's ideas, only to safeguard "the ladies."

I hope things go well for your group, whether in America or by that pleasant lake.

Yours,
Gerhard Lanz

He puts it in an envelope, writes *Rose*, realizes he doesn't know her last name, and adds *(The Painter), Sunland, Langenhain.* For his return address he uses the telephone factory, where he receives occasional updates on regional wiring protocols, always in plain brown wrappers.

Three days later he gets her reply, in a handmade envelope addressed in angular pen and ink.

A letter from Gerhard! And you remembered the hens!

How is Anna? How is Lilli, the heiress to a fortune in helical designs? How is her brother, the dour angel?

It was our pleasure to host you, the nicest family and hardest workers. The field you plowed has attracted many distinguished visitors from the world of science. A drawing like an illustration in Hoffmann's Tales shows two bearded men on their knees, measuring the furrows with calipers. *Your thoughts about the henhouse are greatly appreciated. Are you versed in building as well as electricity?*

I will pass your drawing on to Frederick. He drew his plans on a bag of nails, whose contours may have influenced the outcome.

Fondly,
Rose

Gerhard enjoys the insult to Frederick and spends three streetcar rides on his answer:

Dear Rose,

Thank you for your letter, with its kind words and fine drawings.

About your question: I worked in construction when I first came to Berlin, but my interest in electricity came earlier, when I was a boy and saw a light bulb. The man whose store it was in explained it to me, after a fashion. Till then I thought the world was mud, manure, and weeds. Imagine learning that there was lightning in all of it.

A few years later I followed this news into the army telegraph battalion, where I spent my spare time taking apart any equipment not being watched. When I was discharged I went home and told my family I was going to Berlin. My father and uncle said I'd wind up in a workhouse. I told them that they were called factories and that winding up in one was the objective. My mother said nothing, which at the time disappointed me but which I later realized was her greatest kindness yet, letting me leave her there with the two of them. I wish I'd worked it out in time to thank her.

He puts his pen aside and stares at the paper. What do I think I'm doing, telling my life story to a woman I barely know? Everyone has a mother. Who cares about mine? But to answer Rose's question:

In Berlin I found work on an apartment building in Wilmersdorf. The electricians kept failing to show up, so I did some wiring myself. When the city regulator came I was afraid he'd tear it out. Instead he told me that he and three friends were starting a new business and asked me to join them. This began my present course.

I see this is more than you asked for, but one thing leads to another, at least in one's early years.

Hoping this finds you well.

Fondly also,
Gerhard

Rose's answer comes two days later:

Dear Gerhard,

Thank you for your letter, even though it ends in suspense. The man who invited you to join his business was— Alessandro Volta? Henry Ford? Otto Fresser, inventor of the self-exciting luck switch?

Our dream of going to California seems faint at present. We asked the owners of the adjoining resort if they wanted to expand. They came to see our property and everyone kept their clothes on, but there was still the question of the buildings. They backed away smiling and promised to be in touch.

Nonetheless, our Astrid—you may remember her glass jewels and her influence on the sunrise—has immersed herself in California history. She says the place was once ruled by a Negro queen with an army of Moslem Amazons whose trained griffins tore Christians to shreds. A drawing shows a gleeful winged lion making off with a terrified man who's naked except for a crucifix. *This picture scares the piss out of your correspondent, regardless that I drew it myself. A testament to Astrid's powers.*

Love to you and your family,
Rose

He replies:

Dear Rose,

Thank you for your letter and your interest in my old stories. I'm sure yours are livelier.

The man who approached me was named Kessler. He and a colleague named Breuer had an ingenious design for small dynamos, and that was to be just the beginning.

There were five of us in the company, bending armatures at a fire in the yard, wiring coils at a table inside, and talking about more ambitious inventions. Breuer had a scheme for sending pictures over the telephone, using piano rolls and lemon-tipped paper. Kessler had plans for cinema in people's houses, using pipes like those for water but with mirrors and lenses to propel the images. I was delighted to be at that table. It was what I'd come to Berlin looking for.

Our dynamos enjoyed good sales. We worked twelve hours a day, but we believed that in the future, with the shackles of time and distance dissolved by these inventions, people would do a minimum of labor and spend their remaining time in parks, cafés, museums and beds.

He crosses out *and beds*, then writes it in again.

Then Werner Siemens and Stromberg-Carlson brought out dynamos with slightly different designs from ours, undercut our prices and hired Breuer and Kessler but not me. This was an education, though not the sort I was hoping for.

A month later I found a job at Dreher Telephone, a factory as hot as Egypt and as loud as if all the phone calls in Germany had backed up to their source. I started out standing at an assembly table between two Silesian women. A telephone is two wires, as simple as shoveling, but in fifteen minutes I was three pieces behind. In time I realized that the Silesian women were a kind of genius and that Breuer and Kessler were a kind of idiot, because time and distance are with us always, bearing down with a special heaviness in telephone factories.

I hope this answers your questions, and that all is well with you.

Yours,
Gerhard

Her next letter comes folded around a watercolor painting of a yellow building with scalloped beams thrusting out of it, set on a hillside of oak trees and wildflowers. People sit in slant-backed chairs on a porch that wraps around it.

Dear Gerhard,

You have so much in your mind! Does it want to burst free sometimes?

There's a cartoon of his brain in cross-section, with sections labeled PLOWING, DYNAMOS, TELEPHONES, CAFÉS, and BEDS.

California is still up in the air (perhaps literally—I should ask Astrid), but I've been making sketches of buildings we might construct there if we had sufficient guidance. Enclosed please find a dining and social hall. You may recognize some of the people on the porch, all of them prized, aggravating, and irreplaceable.

Could this building exist in three dimensions? Are you having luck with Rosa Luxemburg and her strike?

I hope you are happy today.

Love to you all,
Rose

He writes back:

Dear Rose,

Rosa Luxemburg is going to prison for trying to stop the war. Her sentencing is the ruling class's worst blunder yet.

I first heard her speak during my second year at the telephone factory. When she came onto the stage of the meeting hall I couldn't believe this was the "Red Menace" the newspapers wrote about—a short woman with a bad leg and floppy hat, limping out of Poland to stop German history. But then she spoke.

Her speech that night was a call to riot wrapped in a tribute to the life the owners had stolen from the workers, a life of joy and safety. The meeting hall looked like an infirmary, rows of people wrecked by work. By the end of her speech I imagined myself in the future telling the history of the revolution in one sentence: "It was overthrow the world or make her angry."

I joined her party that night and went on their Sunday Suffrage Promenades, demanding the vote for workers. My third time, the police rode down on us with horses and knocked me to the ground. A horse reared up over me, about to put my brains out, till two of the most wrecked-by-work people pulled me out. I went back every Sunday till Anna made me stop.

I hope you are happy, too.

Fondly,
Gerhard

He burns that letter as soon as he finishes it, in case the mail's being read. He burns Rose's too, and writes back:

Dear Rose,

I'm afraid I haven't kept up with the news and know little about Rosa Luxemburg. I believe she is with the Social Democrats?

The yellow building looks very handsome. Care will have to be taken with the placement of the foundation on inclined ground, and sufficient sealing of the stucco where the beams project.

Yours,
Gerhard

Who writes letters just to burn them? Who tells all his history this way and looks for mail at work every morning? It's ridiculous.

And yet—isn't this just the shock to the system Rosa talks about, that we, the milked-dry workers, have dared to start thinking about our happiness the way the bourgeoisie do? And what if happiness consists in having a *story*, which of all things turns out to be touching? The Sorrows of Young Gerhard, Gerhard's Adventures Underground, even Gerhard Agonistes, but *not yet* Twilight of the Gerhards. How do you stop such a force? It's like having the streetcar you're writing your letters on hit you from behind and push you straight across Berlin.

Still, he resolves to stop writing to her, or at least slow down.

Two evenings later he comes home and finds Anna heating up veal from work. She says a short hello, then nothing through supper. When the children are asleep she opens her dresser drawer, takes out a thick brown envelope and hands it to him, her expression almost grave. "This came," she says.

It's addressed to *LANZ*, with the return address *SUNLAND, LANGENHAIN* in penciled capitals, a man's handwriting. Frederick the idiot carpenter, Gerhard thinks, feeling sweat go down his neck. You'd think there'd be none left after work.

His letters to Rose aren't in there, though. Instead he pulls out a thick newsprint booklet. His English from school is modest but he understands *CROPS, 1912*, and *United States Government.* A dog-eared page is headed *CALIFORNIA*, with columns for *Lettuce, Oranges,* and *Peppers (Bell).*

He empties the envelope. There's another crop report and a brochure titled *San Bernardino, County of To-Morrow,* with colored drawings of schools, parks and a squat brick opera house.

At the bottom of the pile is a letter in pencil on lined paper:

Dear Anna and Gerhard,

I hope this finds you and your children well. Gerhard, thank you for your advice about the henhouse, which will be put to use when the building is realized in California. We have had an offer for our land from a hotel company in Belgium.

I enclose documents. Growing conditions in California appear excellent. We'll have nearly the same number of workers, losing only Clothilde and Franz, who feel they're too old to change countries. Franz's violin in the string quartet will be missed.

We sail from Bremen in the spring. Would you and your children like to join us? Richard says that funds are in place and we can pay your passage. Our practice is to pool our savings for common expenses, except 50 marks a person to be held back each year for individual needs.

There are of course no guarantees of the outcome, but the adventure should be interesting, and I have great hopes for the fruit.

Yours faithfully,
Manfred (farmer)

Gerhard looks up from the letter at Anna. "What do you think?" he says.

"About them going there?"

"About us going with them."

She looks confused. "Are you thinking of it?"

He shrugs. "Maybe."

"Why?"

"The war. The children."

"Yes, but"—she gestures at Manfred's letter—"I thought you thought they were silly."

"You like them, don't you?"

"Yes, but—I couldn't keep up."

"With who?"

"With Rose. With all of them."

He closes his eyes for a second. "Of course you could," he says. "You could play in that quartet."

"I'm too normal for them," she says.

"You're not." He takes her in his arms. "You're as strange as anyone."

"You just say that," she says, but laughs a little, her tears warm on his neck.

"You're as *good* as anyone," he says. "Better."

He means every word. What a relief to do something for her, to make things better. All at once, he's back to when these things came naturally and filled him with love. A little kindness. That's my only reason for going, he thinks. What more would I need?

"We don't have to decide tonight," he says. "We can talk in the morning."

They get into bed. He opens the government booklet and turns to the dog-eared page. *Do you see this?* he asks Rose, imagining she does because he can see her in that room she pointed to. *It's the crop report from California. Your friend Manfred sent it to us. I'm staying up reading it, every last bushel of green beans and avocado pears. Anna's sleeping but I can't.*

Ten

The proletariat of Europe, cutting their own throats: Gerhard and ten others in the men's toilets, trying to shave while the ship pitches on the first morning at sea. There's one metal mirror on the wall and everyone crowds around it, a tangle of elbows, mugs and razors. When Gerhard grows a beard he looks seventy and violent, and there'd be dissolute stubble like Frederick's along the way. He gets out with two nicks and a slit, not the best in the room but not the worst either.

He walks out on deck and looks around. The ship's as tall as the Kaiser-Gallerie, painted purple, with *Saxonia* in yellow letters on the prow. Gerhard backs up against the rail and cranes to see the upper decks. High above, First Class passengers in topcoats stroll around browsing the ocean as if it's a street of high-priced stores: those white-caps look cunning, but simply everyone's doing them. In Second Class a man in athletic clothes walks determined laps around the deck, checking a stopwatch as he passes a funnel. Here in Third Class a few people in black huddle at the rail, staring at the horizon as if they can make their future reveal itself if they look hard enough.

Gerhard goes into Third Class Married and Family, a vast airless room crammed with three tiers of bunk beds. In the aisles he slips past people dressing for breakfast. A woman struggles into a girdle, a man adjusts a hairpiece, and a little girl giggles at both of them and gets slapped.

Anna and the children have left. Gerhard's putting his shaving things away when Jorgen, the Bible-prophet one, comes over with his younger daughter Trudy. "Are you people Catholic?" he asks.

Gerhard shakes his head. "Communist."

"That won't help," Jorgen says. "The Uzbeks over there have raisin wine. They'll take any kind of icon. A prayer card would do it."

"Sorry," Gerhard says.

"Did Lilli bring her dolls?" Trudy asks.

"They gave those things away," Gerhard says.

"Communist," Jorgen explains to Trudy as they walk on.

In the Third Class dining room the color scheme is jaundice and bathwater. From the doorway Gerhard surveys the Sunlanders, two tables full of attic-raiding costumes under a canopy of long hair and feathers. The other passengers have left a row of empty seats on either side of them.

"Have you seen this menagerie?" a voice next to Gerhard says.

He turns, sees one of the men he shaved with, and says, "I think I'll sit with them."

"Be serious," the man says.

Gerhard shrugs. "What's the worst they can do to me?"

He gets his tray of breakfast—hard cheese, a roll, stewed prunes and coffee stretched with barley. Anna's sitting with the woman who scarred Benji for life by undoing her overalls.

They wave Gerhard over. He pulls on a chair. It weighs thirty kilos and he almost drops his tray.

"It's to keep them from sliding," Anna says. "Gerhard, this is Frieda. We're going to sew later. I'm making school clothes for Benji."

She opens the *County of To-Morrow* brochure Manfred sent them and points to a picture of children outside a school. "They want dark suits with knee pants," she says.

"But not a uniform," Frieda says. "That's already American."

The boys in the picture look twice as big as Benji. They'll use him for a football, Gerhard thinks. When he finishes eating he gets up, finds Benji eating by himself with two books open in front of him, and leaves his roll on the boy's plate.

Manfred and Tilda are poring over papers at the next table. "Gerhard. Please join us," Manfred says. "We're planning crops."

Gerhard sits down. "We need to get things in the ground before it's too hot," he says. "Beans and tomatoes, I think."

"And corn," Tilda says. "Maybe peppers. Look at this."

She hands Gerhard a pamphlet with a colored photograph on the cover, a bulging tomato with water beading on its skin and leaves curled around its thick stem. It's a seed catalogue from California, fancier than the ones in Gerhard's childhood. He understands half the English— SETS FRUIT LIKE CRAZY, MONARCH OF THE LIMAS—but the catalogue's strength is in the pictures: voluptuous produce with straining stalks and deep-set carpels, like pornography for bees. Or for Manfred and Tilda: the pages are limp from rereading, with circles drawn around half the plants. "Their strawberries are bigger than our apples," Tilda says.

Of course they are, Gerhard thinks, and why stop there? With this catalogue's trick photography and your trusting natures, you can have melons big enough to live in. There go your food and housing problems, all in one.

"Did you bring tools?" he says.

"Hoes and hammers," Manfred says, "in people's luggage. For bigger things—" He passes Gerhard a thick book called SEARS AND ROEBUCK—THE GREAT PRICE MAKER.

Where the seed catalogue is prurient this one is clinical, detailing every nut and screw on the Little Jap Cultivator and Bonanza Manure Spreader. Hundreds of dollars in goods are circled in pencil.

Gerhard closes it. "The first thing we'll need is shelter," he says. "A pole barn to sleep in."

"We should talk to Rose about that," Tilda says.

We should talk to her and I shouldn't, Gerhard thinks. He's said hello to Rose a few times on the ship, but there's no sign that they're picking up where their letters stopped, or even from her teasing him in Langenhain. That's for the best, he reminds himself every time.

"How much money do we have?" he says.

"Not as much as we thought, after the boat tickets," Manfred says. "Six hundred sixty American dollars."

"Have you made a budget?"

"Yes. We're short but we could forage for a while, and when these come in—" Manfred puts his hand on the lying seed catalogue as if to swear by it.

Gerhard takes their budget back to his bunk and reads it. No matter what he cuts he can't get under $1280.

He goes to Single Men's, which looks even grimmer than Family and smells like feet, mops, cigars, the sea and its sickness. Men coming back from breakfast are knocking into one another in the aisles as a kind of sport.

Richard's lying on a lower bunk, writing in a notebook. Gerhard stands over him till he looks up.

"Gerhard," he says. "How's your crossing?"

"Bumpy. According to Manfred, you said funds were in place. What happened to them?"

Richard returns his look evenly. "The fares went up, Gerhard."

"Did they?"

"You could complain to the ship's bursar or whatever he's called. You might learn some nice nautical slang that way."

"There's not enough money."

"We had to get out of Germany," Richard says. "It's like a burning building. You don't get to dress for that."

"I suppose people could get jobs in the town."

"Jorgen's getting a job?"

"No," Gerhard concedes.

"So much is improvisation, Gerhard."

Gerhard waits a moment, realizes nothing more is coming, says, "Thank you" and walks away. He runs into Manfred by the stairs, nods toward Richard and says, "Is he any practical use?"

Manfred considers. "He got me out of Berlin a few years ago. Saved my life." His expression is mild but unshakeable.

They go out on the Third Class deck. People are crowding the sunny spots, sitting by nationality, a caravansary of black dresses, balloon pants, headscarves, skullcaps, and vests with bits of mirror on them. They're busy with gossip, knitting, smoking, books, letters, chess and parcheesi, but here and there Gerhard sees the nervous glances of people traveling from one catastrophe to what they hope won't be another.

Tilda's playing cards with three sailors at the base of a funnel. She folds her hand and leads Gerhard and Manfred to Rose and Frederick, who are working on drawings with a stack of books between them, some in German and some in English: *California Chaparral, The Mission Style of Building, Farms and Ranches of the San Joaquin.*

"May we talk about shelter?" Gerhard says.

"Please," Rose says, moving over. She's wearing a fisherman's sweater, thick straw-colored yarn with stitches a finger's width apart. Her red hair spills down behind her from its silver ring.

"I have a barn," she says, handing Tilda a drawing of a grand one, with a stonework facade, peaked dormers, and a portico whose columns are stripped and polished redwood trunks.

"It's beautiful," Tilda says.

"Yes," Frederick says, putting an idle hand on Rose's arm. She gives him a cigarette and takes out more paintings: an even fancier henhouse than before, the yellow dining hall, a corn mill like a stone cottage, a greenhouse like the Crystal Palace, and a building beyond modern architecture, with corrugated steel walls and a bright red roof slashing up at the sky. "That's the carpentry shop," she says.

All to be built without powered machinery, sufficient materials or money, Gerhard thinks. Frederick's put his cigarette down on the edge of the chaparral book. Gerhard picks it up before it starts a fire and holds it out to Frederick, who takes it from him without blinking.

"Here's the toolshed," Rose says.

She leans across Gerhard to pass the drawing. Her hair falls away from the back of her neck, just under his face, with sunshine on its copper down. He's still breathing her clean smell as she sits up and smiles at him.

Maybe I'm being too harsh about the buildings, he thinks. Some of them could be built plain, with a kind of stage set on the outside. I could show her.

He points at the dining hall. "Do you have plans for that?"

"Here," Frederick says. He digs through a paper bag, brings out three pages of rumpled notebook paper, and hands them to Gerhard.

"Thank you. May I take them with me?"

Frederick shrugs. Gerhard puts the plans in his pocket. The smell of Latakia tobacco drifts over from some Arabs by the rail, making him think of roofing tar and what it might cost in America.

He goes to lunch by himself and starts to unfold Frederick's plans till Anna sits down next to him. "I've had the *best* morning," she says. "Sewing with everyone. I talked to that Suzanne, the cello in the quartet? She came to Berlin last year for the Ernst Kirchner exhibit. She said she ran through the city to get there and then the paintings were exactly what she'd just run through, if only she'd known how to look. These pictures of prostitutes, with men hanging around them—and then Frieda said she'd been up to his studio for these twenty-minute paintings they do. The girl who models is fifteen." She lowers her voice. "People make love in his studio and he paints *that*.

"Anyway"—a pause before news—"I'm going to try and play with them. Frieda asked me. She's the first violin. It's horrible practicing after this long. You feel like a gorilla. I'm going to try, though."

Stop, Gerhard thinks. The happier she sounds, the harder it is for him to breathe. It shouldn't irritate me, he thinks, but she has no idea of the work ahead of us, and her happiness isn't just joy, it comes wrapped in all the unhappiness that came before it. Unhappiness can live on a modest diet forever but happiness eats everything in its path.

"It's not going to be like that," he says. "Not for a long time. We're going to need everyone clearing the land and getting crops in. No one's playing music yet."

"No," she says, stung. "Of course—"

He lowers his voice. "They don't know anything. They're expecting giant strawberries and who knows what else."

"I'm sorry."

He holds up Frederick's papers. "I have to look at these plans. We have to see if all this can work."

"Yes," Anna says.

He pats her hand, goes to a chair at the end of the table, reads Frederick's plans, gets up and goes to Single Men's. Frederick is lying on his bunk, reading a book called *Inca Psychology—Portal to the Hidden Plane.*

"I've looked at these," Gerhard says, unrolling the plans.

"Do they meet your approval?"

"I'm afraid not. These footers are off center. The foundation could crack."

Frederick closes his book and sits up. "There aren't enough posts for the roof," Gerhard says. "For the weight on the headers."

Frederick looks blank. Gerhard turns the page. "Did you read about the earthquake at San Francisco? These are the kind of walls that collapsed." He holds up the exterior elevation. "We're on the wrong part of the slope here. Floods."

"All right," Frederick says. "Do you want to draw them?"

"I think that might be best."

"Fine." He lights one of Rose's cigarettes. "You don't need to be competitive about it. It's not a *sport.*"

He leaves the cigarette burning on a bunk post and goes back to his book. Frederick growing to adulthood without getting murdered, Gerhard thinks: there's a story. I'd love to hear it, some other time.

He finds Rose on deck by a ship funnel, drawing a granary like a Greek rotunda with her pastels. "I spoke with Frederick," he says. "We think I should draw the plans."

"Oh, good. I'm glad you two talked. Here." She pats the space next to her but he stays standing.

"Can these people work?" he says.

"Artists? They work harder than the upright townfolk. Don't let the nervous breakdowns fool you."

"There's not enough money."

"Money's not their strength. Tell them what you need and they'll find it in an alley."

"You believe in them."

She nods. "Don't you have people like that?"

"I used to."

"That's sad. Here." She pats the place next to her again. Don't sit down, he thinks, but there's never been a *What am I doing?* that can stand up against a *Look! I'm doing it well!*

He sits. The deck is so crowded their shoulders touch. Whose fault is that? No one's but the shipping profiteers.

"Blueprints weren't Frederick's gift," she says. "He can ask what people want for their houses and sketch them."

"Houses?"

"Everyone gets their dream house. A beer hall, an ashram—whatever they like."

"No, they— I was thinking of a pole barn first, then cabins. Square beams and planks. That's what you do in the woods."

She shakes her head. "If we're going to draw together we have to dream. Cabins aren't dreaming. Look." She shows him a drawing of an orange adobe house, with slate paths and cactus plants. "Mine's Mexican. What about yours? For your family?"

"I don't know."

"You come home from working and what does it look like?"

She turns a page in the sketchbook. Her shoulder presses against his. "Name a style," she says.

Gerhard shrugs, feeling the thick stitches of her sweater and by implication the inviting spaces between them. "Japanese?" he says. If you're heading for ruin you might as well have manners.

"Good," she says, and starts drawing.

"We could starve."

"We won't, though," she says. "We have you." In a minute she's sketched a Japanese room, with blond wood and blue cloth hangings. Her hand pauses, then moves again. A bed takes shape on the floor, sized for two people, its covers barely made up, as if everyone knows it's getting mussed again soon.

Eleven

Benji walks out on deck with his book bag, sits down against the rail and gets out his English grammar book. Tucked inside it is a ten-pfennig novel called *Dusty the Wranglercowboy*, published in Hamburg. He bought it for information about the American West but it's baseless trash, or at least he hopes it is. The story starts with a train robbery, poisoned wells and a range war, all in the first morning. Every illustration shows Dusty laughing with his hands on his hips, even when a gang of hook-nosed Indians tie him to crossbars and set him on fire.

There are other drawings, salacious ones, that don't even go with the story. They show women with their skirts bunched up between their legs so the folds look like hair. Benji's thrown the book away twice but, to his shame, rescued it both times, for those drawings. I'd be more likely to discipline myself, he thinks, if Mother and Father weren't throwing my future away for a trip to the desert wastes. Father's spent years wiring circuits but electricity's behind us, now that he's finished with it and I haven't started.

He opens his English grammar and starts declining verbs out loud: "I sell brooms. Yesterday I sold brooms. I am selling a broom today."

A shadow falls over the book. Benji looks up to see a swarthy man around thirty in a high-waisted suit. He points at the book and says something Slavic-sounding. From the expression on his face it seems like a request for help. Benji looks uncertainly at him. The man sits down facing Benji and gestures at him to go on.

"Tomorrow I will sell a broom," Benji says in English.

"To borrow high zell boom," the man says.

"No, *sell*," Benji says. "I will sell." The man stares at him. "It means—"

He stops talking, takes his comb and a pfennig out of his pockets, hands the man the comb, then trades the coin for it. "You sell. I buy," he says.

He does it in reverse. The man repeats the words after him, a syllable at a time, till he gets them right.

"I comb," Benji says, showing him. "I comb my hair with my comb." He points at a woman down the way. "She combs her hair."

"High comb!" The man grabs the comb and pulls it through his hair, a disordered mass that starts high on his forehead. The comb snags, pulling out hairs and keeping them. The man offers it back. Benji starts to take it by the edges, sees the man's expression, takes it fully in his fingers and wipes them on the inside of his pocket as he puts it away.

The man holds his wrist out, wiggles his fingers over it, says something in his language, clasps Benji's arm and hits the cover of the English book with his finger.

"I don't know," Benji says in German. He copies the wiggling. "I don't know what that means. I'm sorry."

The man repeats his speech, louder. A sailor hears them and comes over. "It's Serbian," he tells Benji in German.

"Do you speak it?" Benji says.

"A little," the sailor says. "A little of everything."

He speaks Serbian to the man, who does his speech and pantomime again. The sailor repeats it in German: "I fix watches. I can fix any watch you have." He grasps Benji's arm the way the Serbian man did. "Take me!"

Benji pulls his arm free. "It's a little eager," he says.

"Have you looked for work?" the sailor says.

The watchmaker thumps the book again. Benji hesitates, but the man seems even more worried about going to America than Benji is.

He looks up the words in his book. "I can fix any watch you have," he says in English. "Take me *on*." He leads the man through it word by word. After half an hour the man stands up, says what must be "Thank you!" while nodding violently, and goes away.

The next day he comes back with two friends, and the sailor brings a woman over. "Italian," he says.

Benji thinks. "All right," he says, "but they have to pay attention and copy the sentences down." The sailor translates. The people nod.

They work for two hours. Benji helps the Italian woman with *I can sew ladies' gloves* and saves a bookkeeper from working with bees.

After that they meet twice a day. Benji's neglecting his own subjects, but it would be wrong to leave people defenseless in America. Even if *Dusty the Wranglercowboy* is trash, the passages where people get *hornswoggled* by *sharpies* seem real enough.

Soon he has eight students. He gives them a sentence in German: "I am a clean, quiet tenant." The class translates it from Russian to Serbian to Italian to Greek. When it gets back to German it's "In silence I wash myself from your house."

Benji says it the right way in English. They repeat it and move on to the students' own sentences: *Does this place flood? How far is Wisconsin? I am a cook and governess. I want to start a strongman gymnasium.*

Eventually there are fourteen of them, not counting the Sunland people. Manfred and Tilda come most days, along with Mother, Lilli, and a few Benji doesn't know yet. Father comes once and so does Richard, though his English is good already.

"You don't have to keep coming to lessons," Benji tells Lilli one evening. "I can teach you when we get there."

"I like saying it with everyone," Lilli says. She's built up a repertoire: *I can deliver babies, I sharpen miners' drills, I am the only one of my family left.* Benji teaches every day, till one morning a shout goes up and his whole class runs to the front of the ship. He waits a minute before he follows them. He knows they want to see their new country, but he wishes he'd had time to teach them how to count their change.

Twelve

Gerhard comes off the stairway and nearly gets run over by people racing for a look at New York. He works his way to the rail and finds Rose and Frederick, watching the statue of the woman with the torch come into view. A roar goes up in the crowd, but Frederick gives the statue an unimpressed nod and says, "Publicity."

Rose turns from looking at it, surprising Gerhard with a tear in her eye. "Frederick, let someone think something nice for once," she says.

"Think away," Frederick says, and gives Gerhard a curt glance. As he walks away the whole ship cheers, because they're coming about so it looks like the lady with the torch is turning to greet them. People who hunched around nervously through the voyage are grinning, crying, and waving little American flags. When they get past the statue they applaud the skyline, colored black and white as if everything that happens here makes the papers.

The engines go quiet, their noise replaced by the anchor winch paying out chain. Gerhard sees Benji standing at the rail and staring at tall buildings with advertisements for scouring powder and fountain pens painted on their sides. For a second Gerhard's eighteen and seeing Berlin for the first time, knowing one of the thousand windows must be his.

A sailor comes through the crowd shouting, "Bring your things on deck and wait for the ferry" in five languages. The passengers get their luggage, wait an hour and crowd onto a barge. They're quiet now, some still waving flags but nervously.

They dock at an island of brick buildings too friendly-looking to be a government's. In Germany, Gerhard thinks, they'd be decorated with Catherine wheels and rearing jaguars, all steel. Here even the biggest one could be a main post office or a small college. A country with nothing to prove, it says. Has there ever been such a thing?

A man in a uniform calls from the doorway of the big building, "*Saxonias* inside, please."

They follow him into a luggage room, where a man checks their names and pins numbers to their coats, smiling at the children. "*Saxonias* one through sixty upstairs, please," a voice calls from above.

On the next floor a doctor takes ten seconds to inspect Gerhard's neck and scalp, pull his eyelids back with a buttonhook, and send him behind a partition where the men wait in line to have their pricks checked for social disease. Jules, the concertina player in the velvet suit, nods toward the doctor doing the checking and says, "He never forgets a face," which gets a laugh from the other Sunland men. The immigrant in front of Gerhard looks alarmed, but no one's in trouble. America's doing all right so far, Gerhard thinks.

Back in the main room, an officer checks Gerhard's papers and says, "Final destination?"

"California."

"By railroad?"

"Ship."

"Show me your ticket." Gerhard does. "And your money." Gerhard takes out his thin pile of marks. "You can change that for dollars downstairs. Are you married?"

"Yes."

"More than one wife?"

"No."

"Are you a socialist?"

Gerhard pauses a second, which could be too long. Am I on a list, he thinks, or is it a question for everybody, like the extra wives?

"I—"

"Are you a socialist?" the officer next to Gerhard's asks a lady with a little girl.

"No," she says. The officer stamps her papers and sends her along.

They ask everyone, then. But why? It's not smallpox. It's an idea, one that's right in line with these friendly, jaguar-free buildings, the smile on the man pinning numbers—those are as socialist as I am. You'd like it, officer. I could send you some literature.

"No," Gerhard says instead. The man stamps his papers and hands them back.

Downstairs, the Sunlanders are gathering to leave. Lilli's near the exit, where a uniformed woman sits at a desk with a telephone and a register book.

"Thank you for the courtesy you have showed us," Lilli says to her in English from Benji's lessons.

"That's English," the woman says. "That's very good."

Lilli smiles proudly. "I can deliver babies!"

The woman's face turns stern. "No you can't," she says. "That's not a fit thing to tell people."

Lilli looks stricken. Gerhard hurries over, tells the woman, "One moment, please," waves at Benji to join them and says, "She said she can deliver babies."

Lilli points at Benji and says, "He taught us!"

"What did you teach her?" the woman says, her hand on her telephone.

"No—only the words, Miss," Benji says in English. "I mean, there was someone who *does* deliver babies, and—"

"You don't want her going down the street saying that," the woman says. "That won't go well."

"No," Benji says. "I was teaching them—"

"And now I'm teaching you," the woman says. "Do you understand?"

"Yes," Benji says.

"All right then," she says, letting go of her phone. "Welcome to America."

Thirteen

The third morning on the second ship, Anna comes out on deck, falls into a long canvas chair and thinks *Yes, all right, I'm going to live.* Not that I was going to die on the *Saxonia*, but if there was a travel poster for that ship the motto across the top would be *And don't come back!*

This *McKinley*, on the other hand, has clean sheets, portholes that let air in, and room to sew on deck without having your elbows in your bosom. They're steaming down the east coast of America in warm air and rainbow spray. The food changes every day, and last night there was pudding.

Rose is busy drawing buildings with Gerhard, so Anna doesn't see her as much as she'd like, but she's getting to know the other Sunlanders one by one. At the moment, though, her fascination is with the Americans on board and their cheerful goals in California—farming chinchillas, trying out for the movies, or collecting their pensions from the middle of orange groves. Some of them wear traveling clothes so bright the Sunlanders look almost normal in comparison.

Lilli's met two sisters from Ohio who are teaching her to play jacks. Benji studies, sitting upright on a deck chair covered with books, looking at the water only when he's working a problem.

"Why don't you take a rest now and then?" Anna asks him.

"I can't," Benji says. "Do you see that man in the straw hat? He was a teacher in Iowa. He says eighth grade in America is as hard as university anywhere else. He says all his students could write a law, Greek-wrestle, and make hydrogen sulfide. He says the Negroes are moving north so fast there's hardly a place for the white children. He says I'll be lucky to be admitted. He says he's giving it up and moving to Nevada."

"His poor students," Anna says, but she doubts that Benji takes her meaning.

She gets her sewing things and takes a seat in the circle next to Frieda, whose two-year-old son Stefan sits between her legs, batting at the scarf she's knitting. Frieda hasn't heard Anna play a note, but takes it as given that she's going to replace the old man in the string quartet.

"Should we try playing for people on this trip?" she asks.

Anna sticks herself with her needle but says, "That sounds nice."

"I was thinking of Dvořák's Twelfth Quartet," Frieda says. "Do you know it? It's when he came to New York and heard the Negro spirituals. So moving. I'll bring you a score at lunch."

How long since I was that game about music, Anna thinks, and how do you get it back?

That afternoon she opens her suitcase, finds her violin and bow wrapped in a sweater, takes them below decks and finds an alcove near the engines where she can't hear herself talk.

The strings have been loose in storage for years. She calls the engine noise a G, puts her ear to the violin's sound hole and tunes up. The engines vibrate so hard the strings play themselves. She backs away just till they stop and draws the bow, one barely audible note. Then scales, then Kreuzer exercises. If I could hear myself I'd stop right now, she thinks.

She opens the Dvořák score. The opening's simple, a pulse like crickets. Anna plays it six times, slowly and full of mistakes, before going up to supper. She sits with Jules and Suzanne while Gerhard and Rose take their trays to the oil drum they use as a drawing table.

Gerhard comes to bed late. "How is it, working with Rose?" Anna says.

"Her ideas are perverse," he says. "I'm trying to make them come true."

By the time they pass Georgia Anna can play the first movement of the Dvořák through, but soon it's too hot to keep the violin tuned and then too hot to play. "We'll try it on the next ship," Frieda says. The sewing circle becomes a straight line in the shade of a stairway, till one day the thimbles and knitting needles burn their skin and work stops. Lunch is cold soup. At dusk the sailors bring out rope hammocks so people can sleep on deck.

The next day the ship slows down and threads its way through green islands to a pier. They're in Panama, soaked in sweat before they leave the boat. They lug their bags down a wooden dock made lacy by termites, past brown-skinned vendors offering fruit and pitying smiles. Gerhard buys lemon ices for the family.

At the train station they crowd into the shade of a por-tico, dog-breathing in the steamy air. Manfred the farmer comes over, points down a gravel road and says, "They're building the canal down there. Shall we look?"

Gerhard, Anna and the children follow him down the road, the gravel hot underfoot and the air buzzing with gnats. Soon they're at a rail yard where men are loading rock drills and water barrels onto trains. Six of them carry cases marked EXPLOSIVO on their heads.

Benji puts his valise down, gets out his camera, unfolds it and names the big machines in the yard as he photographs them: "Excavator. Crusher. Bucyrus."

"Take me," Lilli says, striking a pose.

"I'm taking the machines," Benji says.

"I'll be holding one. Here." She puts her hand out flat, trying to give the illusion that a steam shovel's in her palm.

"Lower," Benji says. "There." Lilli gawks at her hand as if the shovel's an insect that's crawled into it. Benji snaps the photo.

"We should get back," Manfred says. They reach the station as their train pulls in, five old cars and a wheezing locomotive.

The Sunlanders' car is suffocating, with powdery leather seats and a crate-wood floor. They start out down a street of buildings huddled under eaves and balconies, with American flags and slow-turning fans everywhere.

In a few minutes they're steaming through the jungle alongside the unfinished canal, glimpsing workers through the greenery. A sudden roar shakes the train, the lights go out and Linda's scream cuts through the sound of something smashing into the roof.

"It's dynamite, for the canal," Benji shouts, as dirt rains past the windows. When it clears they're looking at bamboo, flowering vines, and shacks on stilts just above the swamp water. Soon they're staring at groves of hibiscus, blue butterflies, gold frogs and pink-faced monkeys.

They come out of the jungle, climb a steep mountain pass and cheer their first sight of the Pacific, steel-blue and flat to the horizon. Coming down, they cross swamps of white mangrove trees, their branches spread against the sky and trunks dotted with yellow-headed lizards.

Rose draws in her sketchbook, pastels flying as she looks out the window. When she finishes the picture she tears it out and hands it to Lilli, who gasps.

Anna stands up and looks over Lilli's shoulder. It's a cartoon of the frogs, monkeys, and butterflies gaping at the strange creature in the train window: Lilli. *CAN IT BE REAL?* says a scroll across the bottom.

"I *adore* it," Lilli says. Like a while-you-wait caricature, Anna thinks, except for that wild talent and the free flow of love.

଄

On their third ship the blue of the ocean changes all day with the sky, and Anna can play her whole part of the Dvořák down by the engines. The quartet holds its first rehearsal in a storeroom, their chairs wedged between piles of life preservers. Frieda's the first violin. Suzanne, whose sweetheart Jules plays the concertina between their kisses, is the viola. Josef, still wearing his cape in the tropics, is the cello.

First rehearsals are supposed to be bad, but it takes them an hour just to play the first theme together. Each time a note goes wrong one of the women says "Sorry" and Josef looks at her with forbearance, even if the mistake was his. The days that follow are no better.

One day Anna practices alone till her hands cramp, goes up on deck and finds Gerhard and Rose drawing at their oil drum. Rose looks up, smiles at Anna and hands her a page from her sketchbook. "Inside the dining hall," she says.

The walls in the picture are sand-colored, with sheaves of dried flowers hung between windows. A brick fireplace and a serving window are framed in yellow tile. Round and square tables make a mosaic on the polished floor. Anna recognizes Jorgen and Tilda, drinking coffee in late morning sunshine.

"It's beautiful," she says.

"It's a cheap trick, putting coffee in it," Rose says. "But

thank you."

Gerhard's drawings are the schematics, with the coal shine of dark pencil and that high-hipped lettering reserved for architects. "He keeps changing everything," Rose says. "Just so it won't collapse."

"Or bankrupt us first thing," Gerhard says. "When we see the terrain we'll have a whole new set of arguments."

Really they're easy with each other, Anna thinks. It's easy being easy with someone when you don't have to talk about household money, say, or Benji. Still, he and I should be more like that.

She goes below and practices for three more hours, but the next day in rehearsal she's late half the time and her double stops sound like cats. Josef tries to give her cues, but sometimes they're when he nods his head and sometimes when he lifts it first. When Anna mentions it he says, "I don't lift my head," and she sinks into the old misery of someone who shouldn't even try to play but keeps tricking herself into it. Josef's another one, she thinks. That's why we can't stand each other.

Twice she makes the mistake of telling Gerhard about it. "I don't see why you're worried," he says the second time. "It's people who like you and these happy Americans. Hardly a tough audience."

"I'm worried about the *music*," she says, feeling like an ass as soon as the words leave her mouth.

"Couldn't you just play softer than the others?" he says.

"No, it's—thank you," she says, and goes to practice.

Anna's prayed the bad artist's rosary a thousand times. *It's all right, I wasn't born with what the good ones have, it's out of my hands, and really it's enough to be anywhere near this art that's given me such happiness. It would be enough to be a bug on the windshield of an automobile parked three blocks from a concert hall where the program tonight is a lecture on phrenology but there was an evening of Liszt three weeks ago, that's all I need,* but as many times as you pray it you backslide, thinking something will change you, and that's why, like an idiot, she said she would do this.

But at ten one morning, anchored for supplies at a tiny village called Acapulco, they play it and it sounds like music. Anna finally hears what Dvořák must have, the songs breathing out of warm-lit Negro cabins. When they come to the end they're silent for a second, bows in midair, eyebrows up, till a sigh and a laugh pass through the four of them, the best feeling Anna can think of.

They decide to play it on the last night at sea, coming up the coast of California. That evening the crew hangs colored lanterns among the hammocks. Anna wears her best skirt, pearls and a lace-necked blouse, her hair piled up.

It sounds as good as it did at practice, even better once they get underway. Anna tries to keep her eyes on her sheet music but the Americans are right in front of her, closer than a concert audience. She can feel their reaction—entertained, appreciative, interested. Everything but swept away.

When it's over they applaud, a few stamping their feet. Then one of the men says something, and Benji translates: "That was fine. That was the real elegance. Do you happen to know something—" Benji hesitates, then tries for an equivalent: "—*bissig?*"

The American man repeats his word: "Snappy?"

Suzanne laughs, lays her cello aside, says "Jules" and waves her sweetheart over.

Jules looks surprised, but people are clapping. He goes to his hammock, comes back with his concertina, stands in front of the quartet and plays a jig, two rags and a polka. He bashes away at the tunes but smiles and throws his head around. The Americans get up to dance and won't let him stop.

All right, Anna thinks, that's what they wanted to hear—a jumble of chords and lots of repetition. That's what "popular" means, or have you forgotten? In a while she goes into the dancing crowd and pulls Lilli out.

"What's wrong?" Lilli says.

"Nothing," Anna says. "But we need to change for bed."

They go inside and put their nightgowns on to sleep in the hammocks. The Americans come out on deck in long shirts or bathing costumes, grinning like children who've wandered from bed to their parents' party. Finally the concertina stops.

Gerhard lies down in a hammock. Rose and Lilli take the one next to it, one head at each end, the soles of their stocking feet pressed together.

Frederick sees Benji looking for a place and says, "University, here. I don't snore or any of that." Benji hesitates but gets in feet-to-feet with him, keeping his shoes on.

Anna gets in with Gerhard and fits her front to his back, still telling her mind to be quiet about the music. There are quartets who leave people too transported to want two hours of jigs, but that's another life altogether.

"Let's bump Mother and Father," Lilli says to Rose.

"Gently," Rose says. They make their hammock sway. Gerhard's already asleep. When Rose's body brushes against his he opens his eyes, sees her swinging away from him and says, "Oh—"

Lilli giggles. "Shh," Rose says. She reaches back and squeezes Anna's hand, slowing her hammock to a stop before she lets go.

⋘

When Anna wakes up it's dawn and they're in a harbor, smaller than New York's but crowded with ships. She slips out of the hammock and stands at the rail, watching cliffs come out of the mist. Soon everyone from Sunland is looking with her, too excited to talk.

They take their luggage from the dock and follow a paved path through a rail yard busy with near-disasters, the trains just missing one another and men with carts going straight toward men with crates. Lilli holds onto Anna, shying from the noise and smoke, but when they come out of the yard they're at the foot of a beautiful hillside town.

White walls, red roofs and palm trees climb the avenues. The haze gives way to gold sun and the smells of flowers and breakfast. An arch over the widest street says SAN PEDRO—PORT OF LOS ANGELES.

"Oh, Richard," Suzanne says. "It's like Italy."

"Better," Richard says. "Let's see where the streetcar goes from."

He leads them across the road. Even the modest houses are beautiful. Who gets to live like this, Anna thinks? Workday hedonists, who retire to California every time they come home. A few of them stroll past the Sunlanders, saying "Morning" with their faces up to catch the sun and sea air. Gerhard points at a building up the hill and Rose starts drawing it. "This isn't a city," Benji says, but Lilli's dazzled.

They walk to a streetcar stop and put their things down under a mimosa tree full of pink blossoms. Anna can't believe she worried so much about the Dvořák. That worry belongs back in Europe, with rust and verdigris and flat wailing people in medieval paintings, not here in the light that falls on Renaissance lambs. Just look how happy everyone is to see it, Astrid and her sun worshipers most of all, like Catholics meeting Jesus without having to die.

Fourteen

Everyone loves California but Lilli loves it more. Just waiting for their streetcar they're surrounded by flowers, some of them as bright as the ones in Panama, others in those same colors but mixed with cream, none of them half as plain and "All right, here's a flower" as the marigolds in Berlin.

If a California streetcar stop has better flowers than a German park, then a California lost-and-found box has better clothes than a German shop, and a California dentist's parlor has funnier magazines than a German library. Lilli bets they do.

Father gives her an American ten-cent piece for her streetcar fare. She trades it for a nickel and five pennies she got in New York, rather than let it go. It's smaller but stronger, she thinks. She kisses it, makes a wish, and puts it deep in her pocket.

A streetcar stops, scarlet with gold lettering, and a handsome conductor with a tanned face leans out. "San Bernardino?" Richard says.

The conductor's the first California person Lilli hears speak and it's like he's singing, even though Benji translates it all in one tone: "That track beside you, change at Do-*ming*-ezz and then at Los *Angle*-ease."

Lilli gets on the first streetcar going their way. Astrid's

teenaged daughter Linda sits next to her on the curved wooden seat, wiggles into place and says, "This feels good on your ass." She leans back, opens the top buttons of her shirt and angles to get the sun on her throat. "We're all on," she says to no one and in German. "Let's go." A second later the streetcar moves out.

The first part of Los Angeles is like a small town, with two-story buildings, men talking on corners and ice-wagon horses dawdling in the heat. Then they pass a field full of big machines dipping at the ground—"oil wells," Benji says—and bad-smelling factories, one of them with hundreds of pigs outside. The Sunland people make faces to show how sick they feel, throttling their own necks and killing themselves with invisible knives. The only other passengers are three California men in coveralls. One scowls at them, one looks straight ahead like he's too tired to care, and the third one smiles at Linda, who smiles back so boldly he blushes and looks away.

The next streets look worn down, like Lilli's neighborhood in Berlin. Girls skip rope by a grocery store. People pour out of a factory and into the beer hall next door. A colored man and lady kiss till his hat knocks hers off, while an echoing voice down the street sings something sad.

They change to a bigger streetcar. Lilli gets a seat by herself and Richard sits in front of her. In a while Jules comes down the aisle, carrying a big flat satchel instead of his concertina, and sits next to Richard.

"New work?" Richard says.

Jules nods. Richard takes the satchel from him but keeps looking out the window. They pass fields of orange trees, then streets that are almost empty—a few houses, a church like a white box, and no trees. "I like this," Richard says. "The money ran out."

"It is nice," Jules says. They watch a fat man in short pants and a jungle hat cross an empty square, his shadow bouncing next to him like balloons. Soon there's nothing but white dirt and a few plants baking in the sun.

"Looks like it's the noble sagebrush for a while," Richard says. He opens Jules's satchel and pulls out a big sheet of paper. Lilli moves up quietly in her seat so she can look over their shoulders.

Jules's paper has bits of other papers stuck to it, half-covering each other—newspaper stories, advertisements, old train tickets and vegetable-can labels, arranged in columns that stop halfway down the page.

"That's so nice, Jules," Richard says.

"Is it?" Jules says.

Richard takes out another one. "Wonderful," he says, but it's just pieces of old maps, letters, bills and cookie wrappers. A face made of photography dots and flyspecks sits on a scrape of yellow paint edged in pencil. The next one has hardly any colors, just five shades of faded brown paper like an old cedar drawer.

"Jules," Richard says, sighing. "You found your way to memory, didn't you? Everyone's memory at once."

"Thank you," Jules says.

What are they talking about, Lilli thinks? They're just jumbles of paper. If those were my memories I'd think I lived in a wastebasket.

Her good feeling from this morning is wearing away. It's been half an hour of white ground with sun blasting down on it. The shadows passing over her make her dizzy. And why is it nice that someone's street ran out of money?

Jules puts his pictures back in the satchel. "I'm glad you got those done," Richard says. "Gerhard says we're going to be clearing the brush for weeks."

"That might be a relief," Jules says.

"Have you talked to him?" Jules shakes his head. "He's terrific. He could build us a city out of aggravation alone."

"Suzanne likes his wife," Jules says. "Suzanne's driving

me crazy, by the way."

Richard looks out the window, pretending not to hear the last part. Maybe saying those weird pieces of paper are wonderful is as nice as he wants to be, Lilli thinks. In a while Jules stands up and goes back to where Suzanne is.

Soon there are trees and telegraph poles, and in another while they come into a town and stop. "San Bernardi-no," the conductor calls out.

Richard steps off with his valise and asks a man, "Hall of Records?"

The man points at a building in the next block. Richard walks over to it while everyone else climbs down into air so hot it gives Lilli chills. There are horses and motor-cars on the street, but almost all the people are under the awnings. The buildings are brick and brown plaster, with waves of heat coming off them as you pass.

A second streetcar brings the rest of the people. Every-one crosses the street to get under the awning of a bank building. Herman and Dara, a skinny couple who like to sit still and stare at things, fold their legs like pretzels on the bank's porch and face a mountain outside the town. Suzanne looks at it and says, "That's an arrow."

"Yes," Herman says.

The mountain has a giant white arrowhead on it, point-ing down. "It's in the book of powerful places," Astrid says. "A sign to the Indians that this was their land."

"The white men kicked them out anyway," Jorgen says. "If it blinked on and off they would have believed them."

Richard comes back from the Hall of Records holding up a piece of paper. "The land is ours," he says, and every-one claps. "They recommended a place to stay, two blocks down and one over."

Lilli walks with Benji as they set out again. "Richard thinks Father's terrific," she says.

"That's fine," Benji says, and points at the buildings.

"Read these signs."

"*Hardware?*" Lilli says in English. "*Core-thowse?*"

"*Courthouse*," Benji says. "Like *haus*."

"*Jail*," Lilli says. "What's that one?"

"*Base Ball Supplies*," Benji reads. "*New York Bakery. Opera House*. Here's an easy one."

"*Y.M.C.A.*," Lilli says, and then sees that Richard's leading them inside.

The Y.M.C.A. is like a school, with the air already breathed. In the lobby Richard talks to a man folding towels, then tells everyone, "We're welcome to stay one night in the transient dormitory, second floor. He says the best food value is in the Chinese district."

Upstairs, past a chapel and a room where men are throwing Indian clubs, there's a long empty hall where the Sunlanders spread their coats on the floor for beds. When they leave for the Chinese neighborhood it's almost dark but still hot, with spirals of bugs in the air. Lilli hopes for pagodas, but it's just wooden houses with no glass in the windows. The Chinese people look like the ones in Berlin but poorer, in long shirts and black pants. One of the men sees Manfred's braid, smiles and holds up his own.

They come to a house with a sign in Chinese and English. Richard reads it out loud: "*Duck Kee Market*. I need the produce experts." He waves Manfred and Tilda over to him.

Lilli asks Tilda, "May I come too?"

"Please do," she says.

The store's dim and cool inside, smelling like mushrooms and the dirt floor. There's no counter, just tables full of plucked chickens and vegetables—carrots, pea pods, and some Lilli's never seen before. The man and lady who work there take some money from Richard for two boxes of vegetables and a bag of rice.

"Thank you," Richard says. "Is there a place where we

can cook?" The man nods. "Will you be our guests?"

"Thank you," the man says.

They go outside, where a few people look at them curiously and follow them down the street. "Where from?" a man asks Richard in English.

"Germany," Richard says.

"Far!" the man says.

"Like you," Richard says. He touches his chest, then gestures around at everyone and says, "Lucky." The man nods at him, smiling, with the last rays of sun on his face. Lilli's California feeling starts coming back. Maybe it's all going to be like this, she thinks—we show up needing food and places to stay and people hand them over.

They stop at an empty lot with a fire pit in the middle, and everyone goes to work at once. Tilda and Patrice get water from a street pump, Father and Rolf build a fire, Herman hangs lanterns in the trees and everyone else cuts up vegetables. Mother and Jorgen stop working for a minute to watch a man play a two-stringed violin that stands up in his lap. A Chinese lady gives Rose a cigarette and she shares it with Frederick.

The Sunland people cook one of their stews, but with the new vegetables instead of squash. The Chinese people let them do it except for criticizing once or twice, and adding a few leaves from plants in the garden behind the lot. When everyone's served themselves Mother pulls Lilli close and says, "If you don't like it you can just eat the rice," but by the time she says it Lilli's licking the last of the sauce from her plate.

Mother and Astrid heat water for washing dishes. Manfred and Tilda are in the garden, following the Chinese people, who go around pointing at plants, shading them with their hats or holding a lantern by them, and motioning with watering cans. Richard buys the leftover rice from the store man for two dollars, the pot included.

As they start off down the street Tilda catches up with Patrice, shows her some packets made of folded newspaper and says, "We got seeds! We can eat those things forever!"

"Oh—may I see those?" Jules says.

He looks at the packets for a second, then runs back toward the yard. In a few minutes he's back, grinning and carrying a roll of Chinese newspaper. He unties the red string around it, unrolls the paper and holds it up. There are columns of black and red Chinese words, a photograph of a graduating class, and advertisements for ladies' dresses and bottled medicines.

All at once Lilli sees what Jules's pictures are about. They're memories, just like Richard said—the way things come back to you, mixed up and faded except for the feelings. That photograph Jules used, a grainy face trying to look at you, is tied up with the sad voice Lilli heard singing in Los Angeles. It always will be.

I know what I'm going to do, she thinks. I'm going to learn about all these Sunland people and what they do, just like I have about Rose and Jules. I'll know a hundred things Benji doesn't, things no one can believe a child knows so well, and when Jules makes a picture with that string in it, the same red as the lanterns, I can go back to that yard any time I like.

Fifteen

The Sunlanders walk down the street at eight the next morning, the air already hot and smelling of onion fields. Richard stops them at a house where a man's trimming hedges, his suit coat folded on a bench by the driveway.

"Excuse me, sir," Richard says in English. "Is there a park nearby?"

The man hesitates, his eyebrows and hedge clippers pointed up.

We look like the circus, Anna thinks. Herman and Dara are the mystic fortune tellers, Patrice the shimmy dancer and Tilda the strong man. Manfred's the clear-eyed weight guesser, Josef the medicine fraud, and Astrid something real and disconcerting. Gerhard and I must do something practical behind the scenes.

The man's eyes go back to Richard, with his clean clothes and calm bearing. He's the circus manager, responsible for any breakage.

"There's a park that way," the man says, pointing. "They're having the Orange Show."

"Do you recommend it?" Richard says.

"I suppose so. Do you like oranges?"

"I've eaten them at Santa Monica," Richard says. "I felt that Adam was had too easily."

The man squints, then nods. "Three blocks down."

He'll talk about us, Anna thinks, at church or a café. *That's right*, people will say one day. *Those were the first ones we saw.*

Richard thanks the man and they walk to the park, which fills a block of downtown. There are white tents on the lawn and a banner Benji translates:

*NATIONAL ORANGE SHOW
TO-DAY FROM 10 A.M.*

The biggest tent's entrance is closed, but the flaps blow open in the breeze. "Let's look," Richard says, and ducks inside.

The others follow him and stop dead. "Does everyone see a train made of oranges?" Jorgen says.

It's a real locomotive, covered in neat rows of halved fruit, rind-side out. The boxcar behind it is armored in half grapefruits and filled with whole ones, their smell so strong it stings Anna's eyes.

The train's on real tracks, mounted on a tall, orange-covered platform. Across the way there's a streetcar like the ones they rode yesterday, plated with tangerines. The passengers are dummies with orange- and lemon-peel hair.

Jules stares at the locomotive. "If artists had balls," he says.

White women in dresses and brown men in work clothes swarm around the displays, putting the last fruits in place. A heap of blemished oranges sits on a tarpaulin. Two workers start to take it away but Patrice smiles at one of the women, points at it and says, "Mrs.?"

The woman looks unsure, then sees the Sunland children. "All right," she says.

"Thank you," Patrice says. The woman turns away, a disdainful look on her face. If anyone but Anna notices it, they don't let it show.

Patrice and Tilda pick up the tarp and lead the others outside. Gerhard's coming out of a tent marked GROWERS' CO-OPERATIVE, looking shocked. "The vegetables," he says. "They're real."

They carry the tarpaulin to the back of the park. Tilda takes a knife from her belt, cuts a bruised orange in half, squeezes the juice onto last night's rice, slices more oranges and gives them to people to squeeze. When there's enough juice, they stir the mixture with their hands. Tilda extends a rice-covered hand palm-down, like a lady in beaded gloves, and says, "*Enchanté*" to make Lilli laugh.

Jules and Suzanne find a rock circle with a grate, gather wood and make a fire. When the rice is warm people dig into it with their hands and eat. Anna's one of the last to get some, and the flavor makes her cough. The rice and oranges are in there, but the principal taste is hands.

They wash the pot at a park tap, fill it with fresh water and put it back on the fire. Manfred has a black tile he bought from the Chinese people last night, with bas-relief trees and clouds on it. He drops it into the water and it blossoms into threads of tea. Rose shares a cup with Anna and Gerhard as she looks around the park.

"We've lost Jorgen and Astrid somewhere," she says. "Linda too, I think." She calls Trudy over. "Dear, do you know where your parents and sister are?"

Trudy shakes her head. "They go off," she says. "In Spain they were gone for three days."

"Tell me you missed them," Rose says.

"All right," Trudy says, and goes back to playing.

When there's no more tea they walk to a horse-cart store, its windows full of shiny carriages with leather seats and fender lamps. A man in shirtsleeves opens the door, looks at them and says, "What's this, now?"

"Excuse us," Benji says in English. "Farm wagons?"

"In back," the man says, closing the door.

He meets them in the yard behind the store and points to a row of sturdy new wagons with steel wheels. "The Paddy Brawler," Benji translates. "Twenty-five dollars each."

Gerhard and Manfred shake their heads. The wagon man says something and Benji translates: "How far are we going?"

"A little past Driscoll," Gerhard says.

"And then?" the man says.

"Clearing the land, farming and hauling."

"Well," the man says, takes them to the end of the yard and points at three old carts whose beds are patched with planks. "They'll take twelve bales of hay in a layer. Twenty dollars for the three."

Rolf and Tilda push down on the wagons' sides and rock them around. "We can brace this," Rolf says. "Build the rims up as well."

"How should we paint them?" Jules says, as Jorgen, Astrid and Linda walk up, their hands full of pale green sprigs.

"It's white sage," Jorgen says. "That whole arrowhead on the mountain is made of it."

"Sacred to the Celts and Indians," Astrid says. "You bind it in a stick and burn it to purify."

"Too late for me," Patrice and Suzanne say at the same time.

"How about divining these carts?" Jules asks.

Astrid holds her sprigs of sage out toward the wagons like dowsing rods. "Boats," she says, and points at the three carts in turn. *"Charon. Trireme. Ship to the Sun."*

"Done," Manfred says, and pays the salesman.

They wheel the carts up the street to the grocery store, where the Sunlanders eat crackers from a barrel as the clerk blinks at them and fills their order: preserves, prunes and dried string beans. "And golden syrup," Rose says. "For the morning bread."

"It's not in the budget," Gerhard says.

"It should be," Rose says. "It's the work ethic of the dissolute." She holds up five fingers for the clerk.

Gerhard surrenders with spread hands, signaling "Do you see what I'm up against?" In its time this gesture has made Anna feel proud and embarrassed at markets like this one, a few bakeries and, once, a shoe store. That's our comedy, she thinks, how we put up with each other. Even Rose shouldn't get to share that.

She takes Lilli to the dry goods store and tells her she can have one thing. After three floors of flannel and cast iron Lilli says, "I think no thank you." When they get outside, Gerhard walks up carrying his own purchases, a compass, a T-square and a book whose title he translates slowly: "*Radford's Portfolio of Building Construction, Showing Every Detail of Structure and Finish for Modern Residences, Barns and Farm Buildings, Also for Miscellaneous Buildings of Every Kind.*"

"What does it mean?" Lilli says.

"Work for all eternity," he says. "Isn't it fine?"

They go back to the Y.M.C.A. for their luggage, fill the Chinese pot with water at a horse pump, and walk east out of town beside the streetcar tracks. A few children run after them laughing but go home when the macadam road turns to dirt.

In no time San Bernardino vanishes from sight, replaced by low hills and unbroken blue sky. Everyone's shoulders loosen, and their walk is light and rolling. Anna feels the ruts and stones underfoot as if she's taking telegraph from the earth itself. Richard's right, she thinks. Cities bear down on the soul.

Gerhard and Herman pull a farm wagon with their suitcases in it, jostling it forward as the road becomes a trace. Patrice yells "Look!" and everyone stops to stare at a red fox till it bolts away into pine scrub.

Then the heat comes in, falling on Anna like ten blankets. After a kilometer her sweat dries and her walk turns unsteady. A shuffle, she decides, stay close to the ground, and then she notices everyone's doing the same and no one's talking.

A streetcar rolls past on the tracks beside the road and a passenger yells something at them. Anna lifts her eyes to the pine trees on the mountain, cool and out of reach. When she looks at the front of the crowd, people shimmer away in the heat waves. This sun's going right through my skin, she thinks, all the way to my blood.

Frieda waves them to a stop. "Can I put my things in a cart if I leave my valise here?" she asks in short breaths.

No one says no. Frieda opens her suitcase, empties it into a cart and drops it beside the road. Other people do the same till the carts are full of belongings.

Anna opens her valise but thinks it's a shame to lose it. Her mother took her to Wertheim's to buy it when she was seventeen, and it's stayed nice because she's never gone anywhere.

Dara the meditator opens her bag and piles the contents neatly in a cart: two pairs of underwear, a dress worn to corn silk, a little Hindu statue, a garden trowel and a bar of soap. She's putting her empty bag on the ground when Frederick calls, "Up here!"

He's at the top of the hillside with five empty pieces of luggage. He leans an open suitcase on a bush so its satin lining catches the sun.

Dara walks up the hill and puts her bag down by the others. "Jules! Collage man!" Frederick calls down. "Help me out!"

Jules carries his empty trunk up the hill, puts it down and starts arranging the luggage into a design. All at once people have energy again, scrambling up the hill with bags for him to place.

Benji dumps his trunk out into a cart, takes it up to Jules, drops it at his feet and walks down again looking angry. "I'll follow procedure," he tells Anna, "but they should consider that some people might want to go home."

Anna takes her suitcase to a cart and adds her things to everyone else's. There are clothes, books, collapsible easels, canvas stretchers, music scores, toe shoes, lederhosen, sun gods, stage makeup, tutus, toys, yarn, fabric, fishing rods, condoms, diapers, zodiac wheels, pots, pans, jars of screws and bolts, fetish underwear, physical culture magazines, Tarot cards, pinochle decks, jewelry pliers, nerve tonics, poppy-seed pods, a hookah, goat canteens, and a stuffed marmot. Frieda's little boy sits on top of the heap like a king. Here and there an axe or a hoe peeks out of the jumble, giving Anna a little reassurance that there's a practical element at work. In less anxious circumstances she'd look right past them to see what everyone's reading.

She takes her suitcase up the hill, where Jules fits it into his mosaic of leather, carpet and cardboard. "Perfect," he says.

They set out again. Anna shies from the sun, a white aspirin vibrating against the blue. Lilli comes over to her with a drugged expression, mouth and eyes half-open. She hooks her hand into the waist of Anna's skirt and stumbles along beside her.

Gerhard and Rolf, the two strongest, pull a cart full of belongings, but it's so heavy they have to stop and let Herman and Tilda take a turn. Gerhard sees Lilli, wets his shirt in the water pot, wipes her head with it and takes her free hand.

Anna thinks of asking Richard to stop the group for a while, but doesn't. We can't slow things down, she thinks. We need to get those mules. Just our family could stop, but we'd be four foreigners on our own, around people like the ones who yelled at us from the streetcar.

At sunset they pull the carts into a clearing by the road and eat a supper of crackers and dried string beans. Anna takes Lilli's head in her lap and wipes salt from her eyes. Gerhard comes over to freshen the cloth on her forehead and asks if she's all right.

"Yes," Lilli says. "It's just my feet."

Gerhard pulls her shoes and socks off, and Anna gasps.

"What is it?" Lilli says. She starts raising her head to look at her feet, but Anna gently pushes it down.

"Nothing," Anna says. "You just have some blisters on there." Really they're so red and swollen she can't believe Lilli hasn't screamed.

Frieda sees the blisters, says a silent "Oh!", walks away and comes back holding a piece of a cactus plant. She cuts it open with a pocket knife, scrapes jelly from it and pats it on the blisters.

Now Lilli does scream. "Sorry," Frieda says.

"No, keep putting it," Lilli says. "It's better."

"*Aloe vera*," Frieda says. "From the Indians. Astrid's got a book about them."

Richard comes over. "What's wrong?" he says. "Oh, those are terrible. Those are expeditionary-force, Lilli."

He kneels next to her, strokes her forehead with the wet cloth, and looks up at Anna and Gerhard. "We would have stopped," he says.

"Yes," Anna says. That lady who let us have the oranges, she thinks, the one whose look said we might let our children go hungry. I thought to hell with her but she was right. About me, anyway.

"We'd have stopped for such amazing blisters," Richard tells Lilli. "We're not like those people in Berlin. Their behavior is shit, but you're done with that now." Lilli's eyes widen at Richard's language, distracted from the pain.

Benji comes over to see what's happening. Anna holds Lilli's hands so her own quit shaking. I have to stop wanting everyone to like me, she thinks. Look how dangerous it is.

In a while they spread their coats on the ground. Anna watches Lilli fall asleep, then lies down next to her. When she closes her eyes she sees the hill where they left their luggage, not now but in a few months, when the sun has turned the suitcases into tatters of wood and fabric that stick in the bushes. It doesn't look like art to people going by, it looks like trash. Anna and Lilli have come to clean it up. Lilli doesn't recognize it and asks what it is. "Work for all eternity," Anna says, "isn't it fine?" but it's blown across the hillsides and they never get it all.

Sixteen

The next morning Benji helps pull the carts, the sun peeling his skin from German white to Indian red. At ten o'clock Manfred waves them to a stop at a long dirt drive where the mailbox is painted with blobby daisies and the words MANNA GROVE. "This is where the mules are," he says.

They walk up the drive through scrub and palm trees to a compound of buildings, all of them whitewashed stucco with tapering domes on top like Russian churches. Even the barn and stable have them, painted in flaking gold or turquoise.

It's so quiet, and the buildings so faded, that Benji thinks the property might be abandoned. Then a man and woman come to meet them, carrying a tub of water with dippers in it. They're in their thirties and thin, the man in a blue tunic and violet pants and the woman in a long white dress, both barefoot. They're smiling but overdoing it, as if their best friends from years ago have just shown up instead of a bunch of strangers.

"Welcome!" the man says. "Nice to see you! I'm Floyd. This is Adeline." They set the tub down. "Please have some water. Have you come a long way?"

"From Germany," Manfred says in English. "I'm Manfred. I wrote to you. You know a friend of Frieda—?" He points to her.

"Of course!" Floyd says. "Germany, my goodness. And you're on your way—"

"We have land on the San Lorenzo Stream," Manfred says. "This is Richard."

"And Ben," Richard says. "He knows the most English." He waves Benji over. Benji comes halfway.

"And you'd like to have mules," Adeline says, smiling.

"Yes," Manfred says.

"We have three that are wonderful. Two geldings and a molly."

"A molly?"

"A girl mule that can have babies," Adeline says. "And geldings are—"

"Yes," Benji says. He turns and gives a digest in German.

"What is the cost?" Father says.

"How about this?" Floyd says. "We're a little short-handed just now. If you'll help us with hay and nectarines today and tomorrow, we'll make you a good price. Is twenty-five dollars a mule all right?"

Manfred looks surprised. "That's very good."

"We'll need to see them," Tilda says.

"Of course," Floyd says. "I think you'll like each other."

"Do you want to rest before work?" Adeline says. "You must be tired."

"I think we can start now," Manfred says.

"Wonderful," Adeline says. "Let's put your things in the long house."

They follow her past a reflecting pool black with algae to a long white building with five blistered domes on top. Adeline opens the door and they walk into a cool, musty room with plaster walls and a soft pine floor. Thirty beds are lined up on one wall, facing a row of curtained windows.

The Sunlanders put their things on the beds and go

outside to work, Lilli and Mother in the orchard, Benji and Father in the hayfield. There are a few windrows started but most of the hay lies flat on the ground, drying with an acid green smell. Benji rakes away from everyone else till Floyd comes and works alongside him.

"Hello, Ben," he says. "This is a fine group of people you have. Is Manfred the leader?"

Benji shakes his head. "Richard."

"Is he a good leader?"

"I don't know," Benji says. "He puts most things to a vote."

Floyd shakes his head, says, "Thank you, Ben," and rakes back the way he came. A few minutes later Adeline comes by, leading the people from the orchard and calling, "Lunch!"

They walk up to a two-story house with a turret and a chipped gold dome. Two long tables are under the trees, set with plates and silverware. As they sit down, three women in white robes and sandals bring food from the house. There's no meat but everything is delicious—melons, nectarines, salad, juice, fresh bread, potatoes, and cutlets made of nuts and beans. Everyone eats seconds and the women bring more, smiling serenely and seeming to glide instead of walking.

"What's on the land you're going to?" Floyd says. "Any buildings?"

"Not yet," Richard says, "but Rose has designs."

"All that and getting crops in?" Floyd says. He finally stops smiling and shakes his head. "So much work."

"They'll have the mules, though," Adeline says.

"Yes," Floyd says, smiling again. "Who's going to see them?"

"I will," Tilda says. "And Benji, for the English?" Benji nods.

"Can I come?" Lilli says.

"Of course," Tilda says before Benji can say no.

"We'll come get you when they're ready," Floyd says.

For dessert there are plums, grapes, verbena tea and cherry ices. As they walk back to work the sun floods down the hills, making the nectarine trees look lit from inside. Benji rakes hay till Floyd comes and says, "Dorothea can show you the mules now, Ben."

Benji finds Tilda and Lilli at the orchard. They get one of their carts and take it up to the paddock, where three mules are tied to the fence. A young woman in denim pants, a checked shirt and boots is combing one of them.

"Hello. I'm Dorothea," she says, and points at the mules. "These are Esther, Luke and Rama." It takes Benji a minute to realize that Dorothea's one of the women who brought them lunch, looking clear-eyed now instead of dreaming. "They're clipped for summer," she says as she unties Luke. "They'll coat up again in the fall."

Tilda kicks a lump of manure. It breaks open bright green. "Good," she says, and goes over to Luke. "His back is straight, you see?" she tells Lilli. "The four legs all the same. The eyes wide awake. This foot, please." She reaches for Luke's foreleg. He lifts it for her, his big eye meeting Lilli's. She smiles shyly at him.

Dorothea gives Luke a piece of carrot and holds his head to her shoulder. "Good boy. He's sixteen hands. He can plow hills where a tractor won't go." She turns to Lilli. "You can pet him if you like."

Lilli puts her hand out and Luke grazes it with his nose. Lilli's mouth falls open and she strokes his neck. She's in love, Benji thinks.

Tilda examines Luke's ears, teeth and eyes. Dorothea hands her a horse collar. "Please," Tilda says to Luke, waits for him to look at her, and slides the collar onto his neck.

"Which harness, please?" Tilda asks Dorothea, who points to one on the fence. As Tilda goes to get it, Luke turns and looks at Benji. His eyes are calm and thoughtful, nothing like Rudy or the bored dray horses in Berlin. He wants someone smart to trade looks with, Benji thinks. I'm not being like Lilli. It's just that those are the most sensible eyes I've seen in weeks.

Tilda brings the harness up next to Luke and says, "Over." Luke steps to the side. Tilda buckles the harness onto him, fits it to the cart's shafts, climbs on the seat, takes the reins and says, "The words?"

"Get *up*," Dorothea says in English. Luke walks around the paddock, pulling the cart's weight easily.

"Good boy," Tilda says. "To stop?"

"*Easy now*," Dorothea says.

Luke stops walking. Lilli pets him and learns how to comb his hair while Tilda tests the other two. "Three champions," she says.

"If you're happy with them they'll be ready to go in the morning," Dorothea says.

"Is it really twenty-five dollars each?" Tilda says.

"We can add in some hay," Dorothea says. "They do fine on grass but they like a few oats if you've got them."

The food at dinner's even better than lunch: spiced mushrooms on soft rolls, three kinds of salad and roasted sweet corn. Dorothea's one of the servers again. She nods at Benji but she's gone back to gliding.

"What did you think of the mules?" Floyd says.

"They're wonderful," Tilda says. "I hate to take them from you."

"Well, you don't have to. We don't turn people away from staying here." He pauses. "Did you come through San Bernardino on your way?" Tilda nods. "Did you see that arrowhead, up on the mountain?"

"Yes," Frederick says. "Why?"

"Because there are signs appearing now that make that arrowhead look like a fluke of nature."

"It is a fluke of nature," Benji says.

"Ben," Floyd says, smiling and shaking his head like he's a wise man. "There have been sixteen ages so far. When the next one starts I want to be under these domes."

"How are you getting sixteen?" Jorgen says.

Benji looks at Richard, who's loading his plate with second helpings and paying no attention to the conversation. "Sleep under them tonight," Floyd says. "See what you think."

"Blessings," Adeline says.

"So blessed," Floyd says.

After dinner they walk up to the long house. Several beds, including Benji's, have big blue books on their pillows. There's a picture in gold ink on the cover, a snake with Hebrew letters in its teeth winding around a circle with four pyramids in it. Behind all that is a big hand with a planet at the end of each finger and a bunch of grapes for the thumb.

Benji lies down on the bed and opens the book. It's densely printed on thin paper and makes no sense at all. A single paragraph refers to lymph, atoms, the Pleiades, Rome, the "living dead," the fourth dimension and the Zoroastrian horoscope. He reads the sentence *Through the Law of Aversion the initiate learns to strive against the Third Light that veils the coefficients of Ptah* and falls fast asleep.

The sound of the door opening wakes him in the middle of the night. No one else stirs.

An old man Benji hasn't seen before comes in, with Floyd and Adeline behind him. He has big staring eyes, a long gray beard streaked with black, and a white robe.

Adeline carries a straw basket. Floyd swings a censer like in church. The smoke smells like burning flowers. Benji pretends he's asleep, with his eyes open just enough to see.

They stand around the first bed, Frieda's. Floyd waves

the censer over her while Adeline sprinkles her with some kind of dust from the basket.

"Better to abide," the old man whispers.

"The heavenly domes," Adeline whispers.

"Dear nectarines," Floyd whispers.

"Location. Location," Adeline whispers. Frieda snores.

Floyd and the others move on to Astrid and Jorgen's bed. Astrid sits up awake as soon as they get there. The old man stares at her. She stares back. "Better to abide," the old man whispers.

"Puh," Astrid says, and nudges Jorgen awake. He blinks at the old man, reaches down on his side of the bed and hands Astrid a match and some of the sage plant they brought down from the mountain. Astrid strikes the match on the bedpost, lights the sage and waves it at the old man, staring him down as her smoke collides with his. He looks away before she does and leads Floyd and Adeline to the next bed down.

A minute later the door opens again, and Rolf and Frederick come in. Each one has his arm around one of the two serving ladies who aren't Dorothea. Their clothes are disarranged. Rolf puts his hand on the bosom of the lady with him. She pushes it away, giggling, till she sees Floyd, Adeline and the old man.

The serving ladies stop where they are, caught in the old man's glare. They pull away from Rolf and Frederick and go over to him. One of them reaches for the dust in the basket but Adeline shoves her hand away.

The old man points at the door and the two serving ladies go outside, looking worried. Rolf and Frederick nod hello to Floyd as if everything's fine, take their pants off and get into their beds.

The old man leads Floyd and Adeline down the row, but they sprinkle the rest of their dust in a hurry and don't whisper anything. Benji keeps his eyes shut when they go past him but lies awake when they're gone.

Breakfast is different from the other meals: overripe nectarines and leftover rolls from the night before. Dorothea's the only one serving. Floyd and Adeline don't say anything. The Sunland people who were asleep last night look puzzled. Rolf, Frederick, Jorgen and Astrid look amused.

After some weak coffee, Floyd and Adeline stand up. "Could you join us, please?" Floyd says. "Richard, Ben and..." He points at Father and Manfred.

Benji and the others go into the house with the turret and climb a spiral staircase to a room with colored windows. The old man with the beard is there, sitting in a high-backed chair under a picture of a moonlit city with a giant gold key hanging over it. He doesn't look as old up close, but his black-eyed stare still bothers Benji. There are boxes of those blue books on the floor.

"Those two girls aren't going anywhere," the old man says. "You can put that out of your mind right now."

"Girls?" Richard says.

"The two you tried to inveigle last night. You're not taking them."

"I know of no such plan," Richard says.

"Two years ago I had thirty-eight people here," the old man says. "You don't know what this valley is like now. Everyone's got a farm here—the White Hindoos, the New Coptics, and now the Yoga Mothers. They've taken almost everyone I had."

"I'm sorry to hear it," Richard says.

"Floyd tells me you people have no beliefs."

"Floyd exaggerates."

"What are your tenets? Tell me one."

"Relax," Richard says.

"Don't tell me how to behave, sir."

"No, that's a tenet. We mean you no harm, believe me.

About the mules—I think the price was..."

"Twenty-five dollars each," Father says.

"That was when we thought you might stay," Adeline says.

"Those mules are worth—" Floyd says.

The old man waves him quiet. "The essence of a deal is unchanging," he says. "It is eternally a deal."

Richard takes out his wallet. "And how much for a book?" he says.

"A book?" the old man says. "You don't want my book."

"I do," Richard says. "I only had it a short time but it looks like it covers some ground."

"Well, yes," the old man says, his eyes softening. "It does. I can do three-fifty."

Richard pays him for everything, picks up a book and leads his group down the stairs, shaking his head. "They're still on yoga here," he says.

When they get outside Lilli's by the reflecting pool, helping Tilda hitch the mules to the carts. There are two bales of hay in each one, along with everyone's belongings. Tilda's on the seat of Luke's cart, Manfred on Rama's and Frieda on Esther's.

Lilli walks next to Luke as they start down the driveway, stroking his neck and speaking endearments. They're by the palm trees when he stops so suddenly he almost throws Tilda off her seat.

Manfred and Frieda stop their carts. Tilda pulls Luke's lines and says, "Get *up*," but Luke stands still and won't look at anyone.

"Get *up*," Benji says in English. "Come on, Luke. Down the road."

"It may be he hasn't been past here before," Manfred says. "That's the problem sometimes."

"Then what do you do?" Benji says.

"We can try some things. Take some hay and walk."

Benji takes an armload of hay from the cart. It weighs more than it looks like and itches his sunburned arms. He backs away from Luke, who doesn't move. Frederick comes up behind the mule, lifting his hands to push. "Don't," Tilda says, and Frederick jumps back a second before Luke kicks.

"Luke, it's fine," Lilli says, and strokes his neck. "We're going to our land. It's beautiful there. Please?"

"Maybe if he sees the other two go?" Manfred says.

"Maybe," Tilda says.

Manfred and Frieda start their carts. Everyone goes down the driveway but Luke, Tilda, Benji and Lilli. Yesterday the mules nickered at one another and rubbed heads, but now Luke watches the others walk away without blinking. In a while Tilda unhitches him. He stands there a minute, then turns and goes back up the drive.

Tilda picks up one of the cart's shafts and looks at Benji, who takes the other. The hay makes it heavier and it doesn't even move till they dig their feet in. After fifty meters Benji's legs are burning. He looks over at Tilda. She nods at how hard it is and smiles to encourage him.

She's more rational than most of them, he thinks. He was scared of her at first, the way she looked like a man with bosoms, but it makes him ashamed to think of that now. When they go through a town she hides in the middle of the group. Who knows what's been done to her for looking the way she does?

He imitates her walk, bringing his bottom down and his knees up. It makes him stronger but he can barely breathe.

People are always saying someone's "a real man" who does "a man's job." Benji wonders if someone will ever say that about him. Herr Fleischer at school said not to say *kerl* because it's slang, like *guy* in English. Of course we should take care with German, Benji thinks, but to have a word that spares you from specifying *man* or *boy*—how often is a language so thoughtful?

The others are waiting under a scorched juniper by the mailbox. Astrid and Jorgen sit in the dust, reading the book Richard bought from the old man.

Benji lets go of the cart, shakes hands with Tilda, and bends over to catch his breath. That was all right, he thinks. I'm stronger than I know. A little, anyway.

They turn onto the road, going east. For a while Lilli walks with her head down, inconsolable about losing Luke, but then Rama walks up next to her. In half an hour she's transferred her affections to him entirely, petting his face and calling him her sweet boy, till Benji thinks Luke got out of this just in time.

Seventeen

"I wish they'd worked us harder," Gerhard tells Anna. "I wanted to see where the talent lies."

They're just behind the group, walking through dry hills at mid-morning. He lowers his voice. "I'd say Rolf and your friend Frieda are the strongest backs. Manfred and Tilda the best organizers. Herman and Dara move the fastest."

"Jules picked a lot of fruit," Anna says. "He said to me you can't make art all the time or you go mad. He said he's done that twice so far."

"That's reassuring," Gerhard says.

"He said Richard pulled him out of it."

That supposed skill of Richard's again, Gerhard thinks. If I start hearing voices I'll tell them to go bother him.

"Suzanne works pretty well," he says. "Josef works if people are watching."

You see, he thinks, everything's in order. My wife and I are in harmony, no one else is in the picture except insofar as we gossip about them, and our children are adjusting to the plans we've made with their interests at heart. Lilli's up ahead, looking happy with her new friends the mules and two pairs of my socks on her feet. Benji's not as cheerful, but he'll have school soon.

Everyone turns quiet as the walk grows long. People

pull filched rolls and nectarines from their pockets but those are gone soon. The heat beats down and Lilli starts wilting again.

Then there's something new up ahead, a mass of green foliage with dots of orange like Christmas balls. When they get closer they see it's a citrus grove on both sides of the road, with a town just beyond it.

Frederick climbs a fence, stretches to reach a tree, tears an orange from it, throws it to Richard and grabs another. The third one goes straight for Gerhard's head, but he catches it and digs his thumb through the peel. The spray of oil turns to pure smell in the heat, like candy crossed with benzene. He digs further and the acid gets under his nails, stinging where he scratched them on hay. When he eats a piece, the taste, the sting and the color fuse into one sensation. This is where water appears in the landscape, he thinks, therefore this flavor, therefore money. He shares the rest of it with Lilli.

A sign says WELCOME TO DRISCOLL as the dirt road becomes a paved, palm-lined street of houses. The town's a California postcard come to life, with a Parthenon of a train station and the green crowns of a thousand palm trees.

"Not a bad place to come for cigarettes," Richard says to Rose as they walk around a corner. A policeman's standing there with his hands up to stop them. A few people bump into each other.

"Hold it there," the policeman says. "Is this a show?"

"No sir," Richard says, stepping forward. "We—"

"Don't tell me it's not a show and then put a tent up."

"We have no tent."

A man in a blue-green business suit and a skimmer hat comes up beside the policeman and puts a hand on his arm. "Bob," he says, then turns to the Sunlanders. "Good afternoon. Tyrus Whitliff. Alderman."

"They say it's not a show," the policeman says.

"Richard Weiss," Richard says. "Farmer." He takes out the sheet of paper he got in San Bernardino and hands it to Whitliff. "The deed to our land."

Whitliff looks the deed over, then the group. "Where do you folks come from?"

"Germany," Richard says.

"Are you a... lodge?"

"Only friends."

A few people have stopped on the sidewalks to watch. Whitliff hands the deed back. "And, now, all the way over in Germany, you decided this was the place for you?"

"Yes," Richard says. "Exactly. Because Germany—" He sighs. "A hundred years ago, Germany had all one needed. Great music and poetry, great thought—but great inventions too, and businesses. You can't eat philosophy."

"What I'm asking—" Whitliff says.

"But that spark never stays in one place, does it?" Richard says. "One day you look around and it's moved on. Where did it go? Well, it's people—that's all it is. When people hear a place is exceptional—"

He planes his hand through the air to trace the light falling on buildings around them. "Tell me about that one," he says, nodding at a brick villa a block long, with an arcade of arches and a gleaming oculus window.

"The public library," Whitliff says.

Richard nods. "And coming outside in the morning here—do you get tired of it?"

"No, I suppose—"

"You see," Richard says. "But more than anything, we're here to farm."

"Have you seen your land?" Richard shakes his head. "You have a lot of work to do," Whitliff says.

"Well—we don't pay one another."

"That might help." Whitliff studies the group again. "I

guess we'll see you here from time to time. Busy though you'll be."

"We look forward to it," Richard says.

"This is a peaceful town," Whitliff says.

"One feels it," Richard says.

"Do you have business here today?"

"The farm supply."

"They'll treat you fairly," Whitliff says. "Two blocks down and one to the right."

"Thank you."

"People on the sidewalk and animals up by the curb," the policeman says.

"Of course," Richard says.

"And I know you'll want to see your land before it's dark," Whitliff says.

The businessman operating the policeman like a lathe, Gerhard thinks. The same as anywhere.

The Sunlanders walk to a big shed with FARM SUP-PLY painted over the door. The farmers going in and out, like the cars and wagons parked in front, look prosperous.

Manfred tucks his braid down the back of his shirt. "Coming in?" Gerhard asks Tilda.

"Better not to," she says, staying deep in the group as a few teenaged boys stare at them from across the street. "Can you see if they have that cultivator in the catalogue— the Little Jap?"

Gerhard nods and follows Manfred inside. The dirt floor is filled with tools, machines and sacks of feed. A man in a string tie stands behind the counter, a rack of farming manuals on the wall in back of him. Gerhard asks him about the Little Jap in his modest English.

"That's Sears and Roebuck," the man says. "You send your money to Chicago and meet the train when it comes. Then one day you come here for fertilizer and we're shut down because everyone's money's in Chicago." He nods at a cultivator on the floor. "Or you can take that one with you today. Does twice the job and we're here when you need us. It's your free will either way."

Gerhard buys the machine and rolls it out of the store, the harrows scraping lines in the dirt. He wheels it over to Tilda.

"This is the Lazy Finn," he says. "The man recommended it."

"Oh," Tilda says. "Well, he must know."

"He said it's better," Gerhard says.

"It's probably true," Tilda says. "He must want us coming back."

"He said he does."

"That's good, then."

"In a way he did."

Tilda rests her hand on the handle. "That enamel's fine," she says.

"Yes," Gerhard says, and puts his hand down next to hers. I'll wind up married to everyone, he thinks.

They go on to the grocery store and then back to the highway, which drops them into a valley of small farms and pastures. On the walk that follows, Gerhard watches the quality of the farmland decline from its high point in Driscoll.

The terrain's been changing like this all along their trip. There are places where his shoes sink nicely into loam, but a short walk later they're on land with no forgiveness for the farmer. Now they're passing through the second-most promising sort of soil, now the third, and he's hoping to get to their land before the water and color dry away altogether.

At five o'clock the people near the front start shouting. When Gerhard and Anna catch up, everyone's standing by a wire fence with a sign that says 2900 HWY. 38 - SOLD. On the other side of the fence are a lumpy meadow and a stream flowing down from green hills to pass under a bridge in the road. Black mountains streaked with snow make a rim in the distance.

Manfred and Rolf take axes from Rama's cart, chop through the fence wires at one of the posts, bend the fence back to make a gate, and walk onto the land. The children run past them, then the grownups, wheeling around to look at the live oaks and outcrops.

Gerhard walks through the weedy grass with Anna. It's possible, he thinks. Just barely.

The crowd climbs the tallest hill, orange dirt crumbling under their feet. They make a ragged line along the crest, looking down at corrugated slopes and muddy washes. The sun shines red on waving grass hillsides in the west. "It's beautiful," Anna says.

Rose walks up next to them, drawing in her sketchbook. She makes a few quick lines for the land in front of them, adds boxes for buildings, holds the drawing up and points to the real places. "The big hall. Richard's house. The drying shed—"

"Dears," Richard says. Everyone turns to look at him. "That's terrific, isn't it?" He points to the hills. "I couldn't have pictured it, but I know it on sight. That's what home is.

"Whatever we do from now on, we have to make room for company. The Americans have half the idea already. Not all of them, but enough. Those children in San Bernardino, running away with us—they turned back, but when they're a little older you won't be able to keep them away.

"Till then"—he waves at the hills again, as if he's presenting a gift—"we wake up every day to this."

He turns to go down to the meadow. "May I add something?" Gerhard says.

Richard hesitates, then turns back around. "Of course."

"Thank you," Gerhard says. He points down at a massive overgrowth of trees, vines and brush that blocks the stream from view. "That's the farm. We need to start clearing it now and not stop till the crops are planted. We need axes, mules and shovels down there, right away."

Everyone looks at Richard. His eyes flicker once, and then the serenity returns. "Yes," he says.

As they walk down the hill Gerhard goes over to him and says, "I hope you didn't mind that."

"Do I mind not being the one to tell them about tiring chores? Not a bit," Richard says, but when they get to the meadow he picks up an axe before Gerhard can hand him one.

They lead ten people to the woods. From the edge of the thicket they can hear the stream but not see it. The wall of vines and branches is meters thick, threaded with trees that died looking for the sun. The good news is a bramble of blackberries, a few weeks from ripe.

Lilli and Tilda bring the mules down with empty carts. "Anything that looks like lumber goes in this one," Gerhard says. "Firewood in there."

Manfred pulls a sampling of weeds and holds them up. "We'll start a compost pile over there with this kind. These two we feed to the mules or plow under."

Gerhard drives his axe through vines and into a tree trunk. A curtain of dead plants crashes at his feet and the relief of work flows into him like a drug. The others go at it just as hard, even Richard and Benji. In an hour the stream sounds louder and twilight shines through the vines, showing twisted trees with bark that hangs in strips.

Lilli and Tilda unhitch the mules and lead them to the stream, squeezing between trees. The water's four meters wide, a spring flow running clear over tan stones. The mules drink, and Frieda and Astrid fill buckets with water.

Gerhard starts up the hill next to Rose. "Where you

talked about putting the big hall—" he says, but then Benji comes over to them.

"Father, may I speak to you for a minute?"

"All right." He stops walking. Rose moves aside and waits.

"I don't know if I should go to school," Benji says.

"You—why not?"

"Because everyone's going to work so hard here. They won't like me being away all day."

Gerhard steals a look at Rose, who's close enough to hear them. We know how these people feel about fathers bossing children around, he thinks. What kind do they wish they had? As different from my father as you can get without being ridiculous.

"Well," he tells Benji. "It's your decision."

Benji blinks. "It is?"

"Yes. You should do what you want"—Benji looks even more confused—"but I don't think people will think badly of you if you go to school and then help out here. They like you."

"Oh."

"You were good with the carts. And the axe."

"Thank you," Benji says, sounding as grateful as he is mystified. In fact this doesn't feel bad, Gerhard thinks. My own father would have knocked me in the dirt by now. You don't want people thinking *ill* of you? *I'll* show you ill.

"So it's settled, then?" he says.

"I'm sorry," Benji says. "It's—?"

"You'll go to school and help when you get home."

"All right. Yes."

Gerhard puts his arm on the boy's shoulder as they walk up the hill. Rose keeps her same distance, possibly impressed.

Back in the meadow there's a fire and supper, hard biscuits with canned beans. When they finish eating Manfred stands and opens a book.

"This is Australian," he says, "from the aborigines," and reads out loud:

"The people are making a camp of branches in that country at Arnhem Bay.

With the forked stick, with the rail for the whole camp, the 'Mandzikai people are making it.

They are thinking of rain, and of storing their clubs in case of a quarrel.

People of the clouds, living there like the mist; like the mist sitting resting with arms on knees..."

He finishes the poem as the sky turns dark. Gerhard follows Anna and Lilli to their sleeping spot, takes his shoes off, lies down between them and asks Anna, "Can you bake bread in a pit?"

"I think so," she says.

"If you can do that we're all right. Because we know the mules are taken care of." He looks at Lilli, who smiles.

Living like mist, he thinks. Hope for corn and tomatoes to come in fast. Anna reaches for his hand. When he turns over to give it to her the stars fly apart like fireworks, a thousand white and one orange, Rose's cigarette across the field.

Eighteen

Benji sits up by the fire worrying about the school entrance examinations. He sees himself standing in a wood-paneled room like a judge's chambers, facing a table where six frowning proctors in dark suits look him over. "Euclid's fourth postulate," one says.

Benji knows it but his throat closes. One proctor leans over to another and Benji hears him whisper, "German curriculum." They stifle a laugh.

The fire's dead. Benji stands up, finds the mule cart with his things in it, gets his school bag and checks its contents: pencils, notebooks, compass, the coat and knee pants Mother made him, and a white shirt whose smell of bluing makes him miss Berlin so much he's dizzy. He puts the bag under his head to sleep.

When he wakes up in the morning he's alone in the meadow. He goes back to the cart for his soap and towel and walks down the hill.

In the woods by the stream Mother and Astrid are mixing dough, using freshly cut stumps for kitchen counters, while Frederick digs a pit. Everyone else is chopping trees and piling the lumber into Rama's cart.

Benji puts his bag on a rock and picks up an axe. "What about school?" Father says.

"I have a little time."

"Don't cut these trees too short. When they're dead a while we can push them over and pull the roots up."

Benji walks through a cut in the vines and finds a tree that's broken itself in half. The top hangs by a hinge of white xylem, too high to reach. He backs up, runs at the tree, jumps, swings the axe and stumbles back. He's running toward it a third time when it comes apart with a noise like gunshots.

Benji jumps back, trips, falls and drops the axe. The top of the tree crashes down a finger's width from his head. Day One of school: the basics of death.

He stands up shaking, wrestles the tree into his arms, and takes it to Rama's cart. He's starting to throw it in when Rolf walks up with one three times as big that makes the cart bounce off the ground.

Benji throws his in after it. Rolf nods at him and he nods back. Frieda comes over, marks an *X* on Rolf's log with an axe, looks Benji's over and marks it too. "For the barn," she says.

The nod and the *X*, Benji thinks. Those are my armor today.

Voices and splashing noises come from the stream. Benji picks up his bag, takes out his towel and soap, shows them to Frederick and asks, "Which way for men?"

Frederick smiles. "Oh, University," he says. "Your prayers have been answered." He points both ways, up the stream and down.

Benji undresses, steps into the water, starts upstream and stops. Patrice and Tilda were hidden by a tree but they're in front of him now, naked and hugging as they soap each other's backs. They see Benji and sing out good mornings.

Benji's penis starts to get stiff. He turns away, furious at himself, and splashes cold water on it eight or ten times. "Refreshing," he says out loud, then hopes they didn't hear him.

He keeps going down the stream. Herman and Dara, the couple who stare at the distance, are washing together. They're both mortally thin but it's still stimulating. That's a husband and wife, Benji thinks. That's sacred. You don't get stiff around that. Herman should beat you up if you do.

He splashes himself again and hurries past them, thinking he's finally alone till he turns a corner and finds Jorgen's daughter Linda, barely older than he is, standing in his way with water on her breasts and soap in her vagina hair. He looks up at the trees.

"What's the matter?" she says. "Don't you like human beings?"

"I have school," he says. She stands aside just enough to let him pass.

He wades thirty meters, washes, walks up on shore, stands on prickly leaves and dries off. I'll get used to it, he thinks. No I won't, and I have ninety minutes till I face the proctors.

He puts his school clothes on and walks out of the woods. "University," Frederick calls, taking a cooking grate out of the pit with four loaves of flat bread on it. "For your studies." He nods toward the stream. "Your *further* studies."

Benji opens his school bag and Frederick slides a loaf into it. Mother comes over, kisses his cheek and fixes his hair with her fingers. "You're so smart," she says. "They won't turn you away."

He walks up to the meadow, where Manfred's writing something on a piece of paper. He puts it down where the sunlight meets the shade and weights it with a rock. Benji reads it: the time of day. There are two others where the sun stopped earlier.

Manfred picks up a handful of dirt, puts it in a drinking

glass and adds liquid from a bottle. The dirt fizzes. He holds the glass up and studies it. "Alkaline," he says. "Also clay. Compost helps with that. Sulfur in extreme cases."

Benji nods at the bottle. "Which chemical, please?"

"Vinegar," Manfred says, and holds the glass where Benji can smell it. "For acid it's baking soda."

"Thank you," Benji says. There's no telling what the proctors might ask.

He walks over the hill and sets out for Driscoll. Irrigation ditches flash silver in the sun. A farmer drives a tractor standing up, the white smoke fluttering into the sky. John Jay, Benji thinks. Potash, Springfield, Brownian motion.

In an hour he's at the school, a green-plastered building surrounded by playing fields. A frieze above the doorway shows a teacher with her hands on the shoulders of a boy and girl, all looking into the distance, a test tube on one side of them and a cow on the other. The real children, boys and girls in separate yards, are throwing balls around, teasing and laughing.

The bell rings. Benji follows the children inside and sees the school office, a yellow room with picture windows onto the corridor. There's no door to knock on so he walks in. The smell of ink and sack lunches makes him even more homesick than his shirt.

A lady with her spectacles on a necklace comes to the counter and asks if she can help him. "Yes, please," he says, handing her his grades from home and a letter he wrote in English and signed Father's name to.

2900 Highway 38, Driscoll, California

Sirs,

This will introduce my son, Benjamin Lanz, who applies to enter your school. I am unable to present him personally due to the press of my business.

He has completed seven years of study in Berlin, Germany, and is versed in mathematics, physics, English, chemistry, literature (including American) and history (also). He is free of illness. Please show him every consideration.

Yours sincerely,
Gerhard Lanz

"How old are you?" the lady says.

"Nearly thirteen."

She looks at his grades. "I'll have to get Mr. Richman to read this. He's the German teacher."

"Thank you," Benji says, and pauses. "I ask only for a chance."

"A chance of what?"

"To be admitted."

The lady looks confused. "Of course you're admitted," she says. "If you don't come here they send an officer for you."

"Oh." She copies his name onto a form. "Is there electrical engineering?" he says.

"In the building?" She looks at a light bulb overhead.

"As a course."

"There's science."

"All sciences in one?"

"Yes."

"I would like to take that, please."

"You *have* to take it," she says, as if he's dense.

"I'm sorry," he says. "A man from Iowa misled me. The Hawkeye State."

The lady looks at him. "I need a doctor and I need a religion," she says.

"Miss?" She points to the form. "Oh. Is Lutheran all right?"

"Certainly."

"We don't have a doctor yet. Is there one you recommend?"

"Your parents know what's best for you," she says. Benji doesn't correct her. "We'll put you in the Ungraded Room for now. Just till we know where you go."

"Thank you."

She directs him to a classroom at the far end of the building. When he walks in, the teacher, a lady of thirty, is asking the students, "Would anyone like to try? No?"

The students turn to look at him. There's a boy with a smirk and a turned-up coat collar, another who's whittling something, and a hulk whose knees rise above either side of his desk. There are girls too, one with a rough red face and one who's asleep.

"Hello," the teacher says.

"Hello, Miss," Benji says. "I'm Benjamin Lanz. I was told to come here."

"All right. Let's welcome Benjamin. Where are you from?"

"Germany."

"Your English is very good."

"Thank you." Someone in the back snorts.

"I'm Miss Riley," the teacher says. "Would you sit here, please?"

She points to a desk in the middle of the room. Benji sits down, gets his notebook out and dips his pen. Miss Riley writes a problem on the board: *12x + (5-2)9 = 87.* "What is *x*?" she says. "You can write it down if you like."

Benji writes *5* in his notebook, then closes it. "Anyone?" Miss Riley says.

The girl behind Benji points at him and says, "He's done it."

"Benjamin?" Miss Riley says. He doesn't answer. "It's all right if you're wrong," she says, and comes to his desk.

He opens his notebook. "*Five*," she says softly. "Yes. Thank you."

The whittling boy turns to scowl at him. Benji keeps quiet for the rest of the morning. At 11:30 a bell rings. "Benjamin, that's our lunchtime," Miss Riley says. "One half-hour."

The students take out lunch pails and paper bags and go into the hall. When Benji comes out, the giant, the whittler and the red-faced girl block his way. "Why didn't you say the answer?" the girl says.

"I'm sorry?" Benji says.

"Sorry for what?" the giant says.

"Was it so we wouldn't look stupid?" the girl says.

"No," Benji says.

"We are stupid," the girl says. "What do you think we're doing in there?"

"I'm sorry," Benji says.

"Stop saying you're sorry or you will be sorry," the whittler says.

"All right," Benji says. They laugh and let him go by.

Outside, children are eating and playing ball. Benji finds a bench by the boys' yard, takes the bread from his book bag with shaking hands, brushes some dust and ash off it and starts to eat.

After a few bites four boys come over, more reasonable-looking than the ones in his class. He slips the bread back into his bag.

"What's your name?" a boy says.

"Benjamin," Benji says. "Ben."

"Where are you from?"

"Germany."

A girl comes over and says, "Are you in the Ungraded Room?"

"Yes."

"They won't keep you there long."

"Thank you," Benji says.

"Boys' side," one of the boys says. The girl shrugs.

Another boy points at a bench nearby. "Do you want to eat with us?"

"Thank you," Benji says, but doesn't move.

"I have liverwurst if you want to trade."

"Thank you," Benji says again, but keeps his dusty bread in his bag.

"All right," the boy says after a minute. "You be good."

The children walk away, and a minute later the bell rings. Back in the Ungraded Room Benji thinks of liverwurst and his stomach rumbles. The giant laughs and Miss Riley says "*James*" so sharply that for a second it's like being back in Berlin.

When he gets back to Sunland, people are unloading timber from a mule cart while Father and Rose make string lines for a building. Benji changes into old clothes, washes his good shirt in the stream, hangs it in a tree, pulls brush for an hour, adds it to the compost pile and asks Father what to do next.

"Digging is in fashion," Father says. "Outhouses, ditches and a saw pit. Your choice."

He gives Benji a shovel with a splintered handle and the front of the blade worn off. Benji digs on the saw pit past dark, stops when he's exhausted, and gets the last plate of supper. I'll bet that's as hard as any of those kids at school work, he thinks.

The next day he makes a golden syrup sandwich and eats all of it at lunch, returning any looks that come his way. In class he answers Miss Riley's questions and ignores the other children's stares. At the end of the day a lady comes in and says, "Benjamin Lanz? I have your book list and schedule for ninth grade. You'll be moving to the high school. Come with me, please."

"How old are you, Fritz?" the whittler says.

"Almost thirteen," Benji says. The children make disgusted noises as he leaves.

The lady leads him behind the school to a building marked DISTRICT BOOK STORAGE and leaves him there. He gets the books on the list, then finds the grade-school books and takes as many as he can without making his bag look suspicious. On his way home he stops at the farm supply store and buys a book with some money he changed in New York.

When he gets back to Sunland he helps Rolf drag a log to the pole barn site, where Father and six others are lining foundation trenches with planks. They're starting back to the woods when a man walks up from the road. "Is one of you the manager?" he says in English.

Benji translates. Rolf points at Father.

"My name's Musgrave," the man says. He wears a sackcoat suit, pointed boots and smoked eyeglasses. "You need a well."

"We're going to dig one," Father says.

"I don't think so," Musgrave says. "The water's two to three hundred feet down. You need to drill for it like you drill for oil. You won't last here without it."

"We have the stream."

"Sir, where you come from, you have winter, is that right? When nothing grows, and you eat what you canned? We call that summer here. Your stream's going to be dust. That's when you need the well. I'll be honest, I can't get you enough in summer to irrigate. This area's been drilled to kingdom come. You can drink and wash, though."

"I bring a steam engine, a derrick and a carbonate drill. We use TNT in the end stages, perfectly safe if you know your business. You can ask your neighbors about me. I've drilled every place around here."

Rolf goes to get Richard. If it wasn't for school I could watch them drill, Benji thinks. They might even let me help.

He retrieves his book bag from the woods, looks for Lilli and finds her tying Rama the mule to a tree. "I have some things for you," he says, and hands her the books he stole from the school: *McGuffey's Eclectic Reader, Arithmetic Four* and *The Pilgrim's Progress in Words of One Syllable.* "We're going to have school here."

"I don't want to," she says.

"You have to. If all you learn is what they know here, you'll be hopeless." He brings out *Mules,* the book from the farm supply store, holds it up so Rama can see the mule's face on the cover, then shows Lilli the inside.

"This tells how mules help in the army," he says. "This is how to make them obey. This is what to do when they're sick. This is the story of a mule named Arrow, who was as smart as any man."

"But it's in English," Lilli says.

"You'll learn it," Benji says. "And arithmetic." He shows her a table on weight and feeding. "We'll do a little every day."

"You didn't like me coming to your lessons on the ship," she says.

"I know," he says. "I was stupid." He says it without shame, like the girl from the Ungraded Room, and Lilli looks so surprised you'd think he never admits to anything.

Nineteen

In May everything runs out at once. The well's not finished yet, and Anna has to lay pails on their side in the stream to get water for baking. The last three sacks of flour from town are bought with personal savings and blackberries.

When the flour's gone, Anna goes to the woods and finds Astrid gathering acorns. She drops a pile of them in a pot of boiling water and hands Anna a book called *The Wondrous Forest Pantry*. The page headed *Acorn Flour* calls for the nuts to be boiled, cooled, shelled, soaked, boiled twice more, dried, dehydrated and finally ground, over the course of five days.

"You see?" Astrid says, and waves an arm over the forest floor. "A world made of flour."

Anna gathers acorns till eleven and takes a tray of coffee to the farm. People are bent over in the dirt, weeding vegetables too frail to touch.

That night at supper each person gets one dried pear, three canned string beans and five blackberries. Benji looks reproachful but Lilli's expression hurts Anna more, that soft-eyed bafflement at something like this happening to people who've done nothing wrong.

The food drops into Anna's stomach, worse than not eating at all because the juices start and now she's starving. We've made an awful mistake coming here, she thinks.

I've put off thinking so but we have.

Astrid stands up, opens her book and points to illustrations as she addresses the crowd. "Mustard greens," she says. "I've seen these all over the slopes." Anna has too, but with blighted leaves. "And prickly pear. And this one"—something that looks like private hair with barbed spikes on it—"there's a banquet of this, just up the stream."

In the mornings that follow they gather plants, wait out the worst heat under the oaks, then forage again till dark. A few people sneak over a neighbor's fence at night to get agave stalks. They mix it all into a stringy stew that tastes like hunger itself but gives them enough strength for the next day's search.

Don't take this so hard, Anna thinks. These other women aren't. They've had more practice being hungry. She digs up greens with them, listening to their jokes and trying to take their attitude.

"I came *so* close to going to Basel this summer," Suzanne says.

"*I* could have had an apprenticeship with Laban," Patrice says, putting the back of her wrist to her forehead in mock drama.

"This is the best I could do and these are the only people who'll have me," Rose says. "Top *that*."

When Benji's school lets out he saws planks and digs trenches, staying out in the heat the way Gerhard does. In June the well is running and they run an irrigation line to the crops, but by late July they're taking water to the field in buckets. The weeds in the streambed turn to dust and blow away, and they water the crops from the well till there's only enough to drink.

In August the small children look glassy-eyed and the jokes stop. Frieda, carrying little Stefan, walks up to Richard one night and says, "We can't do this, Richard. We have to go back."

"This is the bad part," Richard says. "We'll get through it. We have food—"

"Stefan can't digest it. He's two years old. He's getting weak." She strokes the boy's arms. "How is this saving the world, exactly? Was there even a plan to begin with?"

Richard closes his eyes. "All right," he says. "You're right. In the morning I'll go to the neighbors, or I'll go into town, and I'll say, 'Please, we didn't know what we were doing, we have children here and—'"

"We'll be arrested," Gerhard says. "The children will be put in a home."

Stefan starts to cry. "Sorry," Gerhard says. "I mean we don't have to do that. We can hire out. There must be a farm that will take a few of us. I'll go, and Rolf..."

Rolf nods. Richard looks at Gerhard but doesn't ask out loud. "...and Richard," Gerhard says. "Meet me at the road at five."

The next night Rolf and Gerhard come home in the dark with three bottles of milk, a bushel of dried apples, a sack of flour and two noisy chickens. Richard trails behind them, sits on a log and says, "*Day's Work is a Grand Chew*" in a dazed monotone.

"What's that?" Jules says.

"An advertisement on the farmer's barn," Rolf says. "For tobacco. It was in our sight all day."

"*Day's Work*," Richard says. Gerhard smiles.

They feed the children milk and apples and go to their coats to sleep. "Rolf was good," Gerhard tells Anna quietly. "Richard was all right. I could see he had to come with us. He says Frieda's child is his. He says every meeting of bodies is a chance at enlightenment." Anna looks at him. "Or some such excuse," he says, and falls asleep so fast she has to take his shoes off.

Near the end of July four little tomatoes appear on the vines and everyone comes out at dawn to stare at them.

When the rest emerge a few days later birds attack them, and gophers pull half the bean plants underground. People stay up three nights making wire cages, which save just enough plants to eat and can. They eat half the corn and dry the rest for soup and flour.

In September, with well water, bartered labor and their own crops, a kind of normal life emerges. On the morning of the twelfth Anna gets up at four and goes to the meadow, hearing owls, coyotes and the snorting mules. She bakes mostly by herself these days because Astrid's making the sun rise and Rose is busy planning buildings with Gerhard, all day and into the night.

The chickens they got for hiring out are in a wire pen, waiting for Rose's grand henhouse to be built. Anna collects six eggs, takes them to the oven, breaks them into a bowl and puts the shells in the compost pile. She fills two bowls at the well, leaves them on the oven to warm, and gets cornmeal and seeds from the storage shed.

At first light she sees people on the hill, putting the sun god back in his cabinet. She scatters yeast on the water, the oven singeing her skin. After sunrise the heat comes in, slowing her down as she mixes dough. When they were eating weeds her skirts got loose, but she's becoming the jolly baker now. You eat what you're making to check the taste, or to clean it off your hands, or because sometimes you just want what's bad for you.

Astrid and Lilli come down from the hill and Anna asks Lilli to stay the morning. "I can't," she says. "We're pulling a stump out." She's barefoot, in a shiny saffron dress Patrice made her that she wears every day. Her hair's in braids, with flower chains like Dara's. Working the mules has made her hands strong. She kneads dough without moving her body, better than Anna can do, but after half an hour she leans down, rubs dust on her hands and leaves.

Astrid brushes egg wash on the rolls. "I think Frieda's

having a liaison," she says. "I don't know who with."

"Where do they find the time?" Anna says. "Everyone's working till they drop."

"That's just when these things happen," Astrid says. "The harder the work, the stronger the animal spirits."

Somehow people have gotten in the habit of leaving their small children with Anna when they go to work. She's putting the first loaves in the oven when Frieda brings Stefan. Rolf comes a little later and leaves three-year-old Karin. By 7:30 there are five lightly raised children chasing one another around, throwing dirt, stealing nuts, crying and needing their diapers changed.

Astrid takes a tray to the people digging beds for Chinese vegetables. Anna carries one to the granary site, fighting to keep the coffee upright as the children run underfoot.

The site's been cleared except for a tree stump in the middle of it. A dozen people watch Lilli and Tilda lead the mules into place on opposite sides of it. There are spikes sticking out of the stump, fastened by chains to two steel poles. Tilda slips the free end of one pole into Esther's harness, and Lilli puts the other into Rama's.

"They're going to walk the mules in a circle and twist that stump out of the ground like you'd take a lid from a jar," Frieda tells Anna. "Look how good she is with him."

Lilli brushes Rama's neck, talking softly. The stump's roots stick up in the dirt, almost to where Anna stands. She puts her tray down and makes the children step back.

"We're just going to walk, now," Tilda tells Esther. "Get *up*."

The mules take a step, feel the chains pull tight, and stop. "That's all right," Tilda says. "Get *up*."

They start walking again, making the poles pull on the stump, but after half a circle they stop and skip backward. Lilli trips. Anna starts toward her without thinking but she rights herself.

"That's fine," Tilda says. "We take our time. Get *up*."

The mules go slower this time, legs bent short and hooves digging in. It takes them a full minute to make a circle, their sides going in and out with each breath.

The stump pulls against the ground. Anna's tray rattles and she picks it up.

The mules dig in harder. Some people clap time, but Tilda stops them with a look. Dirt turns over where the roots are, slowly at first and then as if the world's fastest gophers are burrowing away from the stump. People jump back to where Anna is.

Rama falls to his knees. Lilli wipes his face and says he's a good boy. He gets up, drops his head and keeps walking. The poles and chains vibrate so hard they hum. Lilli has tears in her eyes.

When the stump comes free Anna feels as if the roots are pulled from her chest instead of the ground. The mules pitch forward, braying like wilder animals. Anna barely saves her tray from flying dirt. The stump hops into the air and crashes down, its roots scratching people who stood too close. Everyone applauds.

"That's good," Tilda tells the mules. "Now we rest."

People come to Anna for bread and coffee. Lilli comes last, after taking Rama's harness off. "We knew they could do it," she says. "We wouldn't ask them if we weren't sure." The tears are gone from her eyes. She pours herself coffee. She's twelve, Anna thinks. I had to sneak it till I was seventeen.

The crew goes back to work. Herman and Dara take their shirts off, tie them to their waists and scratch their stomachs, grinning, as they pick up hammers. Everyone's learned to move in the heat but me, Anna thinks.

She takes the children back to the meadow, refills the bread tray and carries it to the henhouse site, where Stefan gets scared of Josef's cape and won't stop crying. When the supper bread's rising she takes the children to the stream and gets splashed till her clothes are soaked. Finally she gets them dressed, returns them to their parents, goes to the pole barn and sleeps for an hour.

When she wakes up she goes down to the woods. Gerhard and Rose are drawing plans at a table made from a cable spool. Lilli sits on a stump next to Rose, reading a book and kicking her feet back and forth. She comes here every day when she's done with the mules.

Rose smiles at Anna and hands her a drawing of a white one-story building with SUNLAND over the door and train tracks running the length of the porch.

"Richard's house," Gerhard says. "He asked for a railway station."

"One and a half *entendres* at most," Rose says, and shows Anna a drawing of the inside, a room with three beds. Train-station signs hang from the ceiling, saying *BEHOLD, YOU ARE BEAUTIFUL* and *WHY SHOULD I BE LIKE ONE WHO VEILS HERSELF?* and *LET HIM KISS ME WITH THE KISSES OF HIS MOUTH.*

Anna gives the drawings back. Rose hands them to Lilli and says, "Would you like to put these on the job board?"

Gerhard built the job board by the stream so he could put up work assignments. The leftover space filled instantly with jokes, sketches, lines from Goethe, anonymous haiku tributes to Frieda's legs, God's-eye trinkets and wildflowers hung to dry.

Rose and Gerhard have pinned up a dozen of their drawings. The carpentry shop's going to be long and gray with no ornaments and a red roof slanting into the sky, like no building Anna's ever seen. Jules and Suzanne's house will be like his collages, faced in strips of billboards and opera posters. Rose's is a Mexican adobe, Herman and Dara's an orange temple, Patrice and Tilda's a camouflage house that vanishes in the landscape. For their own house Gerhard suggested Japanese style, an interest Anna never knew he had. Rose's painting of it is up there now, showing pine floors and blue cloth hangings bathed in sunlight.

"Sit with us," Rose says, moving over on her stump.

"Thank you. I'm going up to the vegetables," Anna says, but still stands there.

Lilli comes back from the job board, sits in the space Rose made, picks up a pencil and puts her free hand on Rose's arm. Now all three of them are drawing.

The harder the work the more animal spirits, Anna thinks. For a place full of harmony I hear a lot of arguing and crying at night. But that's what makes us so much better than the dull citizens, isn't it, the way we go straight to the bottoms of our natures. I know I'm near the bottom of mine.

She starts into the woods and almost walks into Richard, who's been standing there watching for who knows how long. He's got a slip of paper in his hand, one of his meditations written on hotel stationery. "Are we all right?" he says quietly.

"Yes," Anna says. "Thank you."

She walks on but turns to watch him pin his thought up on the board. He has that way of coming out of nowhere and knowing your troubles, she thinks, like Rose when she's your friend.

Anna goes to the vegetable beds, digs rocks out and throws them into piles as if she's shooting them from a gun, till quitting time. A few weeks ago Richard and Gerhard announced the return of lawn hour, on the grass at the dining hall site. Now people change for supper and put on entertainments—Herman juggling weed diggers, Dara waving soap bubbles from an embroidery hoop, Jules and Suzanne playing scenes from *Pandora's Box*, calling the lines to each other from far ends of the lawn.

Two evenings ago, Rose sat down under a tree and Richard joined her. "I saw those houses you drew," he said.

"What do you think?" Rose said as people turned to listen to them.

"I think you and Gerhard are making the fallen people's paradise," Richard said. "This place amazes me. I said all those things but I didn't know we'd *do* them."

"I'm a little shocked myself," Rose said.

"I should give up making predictions and stick to hoeing," Richard said. "We all look so strapping these days. Did you get a mango?"

Rose nodded. The week before, Herman and Josef had hired out unloading fruit in Rialto and taken half their pay in parrot-colored mangos—bad finance but good for morale. You could hear a moan of ecstasy, then laughter, rolling across Sunland as people tasted them.

"We can't grow them but we're close enough to get them, yes?" Richard said.

"Yes," Rose said, as Gerhard walked down from the unfinished dining hall, cleaning a trowel with a brush, his shirt tied around his waist. He squatted at the edge of the lawn and kept scraping.

"I think people will see this place and build them all over America," Richard said.

"That's fairly crazy," Rose said.

"I don't think you know what you're part of till it's done," Richard said. "What does Gerhard think?"

Gerhard glanced up from his trowel and said, "They'll never have our framing crew."

People smiled and some of them cheered. It's true, Anna thought. Everyone works on the farm and buildings all day, then for hours after supper on their own houses, making little crews to help one another. They love the way Gerhard leads them. He listens like he's fed by an underground stream of patience, explaining things the third time as gently as the first.

The problem is that he treats Anna that same way, which leaves out all their years of good and bad luck and the things just the two of them know. Those things are gone from his look, even when they go to the tall grass to make love. You have privacy there if you don't mind hearing other people have it too.

This evening she doesn't go to the lawn but gets her violin out for the first time since the ships. She walks far up the stream and tries the Brahms concerto, the one she watched Lilli listen to at the music store. She makes a hundred mistakes but pushes through to the last movement, the one that's so happy she knows the story can't end there. In fact Brahms wrote a second violin concerto. He burned it as soon as he finished, though. No one's ever heard a note.

Twenty

In July Benji and Jules cut logs into planks at the saw pit. Benji stands in a hole like a grave and holds one end of the saw while Jules stands on the ground holding the other. By afternoon Benji prays that Jules will ask to stop, knowing that Jules is praying the same about him but that neither of them will.

After supper he finds his father at the spool table and says, "I want to build a sawmill."

Father looks up. "It's machinery but it's water-powered," Benji says. "Water's permitted, isn't it?"

"Yes," Father says.

"Are these rules written down someplace?"

"Watch yourself."

"I meant it," Benji says. "I want to know."

Father puts his pencil down. "Sawmills are complicated."

"There's a book at the farm supply."

"The gearing's expensive."

"We'd save months of people sawing."

Father thinks. "All right," he says. "You can try."

"I'll need helpers."

"Helpers?"

"Workers," Benji says. "I'll need fellow workers. Is that better?"

"You can have two."

"Can Rolf be one?" The strongest man at Sunland.

Father nods and says, "And Herman." Quite possibly the weakest, the one who sits cross-legged with his girlfriend and stares at the landscape for hours. He doesn't look like he can dig a pond any better than Benji can.

"All right," Benji says.

As he walks away Father says, "Show Rose your drawings."

"Oh, she's the first one I'd consult," Benji says, not looking back.

The next day, turning compost with Rolf, he asks, "Have you ever built a sawmill?"

"Dug the pond for one," Rolf says. "Built the dam as well. Five years ago, in Rosdorf. We got blood blisters and chigger bites. I was driving planks for the dam one day and this muscle went *pop*." He points to his biceps. "I looked and it was down by my elbow. Only time I passed out. Are you building one? I'd love to get in on it."

"Yes."

"We should dig it now, while the stream's dry. Do you have anyone else?"

"Herman," Benji says.

Rolf thinks. "Good concentration."

Herman, Rolf and Benji meet with shovels at dawn the next day and walk up the stream. "This could be it," Rolf says, stopping by a rise where the water runs straight. "We'd put the pond here." He paces it off. "The dam across there."

They start digging, but in a while they come to clay so hard they have to go back to the tool shed for mauls and pickaxes. Herman and Benji stop every few minutes, blink at each other through sweat, then start again, while Rolf keeps going at twice their speed, his maul like a wheel that barely slows down in the dirt. "We can line the pond with this," he says, heaping the red clay in a pile.

They eat supper together that night, three servings of stew, a pan of cornbread, two pitchers of water, and no talking. In the morning Astrid puts them on her bread route.

It takes three weeks to dig the pond. The longest-worm contest dies out on the second day, but deepening the hole is so interesting that Benji's shocked at how simple his thoughts have become.

One night at supper Rose comes over and looks at his drawing for the millhouse, a plain shed with a water wheel on the side. "Just that?" she says. "You know what people are doing for their houses."

"This isn't a dream," Benji says, but that's just to annoy her. A dream is exactly what it is. Rolf's a giant who's poured steel and pulled barges, Herman stares into space even when he's looking at you, and Benji should be educating himself if he ever wants to see the inside of a university, but the sawmill's like a friendship. In a month of work Herman and Benji put on muscle, and after a day of digging the dam trench Rolf says, "I'm as tired as I've ever been," giving Benji a feeling of triumph just before he passes out.

They line the trench with clay and build the dam on top of it, a wall of wood and concrete with an iron sluice gate. "That's all we can do till it rains," Rolf says.

Benji tells Father the dam's finished. "That's the easy part," Father says.

"I'd like to work on buildings till we get the mill running," Benji says. "After that I'm going back to Berlin." Father looks at him. "It's my decision," Benji says. "Isn't it?"

"What will you do there?"

"Finish school. And then I'm thinking of radio."

"For ships?"

"For houses," Benji says. "You turn a switch and there are symphonies, lectures—anything you like, from all over the world."

"Of course there are," Father says. "Or why not cinema, right in your home? My friends and I used to talk about that all the time. And opera, transmitted through the streetcar lines. It was all going to happen."

"I know," Benji says. "I'd like to work on buildings till then."

"The granary. Lath and plaster. Jorgen will show you."

Two weeks later Benji takes a day off and goes to the Driscoll Public Library, a long brick building with towers, gardens and stained-glass windows. When he asks the librarian for books on electricity, she leads him to a ten-volume set titled *HAWKINS ELECTRICAL GUIDE - THE THOUGHT IS IN THE QUESTION - THE INFORMATION IS IN THE ANSWER*. "These don't circulate," she says, "but you can read them here."

Benji takes the first volume to a table and copies passages into his notebook. He's just finished one on alternator voltage when there's a commotion at the reference desk, people raising their voices even though it's a library. Three men are looking at an afternoon newspaper a boy just brought in. Benji goes over, fits his head between their shoulders, and reads the headline:

GERMANY DECLARES WAR
ALL EUROPE IS IN ARMS

The men shake their heads over it for a moment, and then one of them says, "Lunch?" The others nod and they go outside.

Benji shelves the electrical manual and leaves the library. Downtown Driscoll looks like it always does, with calm pedestrians and light traffic. This country's not at war.

He walks back to Sunland, wondering if people there

know yet. I want to be around Germans, he thinks. Even those.

When he gets there the front page of the newspaper is pinned up on the job board. Under it is a quotation in Richard's handwriting:

Someday that brutal Germanic lust for battle, the savagery of the old warriors, the mad berserker rage, will explode again. When you hear a crash the like of which was never heard before, you'll know the German thunderbolt has reached its mark.

Heine, 1834

Benji sighs. I was stupid to hurry back here, he thinks. At school in Berlin we read centuries of German poetry, but not Heine. Herr Kubler said he wasn't worth reading, not because he was Jewish but because his writing was sarcastic, anti-German, and in the end anti-human. Almost everyone here will like that quotation, though. Only Josef is loyal to Germany, and he's such an ass you can't imagine how Mother plays three notes of music with him.

Benji turns around and bumps into Jules, who's been reading the news over his shoulder. "Fucking hell," Jules says. We agree on that much, Benji thinks, and nods.

For the next few weeks life is almost normal. The newspapers from town predict peace in a few months, when the European monarchs' family peeves have been played out.

Then letters appear on the job board, handwritten on thin paper, and conversation quiets down. The Sunlanders are mostly pacifists, but everyone's got a friend or relative who's gone to fight. Benji reads the letters each morning:

All around us, men and horses have been blown up so badly that the field resembles a morgue for centaurs. I keep my thoughts on God and the Fatherland and there is my comfort.

To be surrounded by young men's bodies full of health and Nature is a thrill second only to knowing that Heaven is close at hand. Regrettably some of the men's talk is coarse, but I know Christ will welcome them anyway, perhaps tonight.

Mud, filth, blood, excrement, and the constant smell of death, but God spares us the lot of our enemies, which is to have black Savages as comrades.

One afternoon Suzanne walks up from the mailbox, crying and waving a letter back and forth in her hand. The next day she pins a note to the job board with a military medal:

My ex-husband
At the Marne
I was the problem
Sweet boy

And more letters:

This war is a great calling and you don't lose faith in it just because you lose your legs. They only carried me into trouble anyway. I have two cheerful crutches, Herr Lefty and Herr Righty, and I will soon be nimble enough on them to return to the front and

For Christ's *sake*, Benji thinks, then feels ashamed. But why do they all think it's such a blessing to die? Why is that better than surviving and making things? Is it possible that Heine had a point?

School starts again. Ninth grade is so simple he wonders how the Americans govern themselves. Studying is subordinated to football games, sack races, dances, parties, fairs, calves, the 4-H Club, mindless chatter about who likes whom, and asking Benji if he knows any Germans who are dead yet. The lessons and textbooks are designed to make time for these priorities.

Each day at lunchtime Benji sneaks to the public library to spend fifteen minutes with the *Hawkins Electrical Guide*. By October he's barely in Volume Two.

One day he's on his way to school when he feels a drop of water on his neck and sees dark circles spatter on the ground. He changes direction and runs back to Sunland.

When he gets to the dam, the rain is steady but vanishing under the rocks in the streambed. It takes two weeks of downpour for it to start running, and another week before the pond starts to fill. Benji, Rolf and Herman sleep in shifts that night, watching the dam for leaks. In the morning the sun is out and the pond's full, with a trickle of excess from the spill pipe.

Rolf crawls along the top of the dam and turns the wheel to raise the sluicegate. Water crashes through it, swelling the stream to its banks for twenty meters. Benji dips a hand in and the flow tries to take his arm off.

Rolf grins, lowers the gate, crawls back to land, takes his clothes off, wades in over his head and comes up spouting water like a hairy Triton. Herman goes in next, then Benji, who floats on his back looking at sun, sky, and oak branches, and doesn't worry about the war or his future for almost an hour.

The next day a dozen people come to swim, then help them start building the millhouse, with a lower story for machine gears and an upper one for the saw. On Halloween six people lift the water wheel onto the hub and set it turning in the stream.

There's a little money at Sunland now, from selling berry preserves in town. Richard holds a vote and gives Benji thirty dollars to order sawmill parts from Denver. When the big gearwheel comes he meets the train in Driscoll with Rolf, Herman, both mules, Lilli and a cart.

The wheel's in a crate that's taller than Rolf. Three railroad men help them get it off the train and into the cart, which cracks in new places but doesn't break. The mules dig their legs in and drive slowly back to Sunland.

They unload the crate by the mill house and open it with pry bars. The wheel glistens blue-black, smells of the foundry, and drives oily iron filings into Benji's palm as he helps roll it.

They push it up a ramp and into the millhouse, next to a stack of smaller parts and the book from the farm supply. Benji goes outside and catches up with Lilli as she walks the mules back to the pasture.

"I have to tell you something," he says. "We'll have that working soon. Once that's done and the war's over I'm going back to Berlin. The papers say it won't go past Christmas."

"You should stay here," she says.

He shakes his head. "You should come with me."

"I like it here. It's beautiful."

"You can't make a life out of scenery."

"People too." She smiles. "You should look some time."

"In the stream?" She shrugs her head. "In the grass? Don't watch people there."

"They don't mind."

"Not for them," Benji says. "For you."

Lilli leads the mules away. Benji goes back to the millhouse, opens the book and starts assembling parts. For the next week he stays home from school and works alone, arranging gears, belts, pulleys and clutches to make the force of the stream move the saw blade up and down.

He follows the instructions precisely, completes the machinery, and throws the lever to start it. A two-foot gearwheel jams, moves again, and flings metal shavings all over the millhouse, cutting a row of red stripes down Benji's arm before he can turn it off.

He picks metal out of his skin while cursing, bandages himself and goes back to work, tightening, loosening, adding spacers, wasting two quarts of oil and another gearwheel before he realizes that the plans in the book don't work.

For a morning he stares at the stream, furious, then goes inside, opens his notebook and starts his own table of loads and ratios. In a week he has a plan. He scrapes the skin off his shins squeezing between mechanisms as he builds them. The next time he tries it, there's a noise like the world ending and he barely saves the pitman wheel.

He starts eating outside so no one will ask how it's coming, and avoids the saw pit, where people look at him with sweaty hope. At night he lies awake on the floor by the big gear, composing angry letters to the publishers of crap American plans.

Think about Germans, then. Think of Werner Siemens, almost ruined when bad insulation on his telegraph wires turned dots into dashes and lost him his business in Prussia. See him rebuilding faith, making meters and dynamos, pacing the stage of a packed theater as he talks up a new model. See people pressing money into his hands to place their orders when he's done.

Benji rearranges the gears over and over. One evening he's wiping oil on them when his ankle seizes with pain. He looks down and sees a scorpion, brown and hideous, skittering away.

Benji sits down hard, grabbing his ankle as a fevered tingling runs up his leg. He stumbles outside with tears in his eyes, dips his rag in the cold stream and wraps it around the sting. It doesn't help.

Who the hell seeks out the desert, he thinks? If there were no cities, Richard would have said, "Let's start one!"

and all these followers of his would have said, "Genius!"

Benji tries to stand up but his ankle buckles under him. He sprawls, crying, and lies there feeling the wound throb till he passes out. When he wakes up it's morning, he's able to stand and he has an idea.

He goes into the millhouse, switches two gearwheels, and throws the lever. The wheels turn like watchworks, nothing touching where it shouldn't. He runs upstairs. The saw blade's flying up and down like a needle in a sewing machine. The noise is beautiful, a smack that shakes the floors once a second.

He tests it twice more, all the way back to the pond. When he shuts it off the calm is absolute. Outside the leaves stand out against the sky in outlines sharper than he's ever seen, a sudden ease overtaking everything.

He goes down to the laundry site, catches Rolf's eye and nods at him. They find Herman, carry a log from the sawpit to the mill, put it on the rails and start it going. A minute later there are two clean lengths of pine and a smell like burned syrup.

"We could cut the whole woods down," Rolf says, "and put it back up as planks."

They run the saw past dark, cutting two logs for framing and one for floors. The next morning people come to watch, and the mules carry logs from the sawpit and planks to the drying shed.

Father comes at midday, stands in the doorway watching, and leaves without saying anything. All right, Benji thinks, I don't need him to like it, but a few minutes later Father comes back carrying the two-man saw from the saw pit. For a minute Benji thinks he wants a contest, man against machine, but then Father takes a hammer from his belt and nails the old saw to the wall through its blade.

That could be taken in different ways, Benji thinks, from *Always remember how hard the first year was* to *We can go back to this when that breaks.* It might even mean the unlikely, but not impossible, *Look what my son has done for us.*

ᚖ

A week later, Benji's walking home from school on a wooded road at the edge of Driscoll when three boys from the Ungraded Room catch up to him. The one who whittles in class is walking a bicycle.

"Say, Fritz," he says, and leans the bike on a fence.

"Hello," Benji says.

"We heard you live with those crazy people out there."

"Which crazy people are those?" Benji says. The whittler goes behind him while the giant and the smirking boy move in from the front.

"The ones that farm with their clothes off," the giant says. "And come in town wearing feathers."

"And Jews," Benji says. "We've got a few of those. Try and keep up, boys."

The smirking one tries to punch him and misses, but the giant hits his temple with a hand like a brick. Benji tries to hit back but they grab his arms. He yanks free, takes a punch in the side and keeps going to the fence.

They snatch at him but he gets hold of the bicycle, starts it rolling and runs next to it. Someone grabs the school bag on his back and half chokes him with the strap. He gets his leg over the bike, breaks away, swerves toward the ditch but steers clear. They try to hit him again but the wheels are going straight now, too fast for them to catch up.

They yell after him that he's stealing, he's a kraut Jew thief and a dead man. He rides as fast as he can, seeing a blur but staying upright.

When he can't hear them anymore he slows to a steady pace and opens his collar. The road is dirt now, and the ruts almost knock him off till he figures out how to charge across them.

I can't go to town anymore, he thinks. The school's not a loss but the library is.

A quarter-mile from Sunland he rides off the road into a grassy field, lays the bike behind a cluster of pinyon trees and walks up to the road, looking back to make sure the hiding place is out of sight.

It's two hours till lawn time. He goes to the art studio site and joins a crew. After a while Linda and her father Jorgen come down the path and walk up to Frederick, who's on his knees nailing floorboards.

"Stand up, shitheel," Jorgen says. Frederick does. Jorgen punches him in the nose.

Frederick falls back, his face in his hands. "Jesus Christ," he says. "What was that for?"

"Think hard," Linda says.

She and Jorgen walk away. Frederick stands there a minute, then leaves in the other direction with blood running down his face. For a minute everyone watches him go. Then Rolf says, "Contrasting views," and they go back to work.

Two hours later, at lawn time, Richard sits on the grass with Jorgen, Astrid, Linda, Trudy, Frederick and Josef gathered around him and everyone else listening. Frederick's nose is bandaged and Josef has a black eye.

"I woke up and he was in my tent," Linda says, pointing at Josef. "He was pulling on the covers and trying to get in with me."

"Is that true?" Richard says.

"I was going to *ask* her," Josef says.

"Sure you were," Linda says.

"And I wouldn't have been there at all if he hadn't said she sent for me," Josef says, pointing at Frederick.

"Complete shit," Frederick says. "Every *letter* of that is shit."

Linda turns toward him and Josef. "I'm going to say this slowly because you're stupid," she says. "The way I act is the way I act, in the stream or anywhere else. It has nothing in the world to do with awful old men coming into my tent."

"I'm thirty-eight," Josef says.

"Clearly you weren't welcome," Richard says.

"I said 'Forgive me' and left," Josef says.

"I don't even forgive that cape," Linda says. "Much less you."

Richard turns to Frederick. "Did you tell him to go there?"

"I had nothing to do with it!"

Richard shakes his head. "All right. A punishment. You're still in love with Germany, is that right?" he asks Josef.

"I'm loyal."

Richard turns to Frederick. "And you'd be some kind of Red if you had the energy." Frederick confirms it with a shrug.

"All right," Richard says. "You're familiar with those sculptures the Kaiser put up, the Hohenzollern emperors?" Benji remembers them, the giant heads of Wilhelm's ancestors lining the Siegesallee in Berlin.

"A hideous display," Frederick says. "People come to laugh at it. 'Even the birdshit is marble.'"

"Keep treating your history that way," Josef says. "Maybe the birds will let you help."

"Asshole," Frederick says.

"I'd like Frederick to sculpt a few of those," Richard says. "Faithful reproductions. Buchard I, Frederick III, those old murderers."

"Jesus, Richard," Frederick says.

"Make them big but use small pieces of wood," Richard says, holding his thumb and forefinger a few centimeters apart. "Eyestrain, glue sickness, whatever happens. When they're finished, Josef burns them down."

"This is vicious, Richard," Josef says.

"No it isn't," Richard says. "If I had any talent for this I'd kick you both out."

True, Benji thinks. He looks at Linda, aiming his thoughts at her: *We're not all like that. I'm not like that. Look how you stood there showing yourself to me in the stream, several times, and I walked around you respectfully. I'd just like to make note of that.*

He catches her eye. Her look back at him says *Oh for God's sake,* and he feels like he's just as bad as Josef, in some way he didn't even know there was.

⁊

The next morning he's at the granary site before dawn, borrowing a tarpaulin. He goes back to the field where he left the bicycle, puts the tarp down next to it, walks the bike to the road, and rides west by moonlight. After a few miles he sits back, fingers loose on the handlebars. It gets light out as the dirt road turns to macadam in Driscoll, where he speeds up to avoid the Ungraded boys.

In San Bernardino he pumps the tires at a filling station and buys a roll for breakfast. Six hours later he sees warehouses and equipment yards. Then he's in Los Angeles, weaving between cars, horses, people and streetcars. He stops at a cafeteria, drinks three glasses of water, and gets swept back outside by a shift of factory workers when their whistle blows.

He takes a street called Santa Monica Boulevard west from downtown. Alongside the road there are miles of tents, some with small, half-finished houses next to them, mixed in with trash heaps, cookfires, dogs and dirty children. It could be a derelict camp, except that the unfinished houses are framed in good lumber and there are fresh ditches with pipe in them.

Benji stops his bike and asks a man working on one of the houses, "Excuse me, sir. What district is this?"

"Francis Brick and Cinder," the man says, pointing proudly at a factory whose chimneys pour black smoke overhead. "If you work there they give you a tent and room to build a house on. From there you trade up and up. I don't know if you can get on, but you could ask." The man's as happy as anyone building a house at Sunland, Benji thinks, but the dreamlike part of his place isn't opera posters or cactus plants. It's the heaven of rising land costs.

"Thank you," Benji says, and rides on. The sun's starting down when he comes to the port where they landed, a lattice of streets running down a hill to the docks. He leans the bicycle in front of a store he saw from the streetcar, with WILLIAMS' BOOKS in gold on the window.

Inside it's like Schropp's in Berlin, with books from floor to ceiling and a smell of leather bindings that puts an acid trickle in his throat. The clerk, a man of about twenty with round glasses and tan hair to his collar, says, "Good afternoon."

"Good—" Benji's leg cramps. He gasps in pain and bends over to knead it. "Pardon me. Good afternoon."

The clerk sees the bicycle outside. "Long ride?"

"From Driscoll."

"That is long."

Benji stands up. "Do you sell the *Hawkins Electrical Guide*?"

"I don't know that one. We could order it." He consults a catalogue on his desk. "It's in ten volumes for ten dollars."

"I only need three through ten."

"It doesn't look like they'll break it up. I can go to nine dollars, though. Half in advance?"

It's most of the money Benji changed in New York. "All right," he says. "Thank you."

The clerk hands him a form and a pencil. "We should have it in four weeks. If you put your address there we'll write you when it comes in. I'm Dan, by the way."

"Benji." They shake hands. "I need something else, for my sister. A book about the solar system, but for children. One that tells why the sun rises."

Dan goes to a shelf and takes down *My First Book of the Stars and Planets*. "And a story, to help her with reading," Benji says.

"How about *Mary Louise Solves a Mystery*?"

"That sounds good." Benji pays him. "Is there a place near here to get supper?"

"Do you have a knife?"

"A small one."

"Two blocks down there's Sailors' Provision," Dan says. "They have the makings for sandwiches. I prefer it to the ones in a restaurant. I like to know what's in them."

Benji finds the store and makes a bologna and cabbage sandwich, the first meat he's had since the ships. He eats it on the sidewalk as the sun sets. It reminds him of the slaughterhouses he passed but tastes wonderful.

He starts home. It's easier crossing the city with the air cooling down, the crowds thinner and the sandwich inside him. At night the road flickers past like a zoetrope, but the ache in his legs keeps him awake. He gets to the field near Sunland at two in the morning, pulls the tarpaulin over the bicycle, and crawls in next to it to sleep.

∞

The next day at lawn hour there's a theatrical. They've been once a week lately, more elaborate each time. Today someone's disguised as a monster, in a costume of rags and a head three times human size, made of books, machine cogs and pieces of concrete.

The monster lumbers around blindly, led by Jules, who wears silk pants, eye goggles and the top of a bathing costume. He talks in a mechanical shout, pressing his hand to his chest and then flinging it outward. "Remit! Remit! These easy terms will expire in an avalanche! The Father, the Son, and the Total Loss!"

Three women in robes and animal masks dance onto the scene and cower by the monster's feet. Then one of them jumps up, pulls a machine cog out of its head, and twirls around with it while the monster groans. "Relax!" Jules shouts. "It's only a tidal wave!" One of the women pulls a book from the monster's head and leaps around reading it.

Benji watches from the edge of the lawn as Patrice walks into the scene on stilts, her tight shirt and trousers striped yellow and black like a bumblebee. Between her legs is a daisy as big as a dinner plate, made of fabric. She smiles, her arms blessing everyone, distracting Benji so he doesn't notice the three boys from the Ungraded Room till they're thirty meters away from him. Benji freezes but the boys have frozen too, watching the actors.

Jules leads the monster over to Patrice. The monster presses his face against the flower between her legs, breathes in and stumbles back, his groans changing to delighted gasps. The Ungraded whittler's mouth hangs open.

One by one the dancers press their faces to Patrice's flower, breathe deeply and fall back sighing. She walks into the crowd and more people put their faces to it.

The boys from school walk up to Benji. "What the hell's that?" the smirking one says.

"A play," Benji says.

"No it ain't," the giant says.

"Where's my bicycle?" the whittler says, but he looks nervous, watching Patrice stilt-walk toward them. She stops in front of Benji.

He hesitates, then presses his face against the flower. The fabric's soft and smells like soap. "Aw Jesus," the whittler says.

Benji looks up at Patrice and says, "Friends from school."

She walks over to them. For a minute he's afraid they'll knock her off her stilts, but they back away instead.

The monster comes over too, with most of its head gone. It's Tilda. When she takes Patrice's hand the boys run all the way to the road.

ᒕ

Two days later Benji's working at the laundry site when Jules comes up and says, "The police are here to see you."

"Always the quiet ones," Jorgen says.

Benji and half the crew follow Jules down the hill. Father's talking to two policemen while a dozen people watch.

"The county agent has been here," Father says in English. "He's examined the well and all the buildings."

"That's a different question," the policeman says. "Son, are you Benjamin?"

"Yes," Benji says.

"Do you speak English?" Benji nods. "A boy says you stole his bicycle."

"No sir."

"He says you did."

"No sir."

"Why aren't you in school?" the other policeman says.

"We have school here," Benji says. "My sister and I and six others."

"Who teaches you?"

Benji hesitates, but Richard comes out of the crowd saying, "I do. Richard Weiss," and shakes hands with the policemen.

"Do you have a license?" one of the policemen says.

"Yes. Dara, would you bring my degree? The one with the ribbons."

Dara goes to get it. "Does your bureau use fingerprints?" Richard asks the policemen. Benji's stomach turns over. His fingerprints must be all over the bicycle.

"They're more up on that in Los Angeles," the policeman says.

"It's wonderful," Richard says. "They've cleared men they were planning to hang."

"It's not scientific," the other policeman says.

"No?" Richard says. Dara comes back with his degree. It's from Erlangen-Nuremberg, in Spanish literature.

"Do you read German?" Richard asks. The policemen shake their heads. "This says I may teach."

"Can we see your school?" the policeman says.

"Of course," Richard says, "this way," but he doesn't know where he's talking about. He puts a hand on Benji's shoulder.

"It's in the barn," Benji says to the policemen. "Is that all right?"

"Let's see it," the policeman says.

Richard leads them to the pole barn and sees the corner where Benji's been trying to teach Lilli and the others. There are mats on the floor, a map of the United States on the wall, the back of some tarpaper for a blackboard, and a crate with a few books in it.

"The one-room schoolhouse," Richard says. "It was good enough for little George Custer."

"This isn't school," the policeman says. "They're going to send someone up here from the one in town."

"If they could bring some chalk," Richard says.

"I mean a truant officer. The kids here have to come down and enroll."

"We like it here," Lilli says. "We learn a lot."

"That's not for you to say," the other policeman says, and turns to Richard. "Some people already don't like having you for neighbors. I wouldn't test things out if I were you."

When the police are gone Benji tells Lilli, "Don't argue like that. It just makes things worse."

"They don't care," she says. "I'm a child. Is there really a bicycle?"

"Down in that field," he says, nodding across the road.

"Good for you."

"They were hitting me when I took it. Don't respect stealing."

"I will if I want to," she says. I know what I want, Benji thinks. It's to be all by myself on that bicycle, or better yet in a crowd in Los Angeles, surrounded by people who don't know me, don't want anything from me and couldn't care less what I do, just as long as I don't crash into them.

1915

Twenty-One

Gerhard leans over Rose to wake her but hesitates, taking in her sleep smell and paint-smudged face. She's in a bed-roll on the ground at her house site, between the framing and the cactus plants. When he puts a hand on her shoulder she opens her eyes wide, sees it's dark and sits up panicked. "My God," she says. "I've slept all day."

"No, no," he says. "Only three hours. It's five in the morning."

"Oh." She takes a breath. "I'm still so behind, though—"

She's wearing a jersey shirt, her breasts sitting up in cocoons of ribbed fabric. She finds her trousers under the blanket and pulls them on. "Are the vases ready?" she says.

"Suzanne's working on them."

"God damn it." She stands up, puts a hand on his arm for balance and twists into her shoes. "My fault, my fault."

"It's fine," he says.

The dining hall's supposed to open tomorrow. Rose stayed up sponging paint on the inside walls till two. He's never seen her worry like this, or had the pleasure of telling her not to.

They walk through the woods and come out facing the building at sunrise. Dew steams off the roof tiles and wildflowers stand out against the yellow stucco. People are bringing slant-backed chairs onto the porch and hanging

Indian blankets on the railings.

They walk into the vestibule, the lacquered floor shining in front of them. "I've still got to place all those tables," she says.

"There's time," he says.

Rolf comes over to them. "You didn't take a bag of concrete, did you?" he asks Gerhard. "One's wandered off."

Gerhard shakes his head. Relations with the town have been friendly enough, but two weeks ago a load of paving stones went missing, and there were lines in the dirt showing where it had been dragged down to the gate.

Another possibility occurs to him, though. "I'll be back," he says.

He goes outside and walks to a clearing on the other side of the woods. Frederick's up on a ladder, troweling concrete onto his unfinished house, a giant replica of the lean-to in Langenhain. Two huge wooden doors, with old glass bowls and wheel rims for doorknobs, lean on three boulders and a pile of junk. Frederick's casting the junk in concrete, from a batch he's mixed in an old wheelbarrow.

That's better than trouble from town, but Gerhard's still annoyed. He picks up the half-full bag of concrete and says, "We need this back."

"Leave it," Frederick says. "We all get materials for our houses."

"This is for the dining hall. Anyway, you're slapping it on. It's too much."

"Not at all. The effluence is the point." He nods at the giant doors. "This is our history. You weren't there."

That's right, Gerhard thinks. I wasn't there, so I had nothing to do with Rose's interest in you fading when the original lean-to was in its glory. Furthermore, nothing has "happened" between her and me in the terms I'm sure you're thinking of, so there's no reason to aggravate me any more than you already have by being exactly the kind of person I was afraid I was getting mixed up with when I—

His thoughts stop as he turns and sees a table with four big heads on it, the Hohenzollern emperors Richard's making Frederick sculpt as punishment. The two that are finished are astonishing. The emperors' cruel inbred features are somehow perfectly realized in tiny chips of wood, gallons of glue and glaring enamel paint. Everything's there, the lazy preening, petty feuds and gout, all leading inevitably to the present war. This is Frederick's "Fuck You" to Wilhelm II, Josef and Richard all at once. Richard won't go through with making Josef burn these. He'll love them. But what does Frederick think he's doing, being talented?

Gerhard can't stand there forever. The sack of concrete's sliding down his shoulder and Frederick's glaring at him from the ladder like the aging delinquent he is.

"I'll bring this back if there's some left," Gerhard says.

He takes the concrete to the dining hall, mixes it, trowels it onto the back steps and then helps Rose till one in the morning, when she moves the same tables back and forth three times.

"Leave them," he says. "You need sleep."

He walks her to her house site, waits while she gets into her bedroll, kneels down and says, "You can rest. You've made the Platonic ideal of a dining hall. I think that means it doesn't sleep with the other buildings."

"Poor dining hall," Rose says, and smiles.

Her hand grips the edge of the blanket. This is it, Gerhard thinks. In a minute she's going to pull that blanket back for me. And then what?

It's not just "Poor dining hall" that led us here. Recently Rose filled up her last sketchbook, bought a new one in town, and decorated its cover with a collage. Gerhard looked at it on the spool table one day when she excused herself. Under the lacquer there were bits of magazine photos, a mountain scene from a cigarette card, and two lines of his own handwriting:

I thought the world was mud, manure, and weeds. Imagine learning that there was lightning in all of it.

He ran his finger over the words. Who saves a letter that long?

I have one second to make up my mind, he thinks, before she moves that blanket. You'd think I'd have a plan, but how could you have one for this?

Rose tucks the blanket around herself, rolls over and closes her eyes.

Gerhard stands up. Of course, he thinks. She's exhausted.

He walks up to the half-built Japanese house. Anna's out baking and the children are asleep. He gets into bed under a roof of beams and tarpaulins, pulls the blanket over himself, pulls it back the way he thought she was going to, just to see how that feels, puts it back again and goes to sleep. When he wakes up there's light in the windows and Anna's home, taking something out of the closet.

"Hello," he says.

"Hello," she says. "It's six."

"I'll get up."

"It took longer with the new oven," she says. "I'm sure we'll all get used to it."

He gets out of bed. Anna's putting a fancy blouse on, the one she wore playing music on the ship. "It's a fine kitchen," she says. "It's just everyone bumping into each other." She picks up her violin in its case. "That's why I wanted the old oven left up, because we're playing and I need time."

"Oh. Yes." He gets out of bed and pulls his trousers on. "I'm sorry. I had to take some bricks from it. Rose wanted—she's being crazy, you know, she's so wound up about this building and she's making everyone—"

"I'm crazy too," Anna says. She lifts the violin case. "I'm as crazy as she is. Do you see?"

Gerhard pauses. "I see what you're saying, yes, but you're not—"

"Yes I am. I'm neurotic. I'm as crazy as Rose is. No one knows what I might do."

"I'm sorry."

"Tell me I'm crazy."

"Yes."

"So I wanted the old oven. I needed the bricks too."

"I—"

"It's Maurice Ravel's string quartet. I bought it when it came out and I still don't know if I can play it right."

"I'm sure you can."

"I suppose we'll see."

She goes out the door. He grabs a shirt and follows her down the path, the angry sway of her ass knocking into the violin case in washed-out early light.

She's right, he thinks. I'm an idiot, risking my family. She should be done with me. Everyone should. They shouldn't even speak to me, except to call me names.

He walks into the dining hall and everyone applauds. The room glows like it's going to take flight, with sunlight on the shiny floors and soft yellow paint on the walls. Everyone's dressed for the occasion, Jules in blue velvet, Frieda in overalls with paisley panels, Manfred in an old suit and cravat. There are eggs, bread, orange juice, and dates from Indio, but Gerhard's lost his appetite.

Suzanne and Frieda are setting up the quartet's chairs

and music stands. Rose is still fretting about the building, wringing people's hands in hers as they congratulate her. "It's lovely," Anna says when she comes over to them.

"Really?" Rose says.

"Yes. It's fine."

"Thank you. If you say it, it's true." She takes Anna's hand and starts to do that wringing, but Anna pulls it away.

"I'm about to play," she says.

"Oh God. I'm sorry," Rose says. "I think I'm tired."

"I think I am too," Anna says, her eyes leveled at Rose's.

Rose pulls her a little away from Gerhard but not nearly out of earshot. "You can be nice to me, you know," she says.

"I am," Anna says.

"I mean there's no reason not to be. Do you believe me?"

"It's no trouble," Anna says. "I'm nice to everyone."

Rose pauses. "Yes. You are."

Anna walks away to join the quartet. She's the last one ready, lifting her violin, taking a breath and nodding. Gerhard catches himself praying it will go all right, that nothing that's happened will disrupt her playing.

Nothing does. The music is an onslaught of longing, almost too much to take. But look at Anna, he thinks, playing in a world untouched by Rose, the new oven, or me. Even Josef sounds good, and Frederick can sculpt, and I wouldn't be shocked if this Maurice Ravel's brain is imploding the way mine is. This must be going on all the time, in theaters and concert halls, bookshops and galleries and well-made dining halls, too—everyone coming off perfect to throw some clammy God off the scent.

Twenty-Two

The children slide down the slope by the road on pieces of cardboard. Anna's got the big ones helping the little ones walk back up, and most of them wait their turns without crying. It's a February afternoon, cloudy for once.

A farmer's truck pulls up and idles at the gate. A man, a woman and two little boys climb down from the bed carrying sacks and old valises. The man waves at the driver, who pulls away.

The woman sees Anna and raises her head, questioning. Anna nods at her. The children stop sliding to watch the family walk up. The man and woman are in their thirties, both thin, in work clothes. Their boys look five and nine.

"Ma'am," the man says to Anna in English. "I understand you're hiring. I'm Roland Durkee. This is my wife Helen."

"Hiring?" Anna says.

"They said you were, in town. We can farm, we and Peter here. Olin's five but he's no trouble." Olin points at the children's cardboard sleds. Helen pushes his hand down.

"I think the people in town were making a joke," Anna says. "Not because of you," she adds quickly. "Because of us. We don't hire people. No one is paid here."

"That's no, then?" Roland says.

"I'm sorry," Anna says, but then she thinks of Richard saying he wants Americans here. "I shouldn't say no," she says. "Maybe."

She leads them up the hill with the Sunland children following. The end of a stringed musical instrument sticks out of Roland's sack, with a shirt sleeve caught on a tuning peg. "Do you play music?" Anna asks him.

"Ma'am, only after work."

At the farm people are hoeing Chinese cabbage. Anna finds Tilda, takes her aside and says, "These people asked about working here."

"We can't pay them," Tilda says.

"I told them," Anna says. "I think they—"

She turns to look at them. Roland and Helen are already hoeing. Peter, pulling weeds a few rows away, slips a cabbage leaf under his shirt. Little Olin's chasing around by the chickens with the Sunland children.

"Would you like some bread?" Anna asks. "It's a while till supper."

Helen looks up at her, says, "Thank you," and goes back to work.

Anna brings them thick slices of bread with syrup and cold coffee. They call their boys over, eat and drink quickly but decline her offer of more. Anna hoes with them till she leaves to take the Sunland children back to their parents. "I'll bring our guests to the lawn," Tilda says.

When Anna gets there the Americans are standing with their things piled neatly under a tree, waiting while Tilda talks to Richard. Helen tries to stop the boys from staring at people, but Roland, kneeling to roll a cigarette, is looking too. His eyes land on Jules, playing a dance tune on his concertina.

Jules raises his eyebrows and nods at Roland's instrument sticking out of the sack. Roland stands up, strikes a match on a trouser button, lights his cigarette and raises his eyebrows in return. Jules waves him over.

Helen puts a hand on Roland's arm, but he pats it and pulls a Spanish guitar from the sack. When he gets to Jules he kneels down, listens to the song for a minute, finds the key on his metal strings, and starts a counterpoint.

The lacquer on the guitar is half dust and Roland picks the strings with fingernails cracked by work, but his lines fit slyly between Jules'. A little crowd forms around them and claps when they finish. Jules smiles at him and says, "Now you one" in English.

Roland plays a simple tune, sounding time on two bass strings with his thumb and stretching the higher strings against the guitar's neck so the notes spring through the air. The timbre sounds like bees, then chimes, then the *boing* of a buckling handsaw. Jules puts some chords in but he can't keep up the way Roland did.

When they finish this time there are more people around them clapping. Roland nods at them, goes back to his family and puts the guitar in its sack. "See, that's all right," he says to Helen, as Richard comes over and offers her his hand.

"Richard Weiss."

The sudden quiet on the lawn startles Helen and her voice comes out scratchy. "I'm Helen Durkee. This is Roland, Olin and Peter."

Richard shakes hands with them. "This is like Columbus meeting the Indians," he says in English.

"Which one's Columbus?" Roland says.

"You're our first Americans," Richard says.

"Yeah, but your side's got the feathers."

Helen looks worried but Richard laughs. "I liked your music," he says.

"Thank you," Roland says, holding his tobacco out to Richard, who shakes his head and takes out a cigar.

"Tilda says you're interested in joining us here."

"We might," Roland says. "We get food for working?"

"Yes. And a house."

"We buy that on time?"

Richard shakes his head. "You build it. We'll help."

"All right."

"There are some other things you should consider, beside the feathers," Richard says. "We're vegetarians."

"Aids digestion," Roland says.

"We don't use money unless we have to. We don't use electricity at all."

"All right."

"People go without clothes sometimes."

"And here she just got the boys to stop that."

Richard pauses. "There's a good deal of sexual activity."

"I think what you're saying is you're poor," Roland says. "I never know why people are shy about it."

Richard smiles. "We need to vote on your staying," he says, and Anna realizes she's anxious about the outcome. "Does anyone have questions for them?"

Jorgen waves for attention. "You've traveled America?" he says.

"Yes sir," Roland says.

"Did you see Chicago? They say it's the future."

"We tried to," Roland says. "Lot of police in the way."

"I'm glad to know you," Jorgen says, and puts his hand up. Everyone else does too, except Josef.

"Against?" Richard says. Josef still doesn't vote. "No objections, then," Richard says. "That's unusual."

"Thank you," Helen says to everyone on the lawn. Anna leads the new family in to supper, the tune Roland played still running through her head. *Snappy*, she thinks.

ଔ

She doesn't see them much for the next week or so, as they move into the pole barn and work on the farm. At supper Roland and Helen speak a little English with Benji or Richard, then let them go back to German while they talk to each other and tease their boys.

In their second week Roland brings his guitar to the lawn again. He plays a few tunes with Jules and eight people gather around. Then he sings one, and twice as many turn to listen.

> *I walked up to Pollard*
> *No work did I find*
> *Bad times before me*
> *And sad ones behind*

He talks like other Americans they've met but sings in a thin, quavery tone, as if an old man's throwing his voice from inside him.

> *I lost my last dollar*
> *In a crooked card game*
> *The sky black with thunder*
> *The wind called my name*

There's no self-pity in it, just facts, as if everyone knows life is like this. Those who don't know English seem to understand it from the sound. When he finishes and looks up he's startled by how many people are looking at him. "Please, more like that?" Dara says.

He sings five songs in all, and more a few days later. That voice is a ghost, Anna thinks. There's nothing more they can do to it, not the landlord, the company store, careless lovers, steel hammers, or the *Titanic*. If he sang in a singing voice you wouldn't believe him.

> *The days of my life*
> *Always having to go*

Always saying goodbye
Just as quick as hello

Two days later she takes her violin up the stream. She has the sound in her head, two notes with the top one just off key, but she draws the bow a hundred times without getting it.

His songs are simple enough. Tick-tock. We rise and we fall. On the one hand, on the other. His voice goes between notes, though. She tries for so long she gets mad at him. He makes it seem so primitive, but those microtones would scare the moderns in Vienna.

I'm never going to get it, she thinks, and stops to take the supper bread out. All these years I've tried to play in tune, and now there's only one right wrong note.

 C3

A week later she stands at the edge of the lawn, the violin in its case, as Roland starts a song about a train wreck, with Jules' concertina wheezing under it. When Anna walks up with the violin, Roland smiles in the middle of singing about women and children dead on the ground.

She plays accompaniment. That crying tone is finally hers, and the tune's so plain she can make her part up as she goes. After a few long bows, Roland cocks his head to look at her. Jules puts his concertina down.

Roland and Anna play four songs together. The last is one she hasn't heard before, about a flood in Ohio, but the tune's the same as Lilli's old school song, so she has no trouble.

At the end of that one they hold their hands still, letting the last notes fade into the trees. While people clap he leans toward her and says, "Should we practice some time?"

Anna nods, looking around. Gerhard's not there but

Lilli gapes, delighted, and Benji's almost impressed. Josef walks up to her afterward, scowling.

"You're talented, you know," he says. "I hate to think you'll use it for this now."

Anna smiles at him. "Oh, Josef—'talented.' *Thank* you."

ॐ

They practice most days, in a clearing up the stream. Roland sits on a stump, leaning over his guitar and tapping his foot in its dirty boot. Anna stands facing him, watching his hands and starting to recognize the chords.

He has so many songs they don't repeat them at the lawn unless someone asks. One day at practice he plays one where the singer really is a ghost, a man who pushed his wife's lover into a waterfall and then fell in after him. He sings, "*We both died for Mary Lee—*" and stops.

"I'm suspicious of that one," he says. "They could be having fun with you. They might not even be from the country. They might be sitting up in an office saying, '*I'll* sell some sheet music.'"

Anna likes the sad songs better after that. If love was lethal, she thinks, then who'd survive?

"Do you like it here?" she asks him one day.

"We do." He rolls a cigarette, draws it through his lips, strikes a match and lights it with a wet flame she worries will take his eyebrows off someday. "In fact we were wondering if we might invite a few people we knew before. Helen was asking about it. Friends, you know."

Anna tries to picture being friends with Helen. When Roland jokes with Richard or Benji, Helen puts her hand on his arm like he's a third little boy who's going to get them in trouble. But if they're Roland's friends I'd like to meet them, Anna thinks. We can play these American songs and make them feel at home.

"I think Richard would like it if people came," she says. "Including colored?"

"Yes," Anna says, and then hopes she's right. Why wouldn't I be, she thinks? We're for everything equitable here.

"We're not like the other Germans, you know," she says. "The ones who put African people in zoos."

"Seen 'em at the Chicago fair," Roland says. "Grass huts and leopard-skin small-clothes. People throwing peanuts." Anna shakes her head. "I'll write some letters," Roland says.

The minute they're done practicing she finds Richard and asks what he thinks about Negroes coming. His face brightens and he says, *"Perfect,"* as if that entire history happened for his purposes.

Two weeks later Patrice tells Anna, "There's another American couple, with two little girls. I saw them working at the laundry site. They seem sweet."

When Anna goes to the clearing that afternoon she hears music before she gets there, Roland's voice and guitar, a second voice, a horn and another stringed instrument. She doesn't know the song.

They finish as she walks up. Helen's there with Peter and Olin, and the new couple with their daughters. The children clap when the song ends.

"Anna," Roland says. "This is Jerome. This is Lois."

"Anna, yes," Lois says. "We've heard all good things about you."

They're not the colored people Roland asked about. Lois is plump and smiling, in a blue dress and two long pigtails, with a mandolin in her lap. She points to the girls. "This is Emmy and Tammy."

"I like your place," Jerome says. He's tall, in work clothes like Roland's, and stands holding a cornet plated in fading nickel. "Helen wrote to us in Wisconsin. This is like summer is there."

"Is there school here?" Lois says.

"Anna's son teaches," Roland says.

"There are schools in town too," Helen says. "Peter's going next year. Yes you are."

"Jack and Jeanne are coming," Roland tells Lois. "Next week, it sounds like."

"What about Bernard?" Jerome says.

"He may," Roland says.

"You get Bernard, you've got an orchestra," Jerome says.

"And then you throw in the rest of us," Roland says, and the others laugh. "'Drover's Farewell'?"

They nod and begin. Jerome plays bright cornet lines between Roland's lyrics in the verses and sings baritone with him on the chorus, their harmony like a train coming. Lois plays arpeggios on the mandolin with a little brown plectrum.

How's Anna supposed to find room in there? Roland's not even looking at her. She gets as nervous as she did the first time she played with him. Finally she adds a few phrases, but when he looks at her for a solo she goes blank and plays the melody. We'll never practice by ourselves again, she thinks, just as Helen smiles for the first time she's seen.

૭૪

A few days later Anna sees Roland and Helen walking in from the gate with a Negro man and woman, carrying valises, the man saying something that makes Roland laugh. When she goes to practice the next day, the man's there. He's thirty and stocky, in canvas pants, brogan shoes and a checked shirt. "This is Bernard," Roland says. "This is Anna."

"Anna," Bernard says, shaking hands. "I think that's

your husband I talked to about the work arrangements." Anna has trouble understanding his speech at first, but repeats it silently to herself. "Is this place socialist?" he says.

"In a way," Anna says.

"You get food and a house," Jerome says.

"But no money," Bernard says.

"You can't go into debt, though," Jerome says. "It's no tenancy. There's no store."

"We'll stay a while," Bernard says. "I like the dry air for Leah. For her health. No money, though, that won't go for long."

"There's no meat either," Roland says.

"I don't mind that," Bernard says. "I worked in a meat plant in Clarewood. I was in the taking out brains division. Then I went to skinning tongues and sizing bladders. That was a step up."

He opens his instrument case, takes out a guitar that makes Roland's look new, puts it down beside him and says, "What have you been playing?"

They play two songs for him, one where a man stabs his sweetheart to death and the other about a shipwreck. When they're done he shakes his head and says, "By this time the audience has gone out and killed themselves."

Lois laughs and says, "Bernard, now..." like they've been teasing each other all their lives.

"No, truly," Bernard says. "Now you have to cheer them back up again. I'll play you what they're playing in Memphis. This was called 'Mister Crump' but they call it 'The Memphis Blues' now. It's one and the same."

He plays. His guitar sounds like two or three musicians, with full chords and silvery notes all at once. "The Memphis Blues" is a suite, one hypnotizing theme after another. The guitar visits, saunters, and tells stories. The meter's like a march but with hesitations, so you'd be marching with your hips swinging. Anna pictures hot weather and old brick buildings. She knows nothing about Memphis, but she'd be shocked if it looked any other way. When it's finished Jerome softly says, "Son of a b., Bernard."

"That one's something," Roland says.

Bernard puts his guitar in his lap and retunes it, lowering some strings and raising others. He plays a chord with his fingers off the frets and takes a tarnished butter knife from his guitar case. "This one's a real blues," he says.

"Are there words?" Roland says.

"Mm. I can't sing them, though," Bernard says.

Anna wonders if he means the words are indecent, but then Jerome says, "Yeah, that's so."

"I heard you hit a right note once," Lois says. "Freeport, six years ago. There should be a marker there."

"Hmp," Bernard says.

"Could you talk it?" Roland says.

Bernard talks the lyrics as he plays, with just enough intonation to get the tune across.

Going to get up in the morning,
Catch that Southern train—

Roland sings the lines after Bernard says them. Bernard stops playing, looks at him and says, "Could you do that when I'm gone?"

"Sorry," Roland says.

Bernard starts again. Roland keeps quiet. The music tells as much of a story as the words do.

Going to get up in the morning,
Catch that Southern train.

That's the I chord, a plain statement: this is how things are. But when the words repeat—

Get up in the morning

—the IV chord comes and puts them in another light, the difference between your outlook at night and in the morning.

Catch that Southern train

He goes back to the I, as if everything's resolved. But now the V chord appears, an unforeseen crisis, the third side of the coin:

Because the way you treat me

Back to the I—

Is just a dirty shame.

—so that the trouble falls back into time but the damage remains.

Now the tune repeats, but on the rest of the verses Bernard runs the edge of the butter knife up his strings. The pitch rises like a siren and sends a chill down Anna's neck. She tries not to stare at him but can't help it.

He starts the song over. The others play their way in, all except Anna. They sound good together, but it's worth your life to find a place between them.

That evening Richard calls for a vote on Bernard and Leah staying. When he asks for questions, Josef gives Bernard a scrutinizing look and says, "Do you think you'll be comfortable here?"

"*Comfortable,*" Bernard says, as if it's a new idea he's never heard about.

Richard calls a vote before the silence goes on too long. Josef abstains, but he abstained about Roland and the other Americans too. Everyone else votes yes.

Anna's glad, but she still has no idea how to play those blues of his. She practices by herself for a week, thinking about him as she plays. When Roland started singing and Bernard said "Do that when I'm gone," did that mean gone to the next town, or just back to the pole barn, or dead? And that lyric, "The way you treat me is a shame"— who's the *you* in there? A woman? A boss? The whole country? He has the right to mean all of them. If that's not a spiritual, Anna thinks, it should be.

Her troubles aren't a tenth of his, but she can picture herself losing Gerhard's and Lilli's affections, and being a fool for thinking about Roland so much. By the time she goes back to practice she's got what the new songs ask for—that walking tempo, those funny flatted notes, that complaint.

1916

Twenty-Three

Lilli walks up the hill in the dark. A dog's howling at the heat, and the crickets rub their wings so fast she's afraid they'll catch fire.

Astrid's waiting at the top of the hill. When the others get there, Dara opens the cabinet and Jorgen pours water into everyone's hands. Lilli loves saying the Egyptian and tasting the water mixed with her skin. We're lucky to live here, she thinks, so close to the sun.

It's light now. The desert goes from night to day before you can catch it. The creation of the world, right where you're standing, every day.

When they're finished she hugs everyone and walks down the hill, her bare feet packed in dust and calluses as good as shoes. At this hour the framing for the laundry has a shadow three stories high, like you're in a city. The road to the gate is finished, a dirt ribbon flying down the hill. Frieda walks past with a back brush, Jules with a roll of posters.

Lilli smells the pasture before she sees it, the haystacks' wet scent and the mules like smoke and leather. Tilda's taking Esther to drink while Rama waits in his stall. Lilli comes in from the side so he can see her. He reaches for her with his head and moves his lips.

"Good morning, handsome," she says, and brushes his

neck. "Lots of work today."

She rakes the manure to the compost pile, spreads fresh straw and picks up his harness. It took her weeks to get strong enough to lift it, and she mixed up the straps so many times he could have stopped trusting her. But she learned it, and now when she says "Over" he moves right away and stands still like a good boy at the barber.

Lilli sits on a stool to buckle him up. When she stands up to walk him out he snorts like he's alarmed, so loud that Tilda comes in.

"Rama, what is it?" Lilli says.

"It's your dress, I think," Tilda says. "In the back."

Lilli looks at Tilda, then pulls her dress around and sees the red stain.

"You go home. I'll walk them down," Tilda says, smiling.

Lilli's never felt cross with Tilda, but she'd rather not be smiled at for this. Pretty much every woman here has given her a talk about how wonderful and natural it will be. She ties a shirt around her waist so she can walk up to her house without getting smiled at the whole way.

When she gets home there's no one there. She washes herself, puts on the belt full of cotton Mother made her, and lies down.

I don't want to be a new person, she thinks. Having a baby before you want one seems like the worst trouble you could be in, and I suppose I have to worry about that forever now. But I don't want to stop loving the mules. I don't want to be like Mary Louise, the girl detective in that book Benji brought me, lying around and dreaming about going to dances when I should be up on the hill for sunrise. I don't want to change how I feel about people, or wear shoes. She keeps checking herself for new attitudes till she's sure there aren't any, and falls asleep.

A week later she takes Rama to the sawmill, where Suzanne helps her load shingles for the library. When she delivers them to the site there's someone new, a boy her age but taller, nailing up lath. She asks him, "Can you help load them out, please?"

"I'm sorry?" he says in English.

Benji hasn't taught her *shingles*. "To take wood out?" she says. He smiles and goes to the cart with her.

The shingles are cedar. "These smell nice," he says. "I'm Oliver."

"I'm Lilli. This is Rama."

"How do you do?" He's fair-skinned with bushy hair, in a striped jersey and blue cap. He talks slowly but carries shingles so fast she can barely keep up.

"That's my father," he says, pointing at a man nailing underlayment with the same quickness. "My mother's in the kitchen. We knew Roland and so on in Michigan." They go back to the cart and Rama nuzzles her. "They wouldn't do that everywhere—let a girl your age work him," Oliver says. "He minds you, though. That's what counts."

When she's done with the mules she spends an hour planting lettuce starts, easing the tiny root hairs into the dirt, watering and shoring them up as she listens to the conversations around her.

"I read all of Ulrich," Jules says. "I read his essays on self-mastery and inner peace, and I said to myself, 'These are saving my life.' Then I found out that when he was writing them he was drinking a liter of vodka every day and screwing his way across Austria."

"Did you feel cheated?" Frederick says.

"Not at all," Jules says. "It's what that old American song says: it's a gift to be shallow."

Lilli doesn't always know what they're talking about, but the hum of their voices makes her happy. Sunland is her heart, a once-in-a-world combination of climbing rocks, spreading oaks, mules, chickens, babies, paintings, nakedness, crazy plays, and those songs of Roland's that Mother plays along on.

Oliver eats with his parents that night, but the next night he sits with her. "Are you going to school in the fall?" he says.

Lilli shakes her head. "My brother teaches. Benji." She nods toward him, sitting by himself with a book. Working on buildings has made him the best-looking man at Sunland, with brown skin and big arms. He could be happy here if he'd relax, Lilli thinks. Linda likes him but he's scared to go near her.

"Did he teach you English?" Oliver says. "He must be smart."

"He is," Lilli says. "He built the sawmill."

"He built that? I was up there this morning. That's fine. That's initiative." She looks at him, puzzled. "Giving yourself urges."

He smiles and she smiles back. She likes him already, the way everything pleases him. Richard says of all the people in the world the Americans are the least troubled by doubt.

"Say, I had news today," he says. "This girl Diana's coming in a few days. With her folks, I mean. We knew her down in Kirby. She's our same age. She's bold as brass. I bet you'll like her."

"Everyone's bold here," Lilli says.

"Sorry?" Oliver says.

"I said she sounds nice," Lilli says.

⁊

Diana comes a week later, with her parents Philip and Gloria. She's not as pretty as Lilli pictured but she looks strong, with big legs and shoulders, reddish skin, and strawberry-blonde hair tied back in a string. The second day she's there, at lawn time, she and Lilli and Oliver go up the hill and sit looking at the road.

"I don't like farms," Diana says. "I like towns." She rolls a cigarette from a pouch like Roland's.

"It's not just a farm," Lilli says.

"Fool me," Diana says. "I just hoed corn for six hours."

"You'll hear Richard talk on the lawn," Lilli says. "You'll see what I mean."

"He does it in English sometimes," Oliver says.

"Boy, you got right on here, didn't you?" Diana says. "What's he say?"

Oliver thinks. "There's no place where you start and other people stop."

"No, they can stop right here," Diana says, putting her hand at the top of her chest. She's developed. "What's town like?"

"There's a place with root beer but they're not friend-ly," Oliver says.

"This isn't promising, Oliver," Diana says.

They go up there every day, talk and look down at the county road. Now and then a car goes by, dust rolling up behind it like wake on the water.

One day two trucks come and park next to the road, with some kind of gold seal painted on their doors. One truck's bed is full of gravel and the other has a black tank full of tar Lilli can smell all the way up on the hill. Three men in overalls get out and start spreading gravel on the road.

"No!" Lilli shouts, standing up. The men don't seem to hear her.

"What's wrong?" Oliver says. "They're just paving."

"The dirt's beautiful," Lilli says. "Why do they want to cover it with something ugly?"

"If we had bikes we could play hockey on there," Di-ana says.

Lilli runs to the spool table. Father's not there but Rose

and Benji are, going over drawings. Benji's never made friends with Rose, but he works on buildings so he's got to be polite to her.

"They're paving the road," Lilli says. "It's all going to be tar."

"Oh sweetheart," Rose says. "That's terrible."

"Can't we stop them?"

"No," Benji says. "It's the county's road, and it's not terrible. It's good for the farmers."

He goes back to drawing. Rose gives Lilli a look that says "What can you do," about Benji, the road or both.

Lilli walks back up the hill. The men are pushing a roller over the gravel. "Benji says we can't do anything about it," she says.

"That's all right," Oliver says. "Here." He pats the space next to him. When she sits down he puts his arm around her shoulder, then kisses her.

Lilli's heart pounds and a few places tingle. When the kiss is over he smiles at her, but she feels too serious to smile back.

Diana pulls on his arm like he's forgetting something. He leans over and kisses her too, for just as long. She gives Lilli a little smirk when it's done. Then they all look straight ahead at the paving men. When the trucks leave, the road's covered in tar past the gate.

Lilli goes down the hill feeling tight in her chest. She tells Rose about it that night.

"Oh, those things are hard," Rose says. "Richard says if two men love the same paintings it makes them friends so why can't they love the same woman, but that's Richard."

"I don't think it's love with us."

"Well, that's easier then."

Lilli thinks about it in bed. Americans want things, even more than Germans do. Diana wants dresses and telephones like the kids in town have. Oliver wants Lilli and Diana, both at once.

The next day she's wondering whether to go up the hill when she hears music coming and going with the breeze. She follows it to the lawn. It's a bigger group of musicians than ever before, on the porch of the dining hall—Roland and Bernard with their guitars, Mother with her violin, Jerome with a cornet, Lois with a mandolin, Oliver's father Jack with a double bass violin, and Diana's father Philip with a trombone.

They're playing the song about the flood, but it's nothing like when Roland plays it by himself. He and Lois sing

It rained on the road till the ditches overflowed,
And the people and the horses lost their lives.
Lost their LI-I-I-I-I-I-IVES

—and on every other one of those strung-out syllables Bernard makes his butter knife quiver on his strings. It's like an electric shock, something you hear down your neck and legs before your ears have even had a chance at it.

Lilli closes her eyes. I love this music, she thinks, but I want everyone to love it and I'm scared they won't.

Then she opens her eyes and sees everyone coming to the lawn to listen, a bigger crowd than Mother and Roland ever got by themselves. People turn their faces up to the sound and let it pour over them.

The depot it burned and the houses overturned,
With their timbers all in splinters from the flood.
From the FLOO-OO-OO-OO-OO-OO-OOD

—and there's that sound of Bernard's again, like a stake going straight through the doom in the words. It's all right singing songs where everyone's happy, Lilli thinks, but that's just one side of life. It's standing up to the bad side that means something. Mother's the proof of it, standing up there playing violin parts that go swerving all over the place, barely in control but safe with her friends. You'd never know how sad she looks sometimes.

Patrice comes twirling through the crowd, doing some kind of dance that fits the music. She holds her hand out and Lilli takes it. They turn together a few times, and then Patrice pulls in Linda, Lilli pulls in Jules, and more and more people join them.

Everyone reads the war news on the job board every day and it makes them sick. It's like the flood in the song. You can know about it but still dance. You *have* to.

When the song ends, Lilli goes over to Oliver and Diana. He stands between them and puts an arm around each one's shoulders. Lilli stays stiff for a second, then lets her side press against his.

The band starts up again, a song about a ghost, with the trombone and cornet flying over the words. The dancing spreads through the crowd like a panic. "We're going to be stuck here forever," Diana says, and Oliver smiles.

Twenty-Four

Benji bicycles to Los Angeles for the fifth volume of the *Hawkins Electrical Guide* in the hottest week of the year. His breathing mixes with the sound of his tires peeling tar off the road. In the bookstore his drying sweat makes him shiver.

"I need something new for Lilli," he says. "Something about normal families."

"I don't suppose Freud," Dan says, looking over the shelves.

"The psychoanalyst?"

"Mm."

"Richard knows him."

"I'm coming out there whether you invite me or not," Dan says, and hands Benji a book called *Little Women*. "Try this."

"It's a long drive," Benji says. "Then you'll see a lot of half-naked people holding up carrots with a big smile, like no one's ever grown carrots before."

"I'll steel myself," Dan says. "Look for me some Sunday."

Ϩ

A few days later, Benji's working by himself on the art studio roof at lawn hour when Rose walks up. "Come to this meeting with me," she says.

"What meeting?"

She looks up at him, shading her eyes with her sketch-book. "About the gatehouse or whatever it is."

There have been more cars going by since the road was paved. Sometimes they stop. The first few incidents weren't too bad. One day a man came through the gate, ran up to Mother's friend Roland and said, "Look, I've had a misunderstanding over in Banning. No one can come after me here because this is its own nation, is that right?"

"Banning?" Roland said. "Banning's got our pope in jail. How bad do they want you?"

The man ran away. A few days later a lady drove up in a car, left the engine running, walked in, grabbed Lilli's friend Diana by the arm and said, "We're getting you out of here, dear. Whatever they've done to you, that's over now. Just hold onto me and keep walking." Diana said something rude in English and the lady let go of her arm to slap her.

But as the summer went on things got worse. One morning three metal signs appeared on the fence, facing the road and saying FOR SALE - FORECLOSURE with a telephone number.

Father took the signs down. Benji called the number from a telephone booth in town and said he was inquiring about the land.

"I can hear your accent," the woman on the other end said. "Do you live out there? If you live out there then this is for you. It's not the bank that's foreclosing on you, it's God. How dare you come into our land and do these things?" Benji wanted to ask what things, but the woman hung up.

A week later, someone drove past and yelled a race insult at Bernard and Leah when they were getting their mail. That same week, at lawn hour, Richard passed around a letter that came with no return address. It was folded around a photograph, taken from above, of six blurry bodies in the stream. *We are sending this picture to the POLICE*, the letter said. *You are WARNED.*

Jules looked over the photo, said, "You couldn't even jerk off to that," and passed it on.

"Oh, the police could," Richard said. Nothing came of it, but the picture could only have been taken from a hill on the property. After a few more incidents, people started talking about a gatehouse, and that's why there's a meeting now.

"Please come down there with me," Rose says. "Everyone's got opinions. I'm going to have to talk."

She's never had any trouble talking that Benji can remember, but he says, "All right." As he comes off the ladder Rose ducks her head and gathers her hair into an elastic, an innocent action that nonetheless lifts her bosom up at him. He takes his shirt from around his waist and puts it on as they walk.

"They're having the music again on Sunday," she says. "Your mother and the Americans."

"I might have a friend visiting then," Benji says.

"Oh? Who?"

"A man from Los Angeles. I buy books from him. He's gotten the idea it's interesting here."

"You should bring him to hear them play. I told your father to go too."

"Why?"

"Because your mother's so beautiful up there," Rose says. "He should see that."

Benji doesn't answer. I didn't know you wanted Father looking at Mother, he thinks. I thought you wanted him looking at you.

When they get to the meeting Richard's saying, "How thick is the traffic?"

"More since the paving," Frieda says. "Usually they just buy some jam and go on their way."

Rose sits under a tree, opens her sketchbook and starts to draw. Benji stays standing. Father's sitting with Rolf and Manfred, Mother with the American musicians. Lilli sits between Oliver and Diana, who are lying down and looking at the clouds.

"It wouldn't have to be a sentry box," Patrice says. "It could look like a house. We could have tea and gifts inside."

"You'd give them *gifts*?" Frederick says.

"Sell them," Patrice says.

"That might help," Rose says. "Spending is a sedative."

"A few people will ask what we're doing here and we'll tell them," Richard says. "A few of them will think, 'It's crazy, yes—but what if it's right?'"

"I'm not here to be put on display," Josef says.

"They'll have to make do with the jelly, then," Rose says. She holds up her drawing, a white cabin at the gate. A second page shows the inside, a room with a counter, tea service and shelves full of jars.

"We could put a back porch on it, with a railing all around," Jack says. "You can see the surroundings but you can't go there."

It's quiet for a moment. "Shall we vote?" Richard says.

Mother, Richard, Rose and the Americans vote yes. Josef, Frederick and a few others vote no. Lilli votes yes and holds her friends' hands up. Benji, Manfred and Father don't vote either way. The yeses win.

Two days later, Rose calls up to Benji on the roof again. "I need something else," she says.

"What?" he says.

"You have to come down. It's confidential."

When he gets off the ladder she leads him into the shade, comes close to him and says, "Electricity."

"I'm sorry?"

"Electric lights. For my house."

"I don't understand."

"For my paintings," she says. "To get the colors I need."

"For your banners?"

She shakes her head. "Those aren't my paintings. The sun is fine for those."

"But you're against electricity."

"Mm." She draws on her cigarette. "Can you do it for me?"

Benji shakes his head, but he's already thinking of batteries, lamps and dynamos. "I can pay for it," Rose says. "I can't paint scenes full of light bulbs if I never see one." She pauses. "May I show you?"

"All right," he says.

They go up to her house, an adobe in the southwest American style, with a slate path winding through cactus plants to the entry. The walls inside are plastered white, with arched doorways. Her bed has a rough pine headboard, white sheets and a red blanket. One wall's covered with pictures from magazines, and the bookshelves are stuffed with scrapbooks.

Across the room there's an easel, and a dozen paintings leaning on the wall with their backs to the room. Rose kneels to pick one up. Her shirt lifts, uncovering an almond shape of skin and backbone.

She stands up and hands Benji the painting, of a nighttime city in chaos—pavements pitching up at violent angles, houses buckling, the sky lit by explosions. Well-dressed people stroll through the scene, smiling as if the danger's for someone else. You can't look at the picture without wanting to shout at them.

"You see?" she says. "I'm not getting the colors."

She hands him another, a line drawing of a downtown in daylight crammed with people, their faces by turns mean, cunning, scared, seductive and cheaply triumphant. Somehow it's all foreground, the horizontal plane shoved up to vertical so all the faces come toward you at once.

"I thought I was moving to the country to paint nature," Rose says. "Well, there is this one."

She hands him a small painting of a naked couple in bed, black brushstrokes on a caramel background. The man's penis lies on his thigh. There are two lines for the woman's vagina. Benji feels his face color as he looks at it.

He points at the paintings. "You don't show these?"

"To Richard and Jules," she says. "For advice."

"Not Father?"

"No." She takes the picture from his hand, presses against him and kisses him for a long time.

He's never done anything but he's seen people do things, in the stream and the tall grass. He wishes he hadn't looked away so much.

He gets on his knees, like he saw Jules do with Suzanne once, and kisses Rose through her skirt. She pushes the skirt down, then her drawers. Her hair's curly, a darker red than on her head.

She sits on the bed and pulls him down with her. When she opens her legs it's not two lines but something complicated. He kisses her in the middle of it. She tastes like the air before a storm.

"Higher," she says. "Here. And fingers."

She guides his hand to the opening. He slips a finger inside, then two. She shows him how to move them in and out. Her thighs close against his ears and everything else goes away. He half-hears her say "*Oh*" in a voice different from her talking one. After a while she backs his mouth and hand away. A high note comes from her mouth, and her vagina flutters in front of him.

She pulls him up next to her, turns him onto his back and kneels over him. He looks up at her breasts and face as she slides his penis inside her and moves up and down, touching herself where his mouth was. Her inside is strong and liquid all at once. He tries to slow himself but his seed gushes out of him in long pulses that make him gasp.

He stays inside her while she keeps moving, touching herself with her eyes closed. It starts to hurt but he waits. She says "*Oh*" again, opens her eyes, rests her weight on him for a minute and then rises, wincing with him as he comes out. They lie looking at each other till they fall asleep.

In the morning he kisses her forehead without waking her and slips out of bed. It feels strange to kiss a grown woman, but maybe he's grown up too now. He stands naked on the wood floor, watching dawn light at the edges of the curtains. How different could it feel to be twenty-five, done with university, having a place in the world? He feels that way already.

He dresses, walks down the hill, gets the bicycle and rides to Los Angeles, enjoying the scenery this time, and the empty ache in his groin. There's an electrical supply store downtown. Even before this it would have been exciting, two long aisles of parts and a brotherhood of clerks and customers talking about rumored inventions and dams coming on line. Now the parts are like jewelry he's buying her.

He makes two trips to get everything: a crank dynamo, soldering iron, wet-cell battery, switchbox, solder, wire, sal ammoniac and four Mazda light bulbs. At one o'clock every morning he sneaks to her house, where they make love, lie in the tangled sheets a while and get up so she can paint and he can wire.

In a week there are four light bulbs hanging from the ceiling. Rose sews orange backing on her curtains so it looks like lanterns from outside. Inside it's the magnesium flash of city nights. She draws a street scene with extra lines around everything, and in electric light it seems to move like cinema.

They tell no one about their relations, not even Lilli. No one's supposed to have secrets here, but they're not supposed to have electricity either. At work they're careful to disagree with each other the way they always have, especially when Father's around.

One Sunday Frieda finds Benji at the sawmill and says, "There's someone at the gate who says he knows you." He goes down and finds Dan from the bookstore staring up at the art studio.

"These buildings are fantastic," he says.

"There are more," Benji says. "Come up this way. The music's going to start."

When they get there the lawn's full of people and the band's getting ready. Benji introduces Dan to Rose and says, "She designed the buildings."

"They're terrific," Dan says. She thanks him and goes to sit with Jules and Suzanne. "*She's* terrific," Dan says. Benji nods. Not telling Dan is the hardest of all, but he manages.

The music starts, a song from the American Civil War. The words say

In my death I will be proud
Flag of freedom be my shroud

but the music says *Let's swing from the ceiling naked! What's there to drink?*

"Who *are* these people?" Dan says.

"That's my mother with the violin," Benji says.

Dan turns to look at him, even more impressed than before. "Would it be all right if I told a few friends about this?" he asks.

"I guess so," Benji says. "Richard seems to like visitors."

Dan surveys the Sunlanders' costumes: fans, boas, antlers, rabbit ears, painted faces and exposed bosoms. Lilli, Patrice and six others are dancing in their shiny clothes and tossing a paper lantern from hand to hand.

"*Sunday Afternoon on the Island of Outer Space*," Dan says.

"We work hard the other days," Benji says. It makes sense to him now. Six months ago he liked hardly anyone here, maybe Tilda and his sawmill friends, but not Rose. It's crazy to think of that now, but nothing stays put these days. No one knows what a map of the world will look like a year from now, or civilization either. It could look like this. Since Rose he knows better than to think anything for sure.

1917

Twenty-Five

Gerhard comes down the hill on a Sunday in February and sees at least two hundred people stretching back from the porch of the Welcome Building. The county road's lined with parked cars. From Los Angeles, he thinks, and more of them every week. The Sunland women have been keeping their shirts on, but that just means people bring their families.

Lilli and her friends are at the front of the crowd, getting ready to dance. Behind them are the other Sunlanders, who've been decorating themselves since dawn—papier-mâché porcupine quills, gold hoop skirts, faces painted with moons and constellations. Farther back are the visitors from the city, spruce young clerks and teachers, and then local boys who come to laugh but get caught up in the music. The smell of joss stick floats on the breeze. If there was an ounce of good news in the world, this would be the celebration.

Anna and the band walk out onto the porch and everyone cheers. They're the stuff of rumor and souvenirs now. Benji took photographs of them playing, bought paper and chemicals in town, developed the pictures in the dark, printed copies with sunlight, and put them out for sale in the Welcome Building. Four different images, three sharp and one blurred on purpose, with Anna's face and scarf moving as she plays.

"Thank you," Roland says as the applause quiets down. "We've got something new this week. All these people down by the front, the people that live here—we're going to bring out the fellow who got them together in the first place. Looking for a new line on how to do things—I can't nearly tell you. He'll do that. Let's just welcome him. Richard Weiss."

The crowd claps as Richard comes forward. On previous Sundays he's stood at the back near Gerhard, scanning the scene as if any minute now he'll understand it, then have a world-historical theory to fit it into, and then have seen it coming all along.

"Thank you," he says, and waits for them to settle down. "I want to welcome our friends from Los Angeles. It's so nice of you to visit us each week. I wonder what that's like. I wonder if you hear the music and see the people and the land, and a crazy question comes to you— what if life was like this?

"But here is the fact: life *is* like this. For so long, life was like this everywhere. Work and rest, art and nature, a few people you'd die for—that was life.

"The question is, who told you otherwise? Who told you that life is what you have in Los Angeles, with the factories and billboards and telegrams? And how did they get away with it?

"They have you thinking, 'What are these crazy new fads—these Sunland people, or the Theosophists in Hollywood, or the raw-food eaters in Glendale? All these strange new ideas.' Because you started your life in the modern world, and you think it's your home.

"But in fact the modern world is the new fad. The guilty religions, the time-clocks, everyone fighting everyone else in a city—*these* are the crazy new ideas."

Some of the Los Angeles people look baffled. They

came for the music but here's this man with a German accent, looking like a professor who gets too close to his students and lecturing them about their lives.

The city people are polite, though, trying to give him a chance. The boys from the nearby towns are another story. "Do you know any songs?" one of them yells.

Richard ignores him and goes on. "We saw what those fads were doing to our country and we walked away. You could walk away too. Someplace where land is cheap, with some people you'd rather make love to than knock over for money—" A few local boys laugh and cheer.

Roland, behind Richard, pats the air with his hands to quiet them down. Richard senses the movement, turns and looks at him. Roland puts his hands down. Richard faces the crowd again.

"I sense I've taken enough of your time," he says. There's modest clapping. Then Roland and the musicians step forward and the real applause starts.

"Thank you," Roland says. "Richard Weiss. Let's thank him again." He turns around, but Richard's already gone through the back doors of the Welcome Building.

Roland plays a chord on his guitar, adjusts a string and plays it again. "This one here, Jerome and Lois made it up. I'm jealous."

He strums and Anna starts the melody, mid-tempo. The crowd recognizes it and claps. Roland sings in his thin tenor:

I walked my shoes to nothing,
A thousand miles it seemed,
But I put down my walking
The day I found the stream.
I love the water
I love the water

Anna dips toward Roland, then away, her scarf moving half a beat behind her.

> *It starts up in the mountains,*
> *It wanders and it bends,*
> *It goes down to the ocean*
> *And the ocean never ends.*
> *I love the water*
> *I love the water*

The audience sings along on the refrain. Richard comes up the side of the crowd past Gerhard, looking at no one. Gerhard turns and watches him walk up the hill. That speech must have sounded better, he thinks, in a Munich coffee house full of people who hadn't already gotten the message from beaches and canyons.

Roland sings:

> *They tell me I should cross it*
> *And see that other shore,*
> *But let that stream run over me*
> *And I won't ask for more.*
> *I love the water*
> *I love the water*

He lets the crowd take over, two hundred voices singing "I love the water" over and over as the sun goes down. Anna follows a long note with a fast phrase, and Roland cocks his ear as if he hears her from a distance.

A young man sitting near Gerhard stares at Anna. Gerhard has to look twice to be sure what he sees: the man's ogling her as if she's an actress. A pretty one.

What a strange human habit, to make musicians our heroes. They don't fight battles or improve working conditions, but people cheer them as if they've just stormed the Bastille, discovered quinine and made dinner for everyone. It's because they shock you with your own emotions, a trick that never grows old. Like Liszt, eighty years ago—he came out on stage and teenaged girls wept, screamed, followed him from the concert hall and saved his cigar butts, feeling everything they were supposed to be too young for.

Another young man, a few meters away, is giving Anna that same look. Roland encourages it, dipping toward her in their duet and grinning at her flurry of notes, his eyes locked to hers.

That's fine, all of you, Gerhard thinks, but that's my wife. And, fantastically, my wife is *that*.

Not that it's news to me. Don't say it is. But wipe away the years, the rooms, the crying babies, the broke ends of the month, and I'm back to when we first met and slept together. *Talk* about lightning being in everything. We went to her parents' house and used her old bed when they were out, then traveled to my boyhood home and took a blanket to the woods. "There," Anna said as we lay still afterward. "Now we've always been together." These little lookers will never know how right they are.

Bernard plays a solo while the crowd keeps singing. He stands at the back, his silver notes curling around their voices in the twilight. Three choruses later Roland comes up and sings again:

If you're in a hurry
You can cross it if you wish
But my dog he likes to paddle
My girl she likes to fish
And I love the water
I love the water

They play two more songs. Gerhard stays till the end,

then walks home past people carrying sleeping children to their cars. In the Japanese house he lights a lantern, turns it low, gets into bed, tries to wait up for Anna but falls asleep. When he wakes up she's there, taking off her scarf and earrings.

"Hello," he says.

"Hello. Were you there tonight?"

"Yes."

"Did you hear Richard? Those people were so rude to him. I worried about it all evening."

"I didn't think it was so important," he says. "I thought you sounded fine."

"No, it was important," she says, undressing to her drawers and camisole. "We all stayed after, talking about it. I thought they'd want to listen to him."

"They heard what he has to say," Gerhard says. "It wouldn't fill books."

She gets into bed. "We played that much harder," she says. "To get through to them."

"You got through to them, all right. I saw that."

He reaches for her but she stays still. "I have to calm down," she says. "I feel like I'm still up there." A minute later she's asleep.

The next morning, by the spool table, Gerhard puts a hand on Rose's shoulder, moves close and tries to kiss her. She turns her head, puts it against his and pats his temple.

"No?" he says.

"I'm afraid not," Rose says. "You're dear to me, you know."

"But because of Anna—?"

"That too."

"Too?"

"But one should always ask," she says. "There might be something there."

He lets go of her and walks up the hill. Two hours later

he finds himself acres away, staring up at the granary with no idea how he got there.

I should be relieved, he thinks. I was going to be sick of myself one way or another, and now I am. I wasn't mistaken, not exactly. She cares for me, but they have ways and ways of doing that here. It's one of their crafts.

In the week that follows he's finally a full citizen of Sunland, poetically sad and mechanically useless. Talking to his family is like mining syllables out of the ground. None of these sensitive people seem to notice the state he's in, though Benji's a little friendlier than usual.

On the eighth night he finally gets some sleep, wakes up at dawn and reaches for Anna, but she's left to bake bread. It's life, he thinks. It was never going to grow wings and turn into something else.

He goes outside. Last night's rain steams off the houses and a starling watches him brush his teeth. At the dining hall he eats breakfast, smiles at Rose and Anna both, walks out onto the porch and almost knocks into Jules, who's back from town with two days' *Los Angeles Times*. He gives them to Gerhard. The first one announces:

REVOLUTIONISTS RULE IN RUSSIA— CZAR ABDICATES

After an almost bloodless revolution, developing unexpectedly out of the shortage of bread in Petrograd, it looks as if the Russian people are acquiring rights beyond their wildest dreams. The red flag of revolt is everywhere.

He sits in a chair, puts his coffee down and opens the second paper:

GERMANY IS NEXT, ALL SIGNS INDICATE
Unrest Is Increasing in Kaiser's Dominion

It is more than probable, was the opinion expressed today, that the world stands upon the verge of a collapse of absolutism in Germany as well as in Russia. Every king in Europe trembles at the din of the mobs of Petrograd.

Gerhard closes his eyes and sees marchers, trash fires, and fists rocking the gates of the Reichstag till the chains come loose. I should be there, he thinks.

Then he sees steerage on the ships, seasick travelers, and the gnats of Panama. When he opens his eyes there's a prism on his coffee and blue sky over the hills.

I'm not going, he thinks. Imagine that. I walked out of my life and lived this one instead. I don't get Rose or the barricades, I get the affection of these weedy people I'm nice to. Revolutions are everywhere—Benji has muscles, Lilli has breasts—but mine was over before it started. Rosa, comrades, I built a gift store.

Twenty-Six

Anna's taking bread to the berry pickers when Suzanne hurries past, saying, "Come to the lawn!"

"What is it?" Anna says.

"War," Suzanne says. "Patrice heard it in town. Do you have guns at your house?"

"What? No."

"People are bringing them," Patrice says. "In case we're attacked first thing."

Anna hurries after her, but it makes no sense. The war's been going on for three years. Has someone started another one?

When they get to the lawn a crowd's forming around Patrice. "Tell them what happened," Dara says.

"I was at the notions store," Patrice says. "I asked the lady for some ribbons and she said, 'I don't know if I can sell you things now.' I said, 'No, it's all right, we have money from selling jelly.' She said, 'It's not that. Don't you know? We're at war with you people. With Germany. The President declared it yesterday.'"

Everyone's here now. Anna goes over to stand with Gerhard and the children. Frieda's holding a shotgun, and Jules and Josef have pistols. Anna hasn't seen guns here before, except the rifle for gophers.

"Are we in trouble?" Herman says.

"We shouldn't be," Richard says. "We're as civilian as

anyone in history."

"They could still arrest us," Frieda says. "As a precaution."

"We can live in the woods," Josef says. "We've done it before."

"If we're doing that we'd better go now," Benji says.

"We could go into town," Suzanne says. "We could ask to be treated as deserters."

"I like that," Jorgen says.

"I'm not getting arrested for anyone," Lilli's friend Diana says.

"Diana," her father says.

"I'm not. No one said prisoner of war."

"Wait," Herman says, holding up a hand.

Everyone listens. An engine shuts off by the gate. Two car doors open and close. Frieda, Jules and Josef raise their guns and point them toward the sound.

In a minute two men walk up, the alderman and the policeman they met on their first day in town. The policeman stops and points a rifle at the Sunlanders. "Guns on the ground," he says. "Now."

For a moment no one moves. Then Frieda, Jules and Josef comply. The two men resume walking up.

"Tyrus Whitliff," the other man says. "Alderman."

"Good to see you again," Richard says.

"You've heard the news, I suppose." Whitliff takes a newspaper from under his arm and holds it up. The headline, *WE'RE IN IT AT LAST*, is flanked by red and blue drawings of soldiers.

"Are we under arrest?" Rolf says.

"Not now," Whitliff says, "but don't count on that lasting. There's concern about spying and sabotage."

"We spy only on each other," Richard says. "We sabotage only ourselves."

"The police will be watching bridges, tunnels, ports,

depots and large groups," Whitliff says. "Anything that goes wrong in the area, the court can order you out of here."

"It's our land," Frederick says.

"I didn't say you can't own it," Whitliff says. "There's nothing about taking property yet. But you might have to disperse."

"We farmed it," Josef says. "For four years. We built—"

"I'm not ordering you," Whitliff says. "I've been the one in town saying live and let live. I'm just telling you what's being discussed." He looks into the crowd. "There are Americans—?"

Roland and the others raise their hands. "I'd think seriously about where your loyalties lie," Whitliff says. "In the meanwhile you ought to be the ones who come into town, for safety's sake."

It's quiet for a moment, and then Oliver says, "Sir? Can we still have the music, on Sundays?"

Whitliff frowns. "You're not having a meeting here with people speaking German. That won't go."

"It's just singing, sir," Oliver says. "In English."

"I don't think you'll have an audience coming from outside here, either," Whitliff says. "You'll be talking to yourselves."

"There are always times like that," Richard says.

"Nobody leaves here without notifying the town clerk where you're going," Whitliff says. "That's all for now. We'll keep you informed."

The policeman keeps his rifle aimed at the crowd as Whitliff picks up the guns. When they've driven away Lilli says, "I didn't know people had guns here."

"Well, now we don't," Gerhard says. "Not even a receipt."

☙

A few days later Anna goes to practice early and Roland's there alone, playing the same few chords over and over. When he sees her he stops. "What's that?" she says.

He shakes his head. "Something I'm fooling with." He gets out his tobacco. "How are your kids doing, with the war and all?"

"They're all right," Anna says. "Yours are little, though."

"Hundred questions a day I can't answer."

"Gerhard explains it with socialism. That it's all about capital and so on."

"I should send my boys over," Roland says. "Catch them asking anything again."

Lois and Jerome arrive, then Bernard and the others. Halfway through practice, Herman and Dara walk past the clearing. They're moving unsteadily, helping each other along, and their clothes are splashed with blue and orange paint.

The band stops playing. "Hey," Jerome yells. "What happened?"

They come over. Dara's crying, her tears mixing with the paint on her face. Herman's cheek is covered by a purple bruise with bloody scratches.

"It's all right," he says in halting English. "Just—in town."

"We bought paint," Dara says. "And some men—"

"Honey, we'll go for you," Lois says. "We'll go any time."

"Thank you," Dara says. "But the colors. We want to see."

"For our house," Herman says.

"Like a temple," Dara says, and starts crying again.

"They made me kiss their flag," Herman says. "They took it down from the post office and made me. I said it's fine. I said the stars are beautiful."

"The one said he has a boy in the war," Dara says. "I

said I'll think about him. I said I'll pray. He said something dirty, I think."

"At the paint store they were kind," Herman says.

"That's good," Philip says. "I'll get you some of that. I'll remember those colors, no question."

Gloria walks to their house site with them. When she gets back Roland cuts practice short. "Seems like it'll be just us folks," he says. "Reaching that multitude is rough on the tonsils anyway."

That evening at lawn hour Richard tells the crowd, "Manfred has something to read to you."

Manfred's talked at the lawn before, always about crop seeding or irrigation. This time he's holding a book and a sheet of paper.

"He doesn't do this, you know," Richard says, "but I asked him to. And I'll translate. My English isn't as good as Ben's but I think it will be all right."

Manfred clears his throat and says, "This is for my friend Georg Hertz. Recently deceased." He reads from the piece of paper:

"Georg, you've finished your education.
You've learned to explode,
your boyhood summers reduced to one smear
in the mud of a forest.
Where do you want the borders, Georg?
I never knew you to care about them
but they're everything to you now,
now that our cellars are open
and mice pour out, squealing for warmth
from a sun long extinguished."

"My God," Anna says.
"What is it?" Benji says.
"Manfred *Scharf.*"

> *"This must be a saint's day*
> *because all these people are here—*
> *proud parents, happy policemen,*
> *sextons in pink chemises,*
> *grocers carrying guns in their teeth,*
> *all of them mostly pus*
> *with tatters of flesh for color,*
> *opening their blood mouths to say, 'Why are you crying?'*
> *The dark around the sun*
> *took years to reach us*
> *but it's here.*
> *I name the darkness after you.*
> *It has your eyes."*

It's quiet for a moment. Then Manfred opens his book, saying, "I have an older one."

"Is he famous?" Lilli whispers.

"Everyone had that book," Anna says. "I still do."

The next day Benji asks her if he can borrow it. "Yes," she says. "I only brought a few books, but that's one of them."

"Thank you," he says. "Really it's for your friend Roland. He asked me to put them into English for him."

Anna almost cries. If you have to live through a war, she thinks, these are the people to do it with: Manfred being Manfred Scharf without talking about it, Roland wanting German poetry and Benji translating it for him. A small sector of the world that hasn't lost its mind.

A few days later two men in suits come into the Welcome Building when Anna and Rolf are working there. "Good morning," Anna says in English.

"We're from the Liberty Loan Society in Yucaipa," the taller man says. "We sell Liberty Bonds and War Savings Stamps. Do you know what those are?"

"No sir," Rolf says.

The man opens his briefcase and takes out certificates, pamphlets, and sheets of stamps. He lays them on the counter, covering Patrice's satin map of Atlantis.

"You should know about them," he says. "They're for defeating Germany."

"Yes sir," Rolf says.

"Are you Germans?"

"Yes sir."

"Do you side with Germany?"

"No sir."

"We have Americans here too," Anna says.

"Miss, I'm talking to the man here."

"If you buy sixteen Thrift Stamps you get a War Savings Stamp," the shorter man says. "When you have ten of those you get a Liberty Bond."

"You buy the stamps from us now," the taller man says. "Let's say a hundred dollars' worth. You sell them here and that's your money back. You can take that to the bank and buy one of these." He holds up a certificate showing the statue in New York Harbor, the one the people on their ship cried over.

"We'd like you to put this on display," he says, taking out a poster that says *BEAT BACK THE HUN WITH LIBERTY BONDS*. The illustration shows a snarling soldier with gray flesh, green eyes, a blood-dripping bayonet and a city in ruins behind him.

"Do you object to that?" the tall man asks Rolf.

"Did you paint it?" Rolf says.

"What? No, of course not. An artist painted it."

"Is it sincere?"

"What?"

"Is the artist sincere in it?"

"Of course he is."

"I can't object to it, then," Rolf says. "It's his work."

"I'm asking you to put it up."

Rolf hesitates. "Generally we have a meeting."

"No, no," the short man says.

"Are we agreed on a hundred dollars for now?" the tall man says.

"You'll have to wait," Anna says.

"All right."

She leaves them with Rolf, goes to Richard's house and finds him writing at his railway ticket counter. "Some men want a hundred dollars," she says. "For the war."

"Will they take thirty?"

"I don't think so."

They collect money from people at the farm and building sites, small sums they've made by hiring out or selling things at the Welcome Building. Anna's apron gets heavy with coins but they're still $18.40 short. They're leaving to get it from the jar in the kitchen when Lilli's friend Diana says, "Do you get anything for it?"

"There are stamps," Anna says.

"How much?"

"Ten cents," Anna says. "But you can't mail letters with them. They're to pay for the war. You put them in a book, I think."

"All right," Diana says.

Her mother Gloria looks embarrassed. "It would say more if no one bought them," she says.

"I'm not trying to say anything," Diana says. "It's my money, from Reedsport."

She goes with Anna to the kitchen and the Welcome Building. The stamp men are waiting with Rolf. They've tacked the Hun poster to a shelf of corn relish.

"I want a stamp, please," Diana says, holding a dime out. "And a book."

The tall man gives her a booklet and a stamp with a soldier on it. The short man counts the money from Anna.

Diana opens the booklet, writes her name and address in a child's scrawl, pastes her stamp in the first blank, closes it and presses it flat.

"You keep buying those stamps and you'll have your own Liberty Bond," the short man says. "That's going to help get this war over with."

Diana shakes her head. "I don't need any more," she says. "I just want to own something clean."

ↄ

The next day at practice Roland plays the song he's written. It's the chords Anna heard him trying, and lyrics. She likes it, they all do, but they have to tell him so for twenty minutes before he asks them to join in. The first few times, they play it angrily to go with the words, but he stops them and says, "Just play it country, like you're happy. They'll know."

For three days they try to get it the way he wants it, till they're so frustrated their sounds crash together like a calliope being knocked down a hill. This is hopeless, Anna thinks, just as Roland says, "That's *it*. Yes. Thank God."

That Sunday the Sunlanders expect no visitors and dress for one another, Patrice in feathered wings and a New Guinea tribal mask, Linda in a shirt of loosely woven cane hoops, Suzanne made up as Pierrot and Rolf as a Mexican sugar skull. By afternoon the crowd and the line of parked cars are as big as ever. Frieda takes Linda a serape and talks her into putting it on.

Twelve of Rose's banners hang from poles around the site, the newest ones showing the band and the city crowd. During the water song Esther the mule walks through the audience pulling a cart rigged with two giant puppets, a man and woman who come together and kiss over and over, driven by the motion of the wheels. Jules, dressed as a drum major, sits in the cart's bed throwing origami animals to the crowd.

As night falls Roland announces, "This next one I made myself," with a nervous catch in his voice. Philip counts it off and Roland sings:

"The mayor's stealing pennies
from the fountain with a rake,
The doctor is a dope fiend
with the eyelids of a snake,
And the welcoming committee
brought a club and knocked me down.
I don't understand it, darling,
It seemed like such a friendly town.

"The preacher wears a raincoat
with nothing underneath,
The grocer goes around
with a revolver in his teeth,
And the honest and the upright,
They've all gone underground.
I can't comprehend it, honey,
It seemed like such a friendly town."

He tears into the word *friendly* like he wants to bite it in half. It makes Anna remember him getting off the truck with Helen and the boys that first day, all of them so thin and dirty.

"They're blacking out the windows
It's darkness all the time
The barber wants to cut me
but the butcher's first in line,
And I get the strangest feeling
They don't want me around.
I can't see no explanation,
It seemed like such a friendly town."

Anna searches the crowd till she sees Herman and Dara, laughing.

"The Methodists play poker
from the bottom of the deck
Five minutes with the Lutherans
and you'll be a nervous wreck
And the Baptists at the river
Hold you under till you drown.
I don't know what happened, honey,
It seemed like such a <u>friendly</u> town."

They run out of verses but keep playing. They've never sounded this good. Roland plays a solo and it's all there in the sound—his clothes, his sons, his broken fingers on his strings and the way he looks down at his shoes and then right back up at you. Anna veers through a long run of notes thinking *But how do I land this aeroplane*, just as Jack's cornet lays down a runway of nickel for her. We could play forever, she thinks, carrying one another like this.

Half the crowd's dancing, and now Anna sees something she can hardly believe: Josef, walking into the ragged lane between the Sunlanders and the Americans. He's never come to a Sunday before. Once at supper he called their music "the shriek from the bush," and Anna thanked God Bernard wasn't there to hear him.

But here he is, with Tilda leading a mule and cart behind him. It takes Anna a minute to recognize what's in the bed of the cart: the four Hohenzollern emperors Richard made Frederick sculpt, gleaming in the moonlight, their pig eyes looking down their offended noses.

The cart stops in the middle of the crowd. Josef, looking angry, pulls his cape back, digs a box of matches from his pocket, strikes one and touches it to the sculptures. When the last one catches fire he goes back into the woods, his punishment complete.

The heads burn fast, with tall chemical flares. Everyone turns to look at them and the band plays louder. These people from Los Angeles can't know anything about Prussian history, but everyone loves a bonfire. Sparks shoot into the sky as the emperors turn black and collapse.

Anna and Roland are in a duet now, going faster and higher, not taking turns anymore but piling onto each other. The tension builds for four choruses till it's too much to bear. They let it crest, the pitch and tempo coming down from the climax as they bend toward each other, sweat running into their eyes and a roar of applause pouring over them.

The music ends but plays on in Anna's head as they walk into the Welcome Building. Jerome says something about the solos in the train song but his words go past her.

She says goodnight, walks out the front door, goes up the path, and hesitates where it forks. Without looking, she feels Roland's eyes on her from the window.

She turns toward the canning shed, a blue wooden building with a boardwalk and moonlit windows. Inside, she pumps water in the sink to wash herself, but Roland's there before she has the chance.

They hold each other, kissing, undress and let their clothes make a bed on the floor. She's seen him in the stream but that was spying. Now she sees him straight on, still thin but beautiful. She pulls him onto her. People are right to be scared of this, she thinks, two people could break the world, but it's long since broken to a hundred worlds or more, their moons shining down from jars of fruit.

Twenty-Seven

Benji stands at the job board, reading the letter again. Last night at the concert he sat with Dan and two of his friends from Los Angeles, Todd the bank teller and Lucy the seamstress. When it got dark, Dan passed Benji his flask of whiskey. It burned, but not as much as it had a week before.

As Benji passed it back Roland started singing a new song, about a town full of "friendly" people who wanted to kill him. The crowd liked it. Benji did too, but a few of its lines bothered him, like the grocer with a gun in his teeth and the Baptists drowning people. After a minute it came to him: those lines were from Manfred's poems, the ones Roland gave Benji a dollar to translate.

You're not supposed to do that, Benji thought—just take someone else's words and say, "This next song I made myself." He craned to look at Manfred, who was sitting with Tilda and Patrice. He gave no sign he recognized his own work.

Then Tilda brought a mule cart through the crowd and Josef set Frederick's sculptures on fire. People crowded around them, pushing and shouting as if they wanted everything to be in one space, the fire, the music and their own bodies, atoms between atoms. The band played faster. Manfred shook his head, ever so slightly.

Now, the next morning, there's a letter in neat slanted handwriting on notebook paper, with an English translation by Richard next to it:

Dear friends,

It seems we are a success. Our Sunday entertainments draw ever more attendance, effecting a truce between two nations at war. We offer useful and beautiful goods, and several crops are at surplus.

I think I am more at home with failure.

Our first year at Langenhain we were hungry. Our radishes were pale pink strings. People had bites on their rashes on their blisters, and the shits were rampant. Still, those are some of my happiest memories.

I am moving to the canyon east of here. Farming is good work, but in this climate a diet for one eater grows wild. The conversations of these years will keep me company a long time.

I love everyone here, without exception.

Manfred

It's my fault, Benji thinks. Part of it, anyway. I could have asked Roland what he wanted those translations for. I could have turned down his dollar.

He finds Rose at her house, drawing with pen and ink. "Did you see Manfred's letter?" he says.

"Yes," she says. "People are going to be furious at him."

"For leaving?"

She shakes her head. "For thinking of it first. It's the next phase. You don't spend all those years fighting your way through the art district without learning something."

"I see."

"And *then* they'll miss him." She looks up from her

drawing. "Do you know what Bernard and Leah want for their house?"

"No. They've been staying in the pole barn since they came."

"Could you ask them? Frederick usually draws the houses, but Bernard likes you."

"He does?"

"Mm."

Benji's surprised. He's talked to Bernard a few times at work, and now and then Bernard looks up from a book in the pole barn when Benji's teaching, but mostly Benji's been shy. He's only spoken to one colored person before Bernard, and that was an African man who asked him directions in Berlin. Benji felt an almost tearful pleasure when the man understood him, but Bernard doesn't seem to need that kind of help.

Benji catches up with him in the woods after supper and asks him what kind of house he and Leah want. "It can be any design you like," he says. "And we all help one another build."

"I think we're all right where we are now," Bernard says.

"It's no cost for the materials," Benji says. "They come out of—"

"I realize. But we don't plan to stay forever. Besides—" He looks Benji over. "That barn has three ways to get out and a couple of spots to hide in. We're not in trouble with anyone, you understand. We've done nothing wrong. But that's no guarantee in this world."

Benji pauses. "All right."

"Thank you, though."

Benji nods. "May I ask you something else? When Roland played you that song about the town—did he say where the words came from?"

Bernard smiles. "Said he made it up. His lack of confidence was touching but he got over it fast."

"Some of it was Manfred's poetry. Roland got me to translate it for him, and then he put it in the song."

Bernard looks puzzled. "*Roland* did that?"

"Yes, he—"

"You're saying *Roland* went and *stole* something for his *music?* What a shock *that* is. *Roland*, you say."

"You're speaking sarcastically," Benji says.

"I can't scratch myself around him, lest he get up there and do it the same."

"Thank you," Benji says.

"Don't tell him I'm not building a house," Bernard says. "Tell him it's a mansion with stain-glass windows. Circular driveway, portico, potted palm trees and Chesterfield sofas. That'll keep him busy."

The next day Benji's walking up to the sawmill when Richard calls him from the porch of his house. "Ben! Come talk to me."

Benji goes up and follows Richard into the main room, with three beds and suggestive signs hanging from the ceiling. Richard sits on a bed, points Benji to another, and lights a cigar.

"Can you go to the canyon tomorrow?" he says.

"The one Manfred moved to?"

"And Rolf, now," Richard says. "It may be a trend."

"They won't come back," Benji says. "Not from me asking."

"No, no. That's fine. But we've had a notice about registering for the army draft. It's in San Bernardino, this Saturday." He hands Benji a letter from the government, giving the details. "Can you go and tell them?"

"Could someone else do it?"

"Why?"

"I think Manfred might have a problem with me."

"What kind of problem?"

Benji has no desire to explain it to Richard, but it's too

late now. He tells about Roland, the poems and the song.

"I see," Richard says, and thinks a moment. "When Manfred lived in Berlin he wrote a poem called 'Falling.'"

Benji nods. "It's in his book."

"He was the first one to write in that style," Richard says. "It came out in *Die Aktion* and people went crazy for it.

"The storm tears voices from mouths
And eyes from faces—"

He frowns and holds up a finger till it comes to him.

"—as actors step down from cinema screens
and spread the contagion of their flicker through the public,
a half-light pulsing under nerveless skin.
New records are set
in the production of gravel and loneliness,
nerves shatter at the slightest music,
and now reports are heard of people breaking apart,
crushed by the careless vise of earth and cloud.

"Just Manfred's luck," Richard says. "There were thousands of people out there as morose as he was. They read that poem out everywhere. I include bicycle races. Or instead of telling someone goodnight, you'd shout a line across the street and they'd shout one back.

"Then there were imitations and parodies and articles about whether some new poem would knock it from its position. Manfred and his friend Georg couldn't go out without people staring at them."

"Georg from the war poem?"

"Mm." Richard draws on his cigar. "Manfred's terror became a commodity. He went a little mad. I had to get him out of Berlin. I told him I was starting a new kind of society in the country. Then I had to go through with it. My point is, this isn't the first time he's needed a change. In any case, don't blame yourself. It's a filthy habit."

"All right," Benji says.

"We think such nice things about art, but up close it's trouble," Richard says. "The blind poet finishes his epic and falls over in a heap. Everyone makes a living off his epic for the next thousand years and no one even stops to sweep him up."

"Manfred's poem," Benji says. "It's true, isn't it?"

Richard looks at him for a moment, then nods. I could almost like him, Benji thinks. I guess I'll go tomorrow after all.

∛

He slips out of Rose's house before dawn, walks to the end of the path, and follows a deer trail into dry hills. By noon he's at the mouth of the canyon, with mountains in front of him and a hazy valley behind. He climbs an upthrust to look for people, doesn't see any, and keeps walking.

The trail rises and falls through fields of rocks, parallel to a stream on the canyon floor. There are boulders big enough to sleep under, but no one's there except lizards.

He goes another hour, past prickly pears and boulders striped like mattress ticking. Ocotillos rattle in the breeze and birds chase each other around spires of rock. Benji's arms itch with dried sweat.

The trail ends at a waterfall thirty feet high, with a pool at the bottom where Rolf's swimming. Manfred, sitting naked on a rock, nods at Benji and says, "That's all right to drink."

Benji kneels, drinks, dips his head in the water and stands up shivering as it runs down his back. "I'm glad you came," Manfred says. "You're well?"

"Fine. Thank you. Do you really have enough food here?"

"It's like a store. Chickweed. Wild dates. Even mugwort, for dreams." He nods at some big rocks by the pool, lined up by size. "Rolf's got me lifting those for exercise."

Benji sits on a rock. "I want to tell you something," he says. "I translated your poems into English for Roland. Before he wrote that song."

"Oh. Do you have the translations?"

"Roland does. I don't think they're very good."

"I'd like to see them. There was going to be an English edition but they kept softening up the despair."

Rolf comes out of the water, nods at Benji and sits down. "Are you joining us here?" he says. "You're welcome to."

"No," Benji says. "Thank you, though. I'm here about the registration for the draft. The American army. All the men from twenty-one to thirty-one have to go to San Bernardino for it."

"When?" Manfred says.

"Saturday," Benji says. "They're leaving from the gate at nine."

"I'm thirty-five but I'll come along," Manfred says. Benji would have guessed fifty-two. "Are you going?"

"I hadn't thought of it," Benji says.

"It'd be nice to have you," Rolf says.

"All right. I'll see you then."

He fills his canteen and starts back. By mid-afternoon he's run out of water, his skin feels on fire, and the cliffs look blurry through sweat and heat waves. He worries about going through town on Saturday and running into the Ungraded boys. Rolf and Jorgen could beat them up but that would make things worse.

He walks into Sunland and over the hill, passing the sun altar. Old offerings are scattered around, moldy orange rinds and rusty pieces of a coffee tin. He bought Lilli that book about the solar system but she's still up here every morning. He walks down the hill, finds a quiet tree and sleeps past supper.

ॐ

On Saturday he meets ten draft-aged men at the gate and they walk to Driscoll for the streetcar. In San Bernardino the main square's crowded with people, flag-covered wagons and free lemonade. A man sees the Sunlanders looking lost, points to a brick building marked *GYMNASIUM* and says, "In there."

Inside there's another crowd, all young men. They're filling out papers and giving them to three officials at a table. One of the officials pushes a stack of forms toward the Sunlanders and says, "Full name, date and place of birth, race, citizenship, occupation, personal characteristics and signature or the letter X. Do you understand?"

Benji translates for those who don't, and they fill in their forms. One of the officials reads Richard's and says, "You realize you're signing up to shoot other Germans."

"We are the other Germans," Richard says. "That's why we're here."

"I can't understand you when you talk," one of the officials says.

"Try me," Jack says. "I passed English four years out of six."

"What are you doing with this bunch?"

"Assembling peaceably."

Bernard hands his form in. "There's a colored division but it's full," an official says.

"Yes sir," Bernard says.

"I'm sure they'll prove themselves brave," the man says. Some of the men in line laugh.

"I don't see the joke," Roland says.

"Just that they're not considered the best at fighting," one of the officials says.

"You haven't seen my friend here when he's aggravated," Roland says. "I've seen him in a few towns by now. Harder towns than this."

"I'd stop there," the man says. It's turned quiet around the table.

They finish handing their forms in and walk out. When they're a few blocks away Bernard comes close to Benji and says, "Now I'm Jack goddamn Johnson," and neither one says anything the rest of the way home.

Twenty-Eight

Tuesday afternoon Lilli goes home early, sits on the door-sill and waits. In a while her mother walks up, her hair pinned back and clothes wet from taking children to the stream.

"Hello," she says, surprised to see Lilli there. "Are you all right?"

"Yes," Lilli says. "How are you?"

Mother looks at her. "What's wrong?"

"I have to tell you something." She nods at the empty house. "It's all right, no one's going to hear."

Mother sits down next to her. "Sunday night, after the music, I went home the long way," Lilli says. "I was up above by the canning shed and I saw you come out, and then a few minutes later Roland did."

Mother hesitates, then says, "All right."

"How is it all right?" Lilli says, so sharply she surprises herself.

"I mean I understand."

"Does Father know?" Mother doesn't answer. "Are you going to tell him?"

"I'm sorry," Mother says.

"You're sorry you did it?"

"No. I'm sorry you know. I'm sorry people—" She sighs and starts over. "I'm sorry people have to do so many things to feel all right. It sounds stupid, why wouldn't you feel all right, but people go all around the world and—"

"—they go around the world and take their children along, whether their children want to or—"

"You love it here."

"I don't know."

"You—"

"Here where we don't have secrets?"

"I said I'm sorry."

"Benji doesn't love it here," Lilli says. "He never wanted to come. He wants to be in school now. Real school, not Driscoll."

"We came here so you'd be—"

"Do you love Father?"

"Yes."

"Do you want to stay with him?"

Mother nods. "You know—it happened. Things happen that nobody plans. It's no reason to hate me."

"I don't hate you," Lilli says. "I just have to get up."

She stands and goes up to the stables, walking unsteadily even though her feet have the ground memorized. "Mother and Roland fuck together," she tells Rama. She thought saying it out loud would feel better than it does. "That's not one you have to remember," she adds.

In a while the bell rings. Lilli starts out for the lawn, but halfway there she hears someone crying.

She follows the sound to the pole barn, where Bernard and his wife Leah are standing outside with Mother and Roland. Leah's crying and leaning on Mother while Bernard shakes his head at the ground.

Someone's died in the war, Lilli thinks. It can't be anything less. She walks over to them and says, "What happened?"

"Telegram from my sister," Bernard says. "East St. Louis, Illinois." He hands it to Lilli. She knows just enough English from Benji's lessons to read it.

WE GOT OUT SAFE ARE AT TANSYS SORRY TO TELL YOU JIM WAS LOST IN IT

"I went to town and telephoned," Bernard says. "She said the white people had a riot there. She said they went into the Negro section, lit the houses on fire and shot the people coming out. She said the police were taking the white people down there to lynch people."

"They—what for?" Lilli says.

"For being colored," Leah says, and puts a hand on Lilli's shoulder to stop her talking. Lilli hands the telegram back to Bernard. He crumples it in his hand.

"We won't play on Sunday," Mother says. "We can't have singing and dancing." She's got one hand in Roland's and the other on Bernard's arm.

"All those people coming, though," Roland says.

"They can go home," Mother says. "We'll put a sign up, 'Out of Respect... Come Back Next Week.'"

"Or we could play some of those songs—" Roland says, and looks at Bernard. "The ones that say what it's like. You know."

Bernard shakes his head. "Those'll go worse than your murder-my-girlfriend songs."

"They could make people think," Roland says.

"Songs?" Bernard says.

"So they know we—" Mother says.

"I'm not going up and doing that," Bernard says.

"All right," Roland says. "But the rest of us—"

"We won't do anything you don't want," Mother says.

Bernard's news is awful enough, Lilli thinks, and on top of it there are Mother and Roland holding hands and thinking they're going to make things better with their music. I don't know what songs they're talking about, but even I can tell they're talking like that mostly to make each other feel glorious, and if you ask me they've done enough of that already.

೮෫

The next day there's a notice on the job board:

THERE WILL BE MUSIC THIS SUNDAY
BUT NO DANCING OR COSTUMES
BUT LOVE FOR OUR VISITORS, AS ALWAYS

On Sunday afternoon Lilli finds Diana and Oliver sitting by the stream. "Come up there with me," she says. "It's going to start soon."

"Do we have to look serious the whole time?" Diana says as she stands up.

"Don't do any favors," Lilli says.

"That reminds me," Diana says. She goes into her pocket, gets out fifteen cents and gives it to Lilli. Oliver gives her a dime. When you work in the Welcome Building you get to keep some of the money, but only Americans can work there now.

When they get near the stage, the crowd's settling in and Rose is taking her banners down from the trees. "Let's sit in front," Oliver says.

"You go ahead," Lilli says. She wants to see the city people. Two nights ago she dreamed about Berlin, the crowds and smart dresses downtown.

She sits behind a man and lady with a picnic basket and swimming towels. They're in their twenties, the lady in a sky-blue dress, the man in a gray suit.

"You said they wore costumes," the lady says.

"They did last time," the man says. "I don't know."

Mother and the others come out on the porch, all except Bernard. When the cheering quiets down Roland says, "We're doing something different today—paying our respects to East St. Louis. This one's called 'The Solstice Hymn.'"

He strums his guitar and Mother plays the melody, a short tune that makes the same sad conclusion over and over. They don't dip towards each other while they play today.

"What's in St. Louis?" the lady on the blanket says.

Lilli leans forward and says, "The riots." The lady startles as if a bug had sneaked up on her. People clap when the hymn finishes, but not like they do for the regular songs.

Lois comes to the front of the porch and sings a song without instruments. It says another man is gone, a man who had a long chain on him.

"Well, this is cheerful," the lady in front of Lilli says.

"I don't know what they're up to today," the man says.

Roland sings the next one, about seeing handwriting on a wall, his voice more ghostly than ever. The band plays softly, without solos.

Then Jerome sings that he's been in the storm too long, and now he needs time to pray.

"It's all colored songs but the colored man isn't there today," the man in front of Lilli says. "It's interesting."

"If you say so," the lady says.

"Let's go in the stream," a man says nearby.

"Shh, no," someone says. When Jerome finishes, a man behind Lilli yells, "Water song!" and other people start yelling it too.

"Thank you," Roland says on the porch. "We'll get on to those next week. We're thinking about East Saint Louis right now. If you saw it in the papers, people lost their houses there. People lost their lives. So—"

"We didn't do it!" the man behind Lilli yells. She's seen him in town.

The man in front of her turns around and says, "Be

quiet, will you?"

"You be quiet," the other man says.

Frieda comes up on stage with her viola. Roland says, "Anna and Frieda are going to play something now."

Mother comes forward on the porch and speaks English, trying to be heard over people talking. "This is by Arnold Schoenberg—"

"German!" someone yells.

"—who is Austrian—"

"No, *you're* German!"

"—called *Transfigured Night*."

Mother and Frieda play the saddest music yet, music like ashes falling on burned-up houses. The longer they play it the more restless some people get, yelling "Aw come *on!*" at the stage and clapping a fast tempo against the music. Roland tries to shush them but it does no good.

Bernard rushes past Lilli toward the Welcome Building, holding his guitar by the neck and looking mad. He disappears around the front of the building, then comes out onto the porch. A few people in the crowd cheer as he goes up front by Mother and Frieda.

He stands there and nods for a moment, like he's appreciating their music, then makes a motion with his hands to stop them. They lower their instruments.

Bernard plays the first chords of the water song on his guitar. There's more cheering from the crowd.

Roland says something to Bernard and gestures at him to stop. Bernard says something back and keeps playing. Lois joins in for a few notes, but no one else does.

Bernard stops. Some people in the crowd groan, others laugh, and the man behind Lilli yells, "Let the black boy play!"

The city man stands up, goes past Lilli to the town man and says, "That's rude."

The town man says, "No, *this* is rude." He punches the

city man in the nose, fast and sudden, and grins as he starts to bleed.

The city man hits the town man on the jaw. A few people rush toward them, knocking into others who are rushing away.

More people start to fight. Roland comes to the edge of the porch and yells, "Hey! Can we stop that? There's no need for it."

No one looks at him. He's always had an arrangement with the audience, Lilli thinks. He makes faces that show he's proud of the other musicians and modest himself, that he's just like the crowd except for standing up there. In exchange they laugh and clap at whatever he does. Now he has no agreement with them at all. He looks terrified.

Lilli looks at the porch a second too long and gets caught in a knot of people fighting. She tries to get away, but a man's knee pushes into her stomach and she can't breathe.

"*Hey*," Roland's saying. "Can somebody—"

Lilli feels a hand on her arm. It's Father, pulling her free. Then he pushes his way back into the crowd, finds the man who started the fighting, twists his arm behind his back and pushes him down on his knees.

Now Mother's there, saying "Come" and pulling Lilli away through the crowd. They get split apart and hit by mistake a few times, but finally make their way to the rise between the lawn and the woods. Mother bends down, gasping for breath. Lilli puts a hand on her back and looks at the crowd.

It's like war, she thinks. There are four fights and everyone's moving, joining the fighting, trying to stop it, or running down the road toward the gate. Most of the fighters are town and city people, but Frederick's hitting someone and Benji's fighting with a boy Lilli hasn't seen before. Father's still at the first fight and Diana's running up to the edge of it, then running backward when it changes shape, like she's playing with waves at the ocean. Oliver's crying, and Patrice too. Richard's at the side of the crowd, yelling "Please," reaching for people's arms and being ignored.

Lilli leaves her hand on Mother's back till she catches her breath and stands up. I'm still mad at her, she thinks, but I have forever for that.

Over by the Welcome Building a man's throwing punches at Bernard, who backs away, shaking his head like he doesn't want to fight. Roland and Jack are trying to get there to help him, but two men fight them back.

It's like pictures, flashing into Lilli's view when there are gaps in the crowd. Now Jorgen's there, grabbing the man who's after Bernard. The man hits Jorgen, who falls backward. Bernard starts to fight. When Lilli gets a look again, everyone's standing still and looking down.

Father pushes through the crowd to get to them, and Lilli follows him before Mother can stop her. When she gets there everyone's leaning over Jorgen, who's on the ground with his eyes closed and his head bleeding. One of the men from town reaches for him but Jack says, "You don't touch him." He and Father take Jorgen's shoulders and lift him to his feet. Jorgen's eyes open, roll back in his head and close again. Lilli thinks she might be sick.

They walk him to the path, his old sandals stubbing in the dirt. A dozen people follow them toward the gate. His mouth opens and moves a little, then stops. Astrid runs up and the men let her get close to him. Linda stays back, pressing little Trudy's face to her side so she doesn't see.

"Lamb?" Astrid says to Jorgen. "Lamb, you're all right. They're going to see to you." Tears start down her face. "You're walking. You see? You're all right."

Her voice breaks and she stops talking. This isn't real, Lilli thinks, don't make it be, but they're all still there, going down the path as if Jorgen's leading them with his eyes closed and his head rolling back on his neck.

Down at the gate there's a crowd of people from the music, four policemen, Mr. Whitliff the alderman, and two police cars. Jack and Father walk Jorgen to one of the cars and help the policemen lift him into the back seat. Astrid gets in next to him, wipes blood from his face and takes his twine headband off. The car drives away with its bell ringing.

For a minute everyone stands watching it go. Then Mr. Whitliff walks up to Richard and says, "That's the last of you here. The court's going to order you out."

"No one here was responsible for that," Richard says. "We tried to stop it."

Mr. Whitliff ignores him and talks to the crowd. "We're going to get everyone's statement on what happened," he says. "If you don't live here you can leave after that. If you do live here you'll be gone soon enough."

Some of the town men who were fighting are talking to the policemen by their car. Lilli hears them laugh. From the corner of her eye she sees something moving in the woods up the hill. It's Bernard and Leah, crouched down but walking fast, a valise in Bernard's hand. A second later they're over a rise and gone.

Lilli wants to talk to Benji but he's not here. She walks up to the house and he's not there either. If she can't talk to him, there's Rose.

The adobe house is dark. Lilli eases the door open and sees Benji and Rose in bed, their bodies curled together. Four electric light bulbs hang on wires from the ceiling. A toy unicyclist is balanced on one wire, a monkey with cymbals and a leering expression on the other. There's a stack of Benji's shirts on a shelf.

Rose wakes up, sees her and says, "Hello?"

"You didn't tell me," Lilli says. "Neither one of you."

Benji blinks awake. "Please don't tell your mother,"

Rose says. "I think she'd be upset with me."

"That's funny," Lilli says, and walks away down the path. Benji comes out and calls her, but she doesn't turn around.

She stops at the house to get a few things and walks up to the deer trails. There's just enough moonlight to climb over the rocks on the north side, scoot down the steep hill on her rear and finally walk out of the woods by the road.

The policemen by the gate could see her but they're not looking. She runs across the road and into the field Benji pointed to. There's the tarpaulin, back by those trees. Lilli lifts it, uncovers the bicycle, walks it through the field and looks over at Sunland. Our safe, special place, she thinks, except for the guns, secrets, fighting, and people pushing over each other to get what they want. You can have all that anywhere, and some places the baths are hot.

Twenty-Nine

"Have you been in the German military?" one of the cops asks Gerhard.

"Yes."

"When was your last contact with them?"

"I was discharged twenty years ago. They never write. In fairness, I don't either."

"Not even to wish them luck?"

"I don't wish them luck." He nods toward the town men laughing with the other police. At least one of them was in the fighting with Jorgen. "Are you going to arrest them?"

"That's not your business," the cop says.

"Are we finished?"

"For the time."

Gerhard turns around and walks up the hillside where the Sunlanders are sitting. Most of them have their knees drawn up, numb faces resting on forearms, looking at the gate and the cops.

He sits next to Anna on a big rock at the side of the crowd. "I feel so bad," she says.

"Don't," he says.

"Bernard didn't even want us to do that."

"It's all right."

"No it isn't. We thought we'd fix things by playing

songs in the desert? It's so stupid—"

"No," Gerhard says. That is, he thinks, I agree with everything else you say, but I don't think you were stupid. I think you were drunk, in a way. You and Roland. I was slow to see it. But you get drunk like that and you think you can do anything. You and I know what that's like.

I could be wrong, of course. This ache in my chest could be mistaken. I could ask her, or I could sit here saying "It's all right" till the stars go out. Would it make a difference?

The police car that went to the hospital drives in through the gate. They hear Astrid wailing before it stops.

A cop opens her door, helps her out and hands her over to Richard. She leans on him as they start up the hill, but falls to her knees. He waits and lifts her up and they go on.

People fall in around them and walk her up the hill in the moonlight. Gerhard and Anna follow them. The police car's headlamps sweep over them as it turns away.

Astrid's children reach her. She holds them close, her face baffled and covered with tears. "Perfect," she says. "He was perfect."

How do you explain someone being perfect, Gerhard thinks, any more than you explain them being gone? Imagine if she and Jorgen hadn't found each other. It's as if they were born the same second, and there was no one else for either one. They'd have wandered in a daze either way, but how much better to wander in it together.

Richard helps Astrid sit on the ground. She rocks back and forth with people's hands on her arms and shoulders.

Anna takes a nervous breath and walks over. Astrid looks up, sees her, takes her hand and presses it to her face. Thank you, Gerhard thinks. You might be half crazy, but the other half forgives Anna for the concert, and that's enough.

Anna comes back beside him. Roland's nearby with his wife and kids, but he and Anna don't look at each other.

Gerhard looks at Astrid, crying at the cold stars. All that could be yours, he tells himself, all that loneliness. All you'd have to do is say it to Anna out loud, how drunk she and her American were.

But you don't really know that, do you? If you want to, you can *almost* know. You can keep that coin in your pocket forever, a coin that stays on its edge because you never spend it. If she wronged you, she'll be making up for it every day. If she didn't, you were lucky not to ask. Either way, you're all the man a family needs.

He pulls Anna away. They walk up to the Japanese house and slip into bed quietly so they won't wake Benji and Lilli.

Where next, Gerhard thinks. Maybe that town where we bought the drill bits, Fullerton. Starting all over, learning a job, a town and people. You can only take so many of those in a lifetime, but Anna's good at it.

He starts to fall asleep but wakes up wondering where Astrid will go. She'll have to leave her house unfinished. That's too bad. It was going to be a mountain hut, homey and gabled, with a garden of tulips in front, the place she and Jorgen always dreamed of stumbling onto after a season sleeping in ditches.

Thirty

Lilli rolls the bicycle from the field into the woods. When she's past Sunland she wheels it up to the road, puts her leg over it and her feet on the pedals, falls over and scrapes her face.

You have to make it go the whole time. She remembers that now. She didn't have one in Berlin but her friend Jutta did, and let her ride it twice.

She tries again, first on the gravel beside the road and then on the pavement. Her bag on the handlebars throws her balance off and the seat hurts her parts, but she keeps going.

The sky lightens. A car coming the other way slows down and the man looks at her. She goes back to walking the bike in the woods, keeping the road just in sight and barking her shins on the pedals when she's careless.

When the woods run out she goes back to the road. An hour later Los Angeles comes to life in front of her, first warehouses, then factories, stables, houses, and suddenly the real city, with stores, crowds, and traffic.

It's so exciting that for a minute she forgets the pain from the bicycle and the trouble she'll be in for running away. All that speed and noise and a hundred new things a second—clothes, shops, taxis, horses, steam from grates, stairs going underground, and *faces*, how you see one for a second and spend the next two blocks steeping in the person's life.

The bicycle's speed is perfect for this, everything rolling past and her mind just keeping up. Awnings and wires, big clocks hanging on corner buildings, and windows displaying adding machines, medicines, and plaster legs with stockings on them. She's so occupied she doesn't see her front wheel getting close to the trolley track till it touches. The tire slips against it and sends the bicycle straight at an automobile coming toward her.

The car blasts its horn. Lilli smashes down on her back pedal, the car brakes too, and they stop a few inches apart. The driver shouts at her, but she's already off the bicycle and running it away, just in front of an ice wagon and up onto the sidewalk.

She leans the bicycle on a long white building, blinding in the sun. Everything hurts so much she can't believe Benji rides here and back in a day.

The palm trees look blurry. Stop it, she thinks. You've barely gotten away and you're already crying. Remember how Benji taught you percentages: you only need to be one percent more determined than you're scared.

She leaves the bicycle there and walks down the street. In the next block a man's catching pigeons and putting them in cages. The people passing by pay no attention.

A woman and a girl Lilli's age come out of a department store carrying parcels. The girl looks at Lilli and stops. Her mother puts a hand on her shoulder and they rush past.

Lilli looks at herself in the store window. She's dirty and her shirt is stringy at the elbows. I'd be scared too, she thinks. I'd better keep moving.

She follows a street called Grand out of the business district into blocks of houses. There's a big one with words painted on the front. The first part says YOUNG WOMEN'S BOARDING HOME. She can hear the women inside, laughing. There's a smell that seems too personal at first and then suddenly smells so good it makes her mouth water—meat cooking.

The next word is long, SALVATION. It has *ation* like *nation* but that's no help, it's just a strange word and she's not going to get it. The word after that, ARMY, she almost knows. In a minute it comes to her—it's in the book about mules Benji bought at the farm supply.

Is it a mule sickness? A kind of feed? That wouldn't be on the front of a house. ARMY—it means soldiers. Mules help the army. That house is full of young women soldiers, killing animals and eating them, getting ready to fight the Germans.

A lady comes out and walks toward her, smiling. "Hello," she says in English. "Are you—?" Yes, Lilli thinks, I'm German, and runs.

Thirty-One

Benji goes to Lilli's room at dawn but she's gone. Up on the ridge for sunrise, he thinks. I wonder if Astrid will be there. If I believed in that religion I'd have slept late and kept today from ever starting.

Last night he went after Lilli and called to her, but she kept walking away. He went back inside and told Rose, "She wouldn't speak to me."

"It's been a shit day all around," Rose said. "Here."

He got back in bed but didn't sleep. At four in the morning he slipped out and went back to the Japanese house, but he couldn't sleep there either.

Now he goes outside. It's cool still, with sunlight coming in low on the ground. Down at the gate the police cars are there, and a black sedan. A few people are gathered around Alderman Whitliff, who's holding up a piece of white paper.

"No one's to leave yet, but you should have your things packed up," he says. "Those taking care of animals, you'll have an extra twenty-four hours."

Benji turns around and walks up the stream. Father and his crew are stacking lumber at the library site. Herman and Dara are at the farm, loading tools into a mule cart. Jules and Suzanne are cutting pieces of signboards off the front of their house and putting them in his portfolio.

He goes up to the sawmill, walks onto the lower floor and takes it in for the last time, the quiet stream and the smell of shavings. He oils the blades and machinery, ties canvas hoods over everything, and walks down to the art studio site to help pack up. People aren't talking or looking at one another. They toss tools into boxes as if they're sick of them, even the new ones from town.

Tilda comes to see him in the afternoon. "Do you know where Lilli is?" she says. "I have a few of her things at the stable."

Benji shakes his head. "I thought she was with you."

"I thought she was packing up at home," Tilda says. "I just went by there, though."

"Let me see," Benji says.

He goes to the house, walks into Lilli's room and looks closer this time. Her bag is gone, and the shoes she never wears. He tries the hill where she goes with Diana and Oliver, then their houses, but doesn't find her.

She's not at the gate, either, where a few people are waiting by the black car from town. Mr. Richman, the German teacher from school, is sitting in the rear seat with a stack of mail next to him. He slits a letter open, reads it, makes notes in a ledger, and opens another. When he's finished he picks up the letters and calls people's names through his half-open window. The third name he calls is Lanz.

Benji steps closer and says hello. Mr. Richman pretends not to recognize him but hands him a letter addressed to *Lanz Family* in Lilli's pencil, with no return address. The postmark is Montclair, halfway between here and Los Angeles. She must have mailed it last night, Benji thinks.

Dear German friends,

I write to tell you I am allright. I am finding a place to live and job. When its time for a visit then Ill let you know.

Thank you for the curtesy you have shown me.

Your friend,
Mary Louise

Benji finds Mother and Father, takes them back to the house and shows them the letter.

"No," Mother says, her voice stricken. "No, we have to find her. We have to tell the police—"

"We can't," Benji says. "You heard what they said. They'd be looking for her for spying."

"But she isn't," Mother says. "She's just—"

"No, he's right," Father says. "Goddamn people. Even if we knew where she is, we'd be leading them to her."

"No. It's terrible," Mother says. "I—" She starts crying.

"It's all right," Father says, taking her in his arms. "She'll come back. She's upset now. She saw Jorgen like that."

Mother shakes her head against his shoulder. "Do you know how many times I ran away?" he says. "Before I was even that old? You get angry, but then you want your mother—"

"No," Mother says, and cries harder.

"Yes you do," Father says. "You do. It's all right."

It's not my fault or Rose's, Benji thinks. It's that you brought Lilli here and let her love it so much. She loves things hard and then hates them harder. You know that.

"She'll come live with us," Father says.

"Where?" Benji says.

"Fullerton. There's work there. Citrus and oil, you can have your choice."

Look at Father, Benji thinks. He's twice the size he was yesterday. Shaking off this place and Richard, predicting the future and deciding where we're all going to live.

"Excuse me," he says. "I'll be back in a few minutes."

He walks up to Rose's house. She's sorting through her

paintings and scrapbooks, her head down and hair more askew than usual.

"How's Lilli?" she says.

"She's gone," Benji says. "She sent a letter saying she's going to find a job and to leave her alone."

Rose sighs. "Are you worried?"

"Some. My mother is, very. My father thinks she'll come live with them."

"Where?"

"Fullerton. They're going there but I don't want to."

"Where do you want to go?"

"Anywhere, just till the war's over. Then Berlin." He pauses. "Will you go with me?"

"Oh. Oh, that's sweet. That's as sweet as you are." She puts a scrapbook down. "I think you should go with them, though. Their English isn't enough."

"But we—"

"Love," she says. "Look at me. You're going to know lots of women. One of them's probably in Berlin right now, wondering why there's no one clever enough for her." She comes close to him. "I love you, you know. I love your whole family, but we all have places to go now."

"Do you?"

She shakes her head. "Really I'm too sad to think."

They kiss. After a minute he goes to the shelf for his shirts. "I'll say I had them out drying," he says, and leaves.

I don't want lots of women, he thinks. I want you, sitting there drawing when I wake up.

He joins Mother and Father, packing up their things at the house. In a few hours the only thing left is a blue Japanese cloth hanging in a doorway, with an oily stain down the middle from people walking into it. A perfectly Sunland thing to leave behind, Benji thinks. Like the Shroud of Turin if Jesus never looked where he was going.

At four o'clock a bell rings by the gate. When they get

down there people are gathered by the back porch of the Welcome Building, where Whitliff's standing with a policeman at his side.

"As you leave, you'll register your names and plans with the officers," Whitliff says. "They'll tell you where to send your new address. You'll do that within ten days after leaving and keep it updated from then on."

Richard speaks up from the crowd. "Send it to me as well, please. To the post office box. Is that all right?" Whitliff nods.

The next morning Benji, Mother and Father bring their things down and join the crowd waiting for police cars and mule carts to take them to town. Everyone looks dazed, as if the lights have come up on a play that took four years to perform. Benji overhears a few people talking about their plans to move to Prague or the Florida Keys, but quietly, so this place won't have its feelings hurt. Everyone's hugging, not the usual Sunland hug that's halfway to sex but a hug that fights against everything scattering away, the people and trees and the poems on the job board. Rose holds Mother that way for a long time, then lets her go.

Tilda returns from a run to town, comes over to them, says, "I can take you, loves," and picks up one of their boxes as lightly as she did the first day at Langenhain. When they get to her cart she looks at them again, doesn't see Lilli and says, "Where—?" but Father cuts her short with a look. She doesn't ask again, even on the road to town. Like spies, Benji thinks, as he puts his box down to wait for the streetcar.

Thirty-Two

Lilli runs away from the woman soldiers for two blocks, turns to see how close behind her they are, and finds no one there. Coward, she thinks, and walks on at a normal pace.

Soon it's dark, and the warm light in transom windows starts her crying again. As she walks on, the houses get smaller, with little alleys between them. She goes down one, thinking she can sleep in a back yard if she's gone by dawn, but when a dog barks at her she runs back to the street. By the time she realizes she's seen a window sign saying ROOM, she's a block past it.

She turns around and finds it, a little box of a house with no porch. When she knocks on the door a lady opens it, looks at her, pulls the door almost shut again and says, "What is it?"

"About the room," Lilli says.

"It's ten o'clock," the lady says.

"Miss, I have money."

"No. I'm sorry." She closes the door.

"I'm Dutch," Lilli calls through it.

The lady opens it a crack again and says, "Don't say that, it's a giveaway. Are you in some kind of trouble?"

"No, Miss. My train was late coming here. I have three dollars and sixty and I'm going to find work."

The lady opens the door and says, "Come in, I guess." She's in her twenties and pretty, with black hair in curls pushed to one side of her head. Her dress is silky white on top and blue on the bottom.

The parlor has two chairs, a painting of a train in a desert, and a photograph of a young man in a uniform. Lilli can't remember being in a room this empty. At Sunland there'd be piles of books, laundry, letters, cigarettes, biscuits and half-cups of tea. This must be the American way, she thinks, to make it seem like waiting at the doctor's.

"You have a lovely home," she says.

"What kind of work can you get?" the lady says.

"In an office?"

"You won't get that. Maybe a factory."

"All right."

"You can stay tonight, anyway. Have a seat. I'll get you a towel to wash with."

She goes down the hall. Lilli sits on the floor, leans against the wall and pulls her knees up in front of her. When the lady comes back she says, "What are you doing?"

Lilli stands up fast and says she's sorry. At Sunland everyone says, "Pull up a floor." What else don't I know, she thinks? Probably everything.

The lady looks at her a minute, then hands her a towel and says, "What's your name?"

"Lilli."

"I'm Alice. The room's down here."

She leads Lilli to a room that smells like mothballs. There's an iron bedstead, an old table, and an empty picnic basket on the floor. "It's very nice," Lilli says, and reaches into her bag.

"You can wait till you get work. You should do that soon, though."

"Yes. Tomorrow."

"I only want someone till my husband gets back. He's in the army."

"Yes."

Alice goes away. Lilli waits till the house is quiet, then goes to the bathroom, stands in the tub and washes herself, her shirt, and her underwear. After one day in the city she smells like oil and cinders. She hangs her clothes in the window of her room to dry.

In bed she feels the bicycle under her, hears the army women's laughter, sees Jorgen's eyes rolling back in his head, and turns over a hundred times trying to sleep. Then a car goes past, and the next thing she knows it's getting light out and her clothes are almost dry.

Alice is drinking coffee in the kitchen, in a flowered dress and blue wrapper. "You can have a piece of toast and some coffee if you want," she says. "Don't use up the milk."

"Thank you," Lilli says.

Alice leaves. The bread has no seeds, oats, or taste. Lilli drinks her coffee black and goes out into the early light. The street is sad except that someone's practicing the piano.

She walks to a streetcar stop and asks a man, "Where are factories, please?"

"All over," he says. "Lots of big ones on Los Angeles Street, down by First. That car there."

Lilli gets on, pays her dime and finds a seat on the inside. The closer they get to Los Angeles Street, the better her worn-out clothes fit in. The men are in grimy pants and jackets and the women wear old dresses and kerchiefs. A few people talk to each other but most of them look like they're still asleep.

On Los Angeles Street there are blocks of brick factories with smokestacks, dirty windows, and train tracks going in the doorways. Lilli goes to all of them, but the men at the doors say, "Only machinists," "Journeyman tool and die," or "White Christian American." Even at one where the air's all cotton dust and everyone's coughing and spitting, they won't let her in.

At three o'clock she walks to the end of the street and sits on a pile of broken concrete. To think I was worried about someone finding me, she thinks. All you have to do is look for work and you'll never be noticed again.

After a while she takes the streetcar back to Alice's and tells her what happened. "Try down in Vernon," Alice says. "The factories there."

"All right." Lilli pauses. "What job do you do?"

"I show houses at a subdivision. They aren't built yet, but I show the model. It's completely legitimate. I've seen wood and cement delivered."

"You show it?"

"It's more than it sounds like. You're describing the future for them and their children."

"How did you get that, please?"

"My husband knows one of the principals. You might get something in Vernon. The smell scares people off."

Lilli sleeps even less than she did the night before. On the streetcar to Vernon there are fewer women but more young boys. She smells the slaughterhouses before she sees them, and spits up in her mouth while the people around her go on talking.

When the streetcar stops she follows people to the factories, a block over from the slaughterhouses. The first three turn her away like yesterday, but at the fourth one a man says, "Talk to him" and points at someone Lilli can barely see in the dark. It's hotter inside but it smells less.

When her eyes are used to the light she sees people working at long tables. Hooks go clattering around the room, hanging from toy-train tracks on the ceiling. The people at the tables put things on the hooks or take them off, always at the last second. A boy Lilli's age grabs onto something going by and almost gets carried away before he pulls it down.

Lilli finds the man the first one pointed at. He's forty, in black trousers and a sweat-stained shirt, his suspenders hanging down by his legs and his mustache curling into his mouth.

"Excuse me?" Lilli shouts over the noise. "I came about a job."

"I have cutting mats. You want it?"

"Yes, please."

He leads her to a table where people are crowded together, each person doing one thing over and over. "Here," he says, and points to a black metal machine with flat sheets of rubber coming out of it on a belt. A woman with a knife slices the sheets off the belt and hands them to a man who cuts them in half with shears. The man next to him fits each half-sheet of rubber into a curved piece of metal. The woman after him singes the rubber to the metal with an iron and puts it up on a hook going by.

The man with the mustache points to the back of the room, shouts "Flanges" at the man with the shears, and waves Lilli into his place. She takes a mat from the knife man, burns her fingers and drops it on the table in front of her. There are marks there for lining the shears up but her first cut goes crooked.

The man with the mustache says "Garbage" and tosses the pieces into a scrap barrel. Lilli starts another one. "In *half*," he says. "We're losing money now." He pulls a red handle. The hooks stop moving, and Lilli feels everyone in the room look around for the trouble.

She cuts two more. The mustached man puts the second pair down in front of the curved-metal man, and Lilli's so relieved her knees are weak. The hooks start moving again. She keeps cutting as if nothing else matters in the world.

In a while the mustached man brings back the man he sent to the flanges and motions at Lilli to follow him. They go up plank stairs to an office.

"Mat cutter," the man says to a lady at the counter.

"Can you write?" the lady says.

"Yes," Lilli says.

The lady puts a printed form in front of her. "Come back down when you're done," the man says, and goes away.

Lilli writes in *Mary Louise Mistree* and Alice's address, puts *Holland* as her place of birth and answers no to eight sicknesses. "I can type as well," she says. "And arithmetic."

"Versatile," the lady says. "Cutter is eight dollars a week, four cents off for spoils. Seven till six, pay on Saturday, Sundays off." She gestures to where the man with the mustache was. "Leonard's going to want a present for putting you on. Seventy-five cents a week is normal."

Lilli goes back to work. At 12:30 they have fifteen minutes for lunch but she didn't bring anything. At four o'clock her hand cramps up and she spoils four mats.

When the bell rings at six she finishes a cut, looks up and sees people streaming out the doors. She walks to the back of the room, where the parts from the tables get made into machines. They're taller than she is, white cabinets full of belts, gears and openings. She looks all around one of them till she finds the curved metal piece with the rubber inside it, low down on the back.

A lady comes by checking things off on a clipboard. "What does it do, please?" Lilli says.

"It makes buttons. Celluloid goes in, buttons come out."

Lilli looks into one of the openings. "It doesn't make them here," the lady says. "It makes them in button factories."

"Yes," Lilli says. "Thank you."

On the streetcar she fingers the buttons on her shirt. They're wood, carved by Herman, and they're gray from sun and water, but she remembers celluloid ones in Berlin, bright blue and smoky tortoise.

If you think about it, some of the biggest decisions in the world are made with buttons. Oliver tried to undo mine but I made him stop. Alice wore two open this morning when she left to show the model homes. Frieda unsnapped the brass ones on her overalls and let her bosoms out when she wanted to. If someone looked too long at me in the stream I'd button mine all the way up for the rest of the day.

All over the world people make decisions with them—who they love, how long to be single, whether they can pay for a baby. Emperors need sons if they're going to conquer the world, and empresses can keep their buttons closed till the conquering stops, but before any of that can happen someone has to make the buttons, and before that someone has to make the machines.

Thirty-Three

Benji and his parents get to Fullerton in the afternoon and step off the streetcar into downtown, a block and a half of stunted brick and wood. A whitewashed building advertising POOL—CIGARS—NEWS AGENTS sits next to one saying SHORT ORDERS—CHILI—NOODLES. It's so quiet they can hear the clack of balls on a billiard table, someone saying "God damn it" and someone else snickering.

"You see?" Father says. "Not bad." A farm truck rattles past. The breeze it stirs smells of oil and oranges, like a mechanic wearing perfume.

Benji waits with their things as Mother and Father go into the cigar store. Father comes out carrying a map and a newspaper. Mother's bought two souvenir postcards showing the street they're on, tinted waxy blue and orange.

Father spreads the newspaper on their boxes, circles advertisements for rental houses, and finds the streets on the map. "There are four for under twenty dollars," he says. "All over that way."

He leads them into a district of small houses and beat-up wagons. When a man opens the door at the first house, Father says, "I see you *haff* a—"

The man shuts the door in his face.

"Let me try," Benji says as they approach the second

one, where an old man's feeding chickens in the yard. "Sir, about the rental?" he asks in his American accent.

"Show you," the man says, and walks them two blocks to a gray cottage with a yard full of weeds and a stub of a porch. Inside there are looming ceilings, glare straining through dirty windows, and grime at the baseboards like sidewalk tar.

"Yes," Father says, and gives the man fifteen dollars.

When the man leaves they look over the rooms. "This one can be yours," Mother tells Benji. "Lilli can stay with you when she comes."

The room is the same size as its closet, but there's a brass ceiling lamp with a two-pin electrical outlet, the first one that's Benji's to use in America. He finds a scrap of steel wool in the kitchen, stands on a chair and rubs tarnish off the lamp till it's almost shiny. When he looks down the black holes it's as if he can see the current waiting inside.

He goes to the kitchen. The postcards Mother bought are on the table, one addressed to the Driscoll town clerk and the other to Richard, both giving their new address. She and Father are standing in the back doorway, looking at a tiny yard with a dead tree in it. "We'll fix up that fence," Father says.

"We could plant passion vine on it," Mother says. "That would do well."

Go ahead, Benji thinks, fix yourself to this spot. I'll be back in Berlin before those vines start to grow.

The newspaper Father bought in town is next to the postcards. Benji reads a few articles, then carefully tears a photo of President Wilson from the paper, finds some putty in the cabinet, and goes into the front room to put the picture in the front window, facing the street. Father walks in as he's doing it and says, "What's that for?"

Benji hands him the newspaper and points to a photograph of some Boy Scouts holding a "Loyalty Day" where they burned bundles of a German-language newspaper and broke Beethoven records. When he's finished putting up the picture of Wilson, he points to another window and says, "I can get an American flag for that one."

"A small one," Father says.

"All right."

"We're thinking of looking for work at the orange groves tomorrow," Father says. "Do you want to come?"

"I was thinking of the oil," Benji says, though he hadn't thought of anything till Father said oranges.

❧

He gets up at four and walks to the oil field, following the smell. It's bigger than the town, with rough wooden derricks spread out in the dark like a hundred Eiffel Towers carved for school. Twice he almost turns back. The smell is strangling and the workers are twice his size, their faces shining black under arc lamps and flares of burning gas.

He goes into a shack marked OFFICE and asks a man in a suit if there's work, sounding as American as he can. The man grabs his arm. Benji thinks it's trouble over being German, but the man's feeling his muscles. He shakes his head, leads Benji outside and says, "Take that mud to 401," pointing to a barrel nearby and a derrick fifty yards away.

Benji tilts the barrel on the ground, gets his hands on the top and bottom, almost falls under it but gets his balance and walks. He's trembling before he's halfway there, taking short steps like the mules, the heat from the gas flares rolling over him.

At the derrick a man like a bear takes the barrel with one hand and sets it down without looking at him. He goes back to the office man, who says, "We'll try you out. Six P.M. to six A.M."

They put him on a crew laying one-foot pipe from the

field to the rail yard. He and a man named Red screw the sections together with three-foot tongs, their rhythm set by a man who hammers on the joints to keep them from sticking. When a joint's almost done it takes six men to turn it, with Red's sweating face an inch from Benji's and the hammer sending shocks down their bodies.

They do that for a week, then bury the pipe in a ditch, shoveling twelve hours a shift. No one says Benji's try-out is over, but he gets paid that Saturday. He saves all the money he makes except for his share of rent, food at Chili-Noodles, and quarts of milk he drinks on the job. He's never eaten this much and he won't ask Mother and Father to pay for it.

After a month he helps build a derrick, nailing six-ty-penny spikes with the flat side of an axe. Red and the others do it with two blows, but Benji needs six. I thought I was strong, he thinks. I'm stronger than collagists. That's not the same thing.

❧

Mother gets a job packing oranges, and Father lines irrigation ditches. They work days and Benji doesn't see them much, but he can tell the two of them are in greater harmony than he can remember. When Mother brings a few oranges home from work, Father acts like it's a Christmas gift. If she remarks on the price of relish at the store he says, "That's right, you're right," and smiles as if there's a breeze in the oily air.

Their happiness seems to rest on two propositions. One is that their time at Sunland barely happened. Occasionally one of them will say something like "I had one, but I left it in the country," and then they retreat to the safe ground of Fullerton civic affairs.

The other proposition is that Lilli's going to come back to them. They've had one letter from her. The outside envelope was from a post office box in New Mexico, with their address typewritten. Inside was another of her penciled envelopes, postmarked Los Angeles and addressed to them in care of Richard's post office box in Driscoll.

Dear Mother, Father, and Benji,
I am still allright.
Mary Louise

One evening Benji wakes up for work and finds a printed flyer his parents have left on his pillow:

UNITED STATES OF AMERICA –
DEPARTMENT OF JUSTICE
REGISTRATION OF ENEMY ALIENS

It says they have to come to a police station and present their fingerprints, photographs, and proof of their peaceful dispositions. Benji buys film and chemicals in town, takes a portrait of each of them, and makes prints in the bathroom.

The next day he goes to the police station. There's one officer there, a man who might be a teenager. He comes to the counter and says, "Can I help you?"

"I came to register," Benji says. "I'm German." He puts the pictures of himself on the counter.

"Could you come back in the evening?" the policeman says. "Chief Lewis has been doing those."

"I work then," Benji says.

"All right." The policeman goes to a desk, comes back with forms and a fountain pen, reads a few of the questions silently, and says, "This doesn't look so bad." He uncaps his pen but hesitates. "It's just that it's federal."

"I'll help if I can," Benji says.

"Well. I've run people in that robbed a store. I guess I

can fill out a paper." He writes in the date and takes Benji's fingerprints, clumsy but careful.

"Now I have to read this to you," he says. "'You cannot own firearms, ammunition, or wireless devices. You cannot foreclose on a mortgage. You cannot leave the country. You cannot go to railroad terminals, warehouses, or Washington, D.C. You need permission to travel or to change your residence.'"

"All right," Benji says.

"I have to put your pictures on here." Benji helps him paste them in straight. The policeman picks up his pen again. "What kind of forehead do you have? Prominent, receding, or average?"

"No one's said," Benji says.

"Average?"

"I think."

"Shape of face?"

"Ordinary."

"Chin?"

"Plain."

"Nose?"

"Commonplace."

"Complexion?"

"Nondescript."

The policeman frowns and writes *Tan*. It's a wonder Rose recognized me from day to day, Benji thinks.

"Do you have permission to enter a forbidden area?" the policeman asks.

"No." Benji pauses. "Does that include oil wells? They seem strategic."

"You'd need to ask Chief Lewis."

Or not, Benji thinks. He gets his Alien Enemy card, goes home, takes a piece of scrap wood from the yard, paints REPAIRS - ELECTRICAL - MECHANICAL on it, stands it on the porch and goes inside to study the *Hawkins Electri-*

cal Guide. When Father comes home from work he says, "What's that outside?"

"I've lost my job," Benji says. "The alien laws."

"Stupid," Father says.

"It's all right. I've saved up money."

Two days later a lady knocks on the door and asks what Benji charges to fix a sewing machine. He says a dollar. "They're not so hard to fix," she says. "My son did it till he went in the Navy." Benji says fifty cents.

The machine's treadle-driven. He takes it apart, diagrams it, makes a new drive rod from wood and a cotter pin from wire, puts it back together and tests it on his blanket. When the lady comes back he asks if she's got anything electric to fix.

"No," she says. "I've got a light bulb, but when it burns out the Edison sends a boy on a bicycle with a new one."

Later Benji opens his notebook and writes *Edison* → *like Siemens* → *light bulbs by bicycle.* The future, he thinks. I'd better hurry up and catch it.

The next week a man brings a vacuum cleaner. Benji finishes fixing it on a hot afternoon, turns it on, holds three sheets of newspaper to the end of the hose with its suction, switches it off and watches them float to the floor. It's as good as the sawmill, he thinks. No, better: electric.

He fills his wall with drawings. Soon he has three repair jobs at once, and a list of parts to buy. He gets up in the dark, packs sandwiches and takes a streetcar. Two towns before Los Angeles he gets off and walks the rest of the way under the power lines, stopping to sketch the coils and transformers on the towers. The lines buzz overhead and lizards dart in the sand, hunting the invisible insects.

As he walks into the outskirts of the city there's a thumping noise. Its source comes into view, a concrete power station with a few windows. The wires he's been walking under go into one end of the building, and lines run from the other toward downtown.

He sees the machinery through the windows, stops walking, and stares at the slowly turning converter. That's not how it looks in *Hawkins*. Those drawings must be out of date already.

He kneels in the dirt, opens his notebook and draws. When he looks up, a man in a uniform is coming out of the power station.

The man sees him. Benji freezes. The man gets into a car.

Idiot, Benji thinks. I'm a registered enemy making drawings of a power station. I'll be held in secret. I'll be lynched, like that German man in the newspaper last week.

The car drives toward him. He stands up and walks as casually as he can, still under the power lines but sneaking looks at the warehouses on his right. As the car comes closer, he sees an alley between two buildings and walks into it as if he'd meant to all along. He turns the corner of a building and runs.

There's a storm drain in the pavement ahead. He tears the drawing out of his notebook, stuffs it through the grate and runs on past warehouses, workmen and rotting cabbage leaves.

When he can't hear the car anymore he climbs a fence, crashes to the ground and runs to a neighborhood of shack houses. He hides on the side of a house, his breath heaving, and watches the corner till a streetcar comes. He runs to catch it and rides back to Fullerton, pretending to look for something in his bag the whole hour.

He walks from the streetcar to the end of their block and watches their house from behind a telegraph pole. When no police come he goes home, takes the REPAIRS sign from the porch to the back yard, makes a fire with it, and burns all his diagrams and the *Hawkins Guide*.

He puts tags on his three unfinished repair jobs say-ing *Sorry, electricity too complex,* and leaves them on the cus-tomers' porches. At sunset he goes home and sits on the porch till Mother walks up, carrying her violin case.

"Hello," she says.

"Hello," Benji says. "Have you been playing?"

"Just practicing. With someone in town."

"That's good. That's wonderful."

She looks at him. "Are you all right?"

"I'm fine," he says. "I'm very good."

I am, he thinks. We all are, if I haven't just ruined it. Who says you have to know everything before you get to university, or be smart to the point of being stupid? You don't need to live your whole life all at once. Look at Mother standing here with her violin, saying she's playing with someone again. Imagine a band like hers and Ro-land's here in Fullerton, with Red and the others coming to the park every week and staring at the goddamnedest thing ever. Or just imagine where we are right now, a mod-est house enhanced immeasurably by the absence of cops. Tell me that's not heaven.

1918

Thirty-Four

One Saturday in March Lilli takes a walk after work as the crowds come out downtown. On Spring Street the stores and restaurants are done up in every style from Moorish domes to Chinese pagodas. Out in the world the countries are killing each other, but in Los Angeles they just fight over customers. She turns onto a busy side street, with electric signs saying SPIRITUAL HEALER and TWI-LIGHT SLEEP DENTIST, and people at card tables selling wind-up toys and plots of land.

A blare of music comes from the next block, horns and a piano. Four horses come around the corner pulling a bandstand on wheels, with men in cowboy hats playing ragtime. A pretty woman stands at the edge of the band-wagon, laughing and handing out flyers.

Lilli pushes through the crowd to get one. It's got a drawing of children playing while their parents watch them from the porch of a rose-covered cottage, and words in racing black letters:

Where Will YOU Spend Your To-morrows?
In the Hectic City? The Lonely Country?
Or at PALMETTO PARK, a Neighborhood combining
the Vitality of one with the Serenity of the other?
PALMETTO PARK—where SCHOOLS,

CHURCHES, STORES and STREETCARS are in Place <u>NOW</u>!
SUNDAYS AT PALMETTO PARK are a
JAMBOREE for the Whole Family.
MUSICALES with Prize Performers—
PONY RIDES for the Little Ones—
GUIDED TOURS of Model Homes—
SANDWICHES for Early Arrivals—
DAISY THE ELEPHANT when available.
If you want to be sure of a home, come as soon
as you can and GET A GRIN!

That's not the one Alice works at, Lilli thinks. Hers is called Roebuck Ridge.

She puts the handbill in her pocket. In the morning she takes two streetcars to where the hills start, north of town. There are signs at the stop pointing to PALMETTO PARK, ROSEWOOD GLEN, and SWALLOW ROCKS.

It's a one-mile walk on a country road, past houses with horses and a tomato farm. A young couple walks past her, the lady with a baby and the man with last night's flyer.

A crowd's gathering at Palmetto Park, a plot of cleared land that covers three low hillsides. The streets are tamped dirt, a straight one up the middle of the property and bean-shaped lanes coming off it. There are lots marked by string lines, pipes in ditches, and trucks and steam shovels parked at the top. The band from last night is playing next to two finished houses and a building that says SALES OFFICE. A man in a buckskin vest is taking a crying little boy for a ride on a badly cared-for pony.

A lady waves people onto the porch of one of the houses. "Come on up," she says. "Nothing to be afraid of."

Lilli joins the crowd around the lady. She looks more serious than the one on the bandwagon last night, and wears a long dress like one of Alice's.

"What a nice group," she says. "My name is Laura and I'm here to show off Palmetto Park. Now, if we had eyes that could see just a little way into the future, we'd see a real all-American neighborhood around us, with people playing ball and gardening and cooking supper." She pretends to smell it. "Let's go inside."

The model house is small but cheerful, with rugs, armchairs, bookshelves, and a bowl in the kitchen with a wooden spoon, as if someone just got called away from stirring it. "This is real enamel paint throughout," Laura says. "I know we ladies like the linoleum for easy cleanup. Well, there are three artistic patterns to choose from."

When she's done giving the tour she walks backwards, leading people toward the sales office, where two men are waiting with clipboards. Then she goes over to the other house and beckons to people coming up the road. That's nothing, Lilli thinks. No wonder Alice can do it.

◌ß

Lilli eats a bologna sandwich on the model house's porch, walks back to the streetcar stop, and follows the signs to Swallow Rocks. It's just like Palmetto Park, except the music is a men's harmony quartet, the sandwiches are cheese and the houses have dormers.

For four Sundays she goes to three developments a day. During the week she practices talking while she cuts mats. "If you'll all follow me. This exposure is a gardener's delight. Let's go into the spacious kitchen." No one at her table notices.

After six weeks she starts asking people at the sales offices if they need someone. No one does. At Dorado Vista a salesman says, "You're a nice-looking girl but you talk like the Kaiser. Come back when the war's over." As she walks away he says, "And the clothes." She stops going, practices sounding American, and spends twenty dollars on an outfit, secondhand.

⁓

One night in September she comes home from work and finds a note and a piece of fabric pinned to Alice's front door. The note says

Lily <u>DON'T</u> come in this door!!

Put this mask on and come in the back.

STAY in that room til I tell you.

Alice

The piece of fabric is black gauze, with a little strap on each end. A blindfold, Lilli thinks. There's something in there she doesn't want me to see. War secrets? Something she's afraid I'll steal? Or maybe her husband's been wounded and come home and it's too awful to look at?

She shudders and goes down the alley. At the back door she covers her eyes with the mask, finds the doorknob by touch and goes inside.

"On your *mouth!*" Alice shouts. "Your mouth and your nose!"

"I'm sorry," Lilli says. She pulls the mask down over her mouth and sees Alice, standing as far away from her as she can and wearing the same kind of mask. "What is it?"

"Stay there," Alice says. "I can project. I project all day long. There's an influenza, the Spanish Influenza. It's killing our soldiers and sailors. Some people think your Germans put it in a bomb."

"I'm sorry."

"They're coming down with it here now. The Army Balloon School and the Naval Station."

"Balloons?" For a second Lilli pictures coughing soldiers making animals for children. "Oh, the ones—"

"*Listen* to me. We can't get near each other. You have to wear that and not let people breathe on you."

"Yes," Lilli says, backing up without realizing it till she knocks into the wall.

Alice cooks her own dinner, takes it to her room and lets Lilli cook next, provided she wears dishwashing gloves, eats off yesterday's newspaper instead of a dish, and washes everything with Borax and vinegar when she's done.

The next day on the streetcar only one other person wears a mask, a lady who stands up the whole way and shies away when people get near her. At lunchtime Lilli asks Leonard if the factory's going to close. "Why?" he says. "Influenza?" He hugs himself. "Oh, I'm buttoning up my overcoat so I don't catch it! I'm *buttoning,* you see? Because I have *buttons.*"

The flu never gets so bad in Los Angeles. "It's too dry here," Alice says the night she takes off her mask, revealing a pale muzzle in a face that's tan from talking to home buyers in the sun. She sounds almost disappointed, Lilli thinks. She stops wearing her mask too, except when the streetcar goes past the slaughterhouses.

One day in November everyone at the factory starts talking at once. When Lilli looks up, they're all rushing out the doors. It's a fire, she thinks. I'm not going to die of flu, I'm going to die in this stupid factory. She drops her work, starts to run, trips on the dirty floor, scrambles to her feet and races for the door.

Outside it's a party. People are laughing and dancing in the street, drinking beer and holding up newspapers with foot-high headlines saying <u>PEACE</u>.

A man from the factory tries to hug her, but she escapes onto a streetcar. The conductor's one she knows but he looks drunk, won't take anyone's money and rings the bell all the way to Los Angeles. There are three times the usual people, holding onto poles and leaning out, singing and shouting into a breeze full of cinders and cigarette ends.

When she gets off downtown, people are crowding the streets, pushing champagne at each other and holding up signs that say KAISER BILL IS SWEET WILLIAM NOW and WHO'S AFRAID OF THE HUN? Lilli smiles, pretends to drink from a champagne bottle, and takes care not to talk so no one will hear her accent and throw her under a streetcar out of happiness.

When she gets home Alice says, "Happy armistice. I guess I shouldn't say that to you. Anyway, Robert's going to be home soon. We'll need the room."

"All right," Lilli says, and starts looking in the paper for a place to stay.

That Sunday she goes back to the developments. Two weeks later the manager at Rosewood Glen gives her a tryout. She already knows the square footages, the optional fruit trees, and the grade-school principal's name, but she adds some touches of her own.

"You spend your days in the city, where people battle one another over everything, where it's all billboards, telegrams and money," she tells her first audience. "But what if, every night, you came home to Rosewood Glen? To where you see what life really is—rest and nature and the people you belong to?

"Your neighbors at Rosewood Glen—it makes you happy to greet the sunrise with neighbors like these. It's so beautiful you might paint a picture of it, or write a poem. Let's go in here, please. Every house comes complete with this electric washer."

It's an offbeat approach, the manager says, but in two months Lilli puts five families in houses. Before long she's making jokes about her accent and finding separate ways to appeal to men, women and children. Sometimes she puts on old clothes after work and helps the landscapers plant trees. Still, when the Sunday crowds go home, she feels something missing from her life. It's a real estate license, she decides, and in the spring she starts night school.

Thirty-Five

When the war ends Benji writes to his friend Pieter and asks if he can stay with him in Berlin. Three weeks later he gets a letter saying yes but warning him that there's no coal or trains, and that people are killing one another over a few pfennigs and cutting up dead horses in the street for meat. Pieter's always liked scaring people but it might be true.

I won't let that stop me, Benji thinks. It means I can get in when there's opportunity. He buys tickets for a train to New York and a ship to Copenhagen, and roadmaps so he can flag down trucks on their way to Berlin.

He says goodbye to his mother and father on the porch in the morning cold. Mother hugs him so long he's afraid he'll miss his train. When she lets go, he turns to Father, who says, "Music and plays at the turn of a switch."

"That's right," Benji says.

"But where's the thrill in that?" Father says, and smiles. Of course, Benji thinks: the first words of encouragement since we came to America, just as I'm leaving. He turns away in case there are tears in his eyes. There must be an age when they can't do this to you anymore.

His train goes up the coast from Los Angeles. At Ventura he eats lunch in the dining car and stares at the ocean, calm blue up to the fevered band of sunlight on the horizon. They pass a beachside village with towels drying on porches and banana trees in the yards. Four years in the desert, Benji thinks. What geniuses we were.

He gets off at San Francisco and takes a ferry to Oakland, a shining green city at the end of the transcontinental railroad. His next train's in the station, coughing steam under skylights full of sunset.

In second class people sleep in their seats. The single travelers have packed light, while the couples and families spread out empires of their things. A man and lady in their fifties nestle under a blanket covered with knitting, cribbage, hot-water bottles and plates of sausage. They look as contented as his mother and father do these days. Benji takes a seat as far from them as possible.

As he pulls his coat over himself, a uniformed boy his age comes down the aisle selling candy and newspapers. Benji buys a Hershey bar, eats it looking out at the dark pines, falls asleep but starts awake a hundred times before morning.

Two days later, coming down the Rocky Mountains, the train stops at a depot with a café, glowing in sun after rain. "Twenty-minute stop," the conductor calls. Most of the passengers get off, but Benji and a few sleeping people stay in their seats.

The candy and newspaper boy comes in, looks around, picks up a discarded box of Cracker Jack, pours what's left of its contents into another box on his tray, then sees Benji watching him. Benji looks away but the boy comes over, leans close and says, "Sir, you won't tell the road, will you?"

"I'm sorry?" Benji says.

"The railroad. About me making fulls out of empties. I'm an independent operator. Just making my costs."

"No, it's all right."

"Sir, I appreciate it. I'll make it worth your while."

"There's no need."

"How far are you riding?"

"New York."

"I've never seen it. I hope to get on that route some-day."

"Actually I'm going back to Berlin."

"Germany? It sounds rough there. Do you think they've learned their lesson? If you don't mind my asking."

"I think so."

"That's good. I'll be back in a while, sir. I'm going to have something for you."

When the boy leaves, Benji takes out Pieter's letter and reads it again. *Father says the "bankers" sabotaged us in the war but that we won't be fooled so easily in the future.* In half an hour the boy comes back, hands Benji a folded newspaper and whispers, "For later. The French packet. It's commonly a dollar but it's yours free."

That night Benji unfolds the newspaper and finds a brown paper package of postcards inside. He holds them by the moonlit window. They're pictures of women, some drawn and some photographed, with the hems of their dresses lifted to the calf or the knees. In one drawing, the woman leans forward so the top of her dress falls open, a faint charcoal line indicating the dip between her breasts.

Is anyone really aroused by that? For a second Benji's annoyed on behalf of everyone who's ever paid a dollar for it, till he remembers that he's seen a lifetime's worth of naked people in the last four years. He puts the postcards deep in the seat pouch for some lucky child to find and goes to sleep.

∞

The next morning he wakes up to Kansas, a full day of featureless earth and sky. The car goes silent except for babies crying. Benji tries to read but the flatness comes in after him. That night he dreams of the land outside littered with those Berlin horses, flayed for food.

In the morning there's scenery again, trees and vines and houses on bluffs. Missouri, the conductor says. Benji buys a Kandy Kake for lunch but has supper in the dining car, sitting with a lady and her eleven-year-old son. As they finish eating, the conductor comes through the car saying, "Ladies and gentlemen, in a few minutes we will cross the Mississippi River. The river will be on both sides of the train."

They go onto a trestle and it comes into view, wide brown water scaled with light by the setting sun. People cheer, the waiters pour more wine, and the lady's son stands staring out the window. His mother leans over to Benji and says, "He's looking for the boys on the raft."

A barge goes by instead, with blocks of cargo under tarpaulins. The winning country, Benji thinks, hip-deep in raw materials. That's all right. Just give Germany a few years to come back into its own. Radio will help.

ଔ

He changes trains in Chicago and two days later he's at Grand Central Terminal in New York, with shops and sculpted ceilings like the Leipzig Hauptbanhof. He tells a policeman the pier number of his ship. "That's the end of Houston Street," the man says. "You can get the subway over there, five cents."

"I haven't been here before," Benji says. "I think I'll walk."

"South and west," the policeman says.

Outside there's cold sun and a crowded sidewalk. The clothes are a sharp new style here, wide lapels on the men and hats shaped like church bells on the women. Benji walks through a square full of vaudeville theaters whose signs rise into the sky, the colored Dixie Duo and the white

Marx Brothers together on a bill.

He has a few hours to spare and takes a detour south-east. The streets descend in class till there are tenements, pushcarts and scrambling children, the air thick with fish, coal, and horse shit. He feels like he's seen some of the people before, then finds himself looking around for a glove maker's or a strongman gymnasium.

He buys a roll and an apple and eats them as he walks toward the piers. The streets turn prosperous again, a commercial district with the tallest building he's ever seen, a limestone tower carved into gargoyles and tracery, with a door like a cathedral's. The sign says WOOLWORTH BUILDING, the same name as the stores in California that sell things for five or ten cents.

Benji goes inside. The ceiling in the lobby is so ornate it seems to swarm. The walls are a frieze of caricatures, including one of a man counting nickels and dimes. A lady sees Benji looking and says, "That's Mr. Woolworth himself."

The money's from those stores, Benji thinks. The tiny profits on thimbles and mouth harps, taken together, are a fortune. He reads the building directory: banks, lawyers, Columbia Records and the Marconi Wireless Telegraph Company of America. When he goes back outside he sees the limestone façade is really terra cotta, a saving in itself.

It's time to get to the pier but he walks slower than ever. When he reaches the ticket office it's sunset, with seagulls screaming in circles overhead. He gets his Copenhagen ticket stamped, starts toward the ship, turns back and asks the clerk, "Does it go again tomorrow?"

"Wednesday, sir."

"May I use the ticket then?"

"Yes sir. Just come in here and change it. It's good for six months."

They're smart to be flexible, Benji thinks. That's the

style here. You make a million dollars but put up a mural of yourself counting nickels like the men with the push-carts, before anyone else can say it about you. You send a boy with the light bulbs. You make fulls out of empties.

"Thank you," he says. "Are there hotels nearby?"

"Up Houston Street," the clerk says.

"Thank you," Benji says. Twenty minutes later he's in one, pinning his ticket to the wall of his room, calculating the date six months from now, and writing it down.

1919

Thirty-Six

One day Gerhard goes to the mailbox and finds another brown envelope with a New Mexico postmark and type-written address. Inside is a letter from Lilli, with a return address this time: *Maltman Bungalow Court # 6, 918 Maltman Avenue, Los Angeles*. It's in English again but on nicer paper than before, and fountain pen instead of pencil.

Dear Mother, Father, and Benji,

I write to let you know I am in Los Angeles and working in home sales. My health is good and I am studying at night for my real estate license.

If you are living somewhere I can reach by street car I would like to visit you.

I hope this finds you well and succeeding at whatever you put your minds to.

Yours,
Lilli

When he shows it to Anna she cries, hugs him, and writes back instantly:

Dear Lilli,

How wonderful to hear from you, and with such good news!

We are in Fullerton, which is on the Pacific Electric streetcar line from Los Angeles. It's a pleasing town with shops as you'll see when you come. Father and I work in citrus. He digs and lines the irrigation ditches and I box oranges.

Benji is staying in New York on his way to Berlin. I know he'll be sorry to miss your visit.

Please let us know when you'd like to come. We'll be so happy to see you!

Love,
Mother

Lilli answers, setting a date on a Sunday evening and giving the arrival time of her streetcar. As the days go by, Anna's excitement is overtaken by worry that the visit will go wrong somehow, or that Lilli won't show up at all.

"Relax," Gerhard says. "It's your own child, and she's the one who asked to see us."

But when Lilli steps off the streetcar on Sunday night it feels like a formal proceeding, a resumption of relations as grudging as France and Germany's. It's been just months but she looks five years older, in a proper dark dress, a wool coat and a hairdo that falls down on one side and pins up on the other. She hugs Gerhard and Anna briskly at shoulder level and gives the main street a quick, unimpressed survey.

"Was it hard getting here?" Anna says.

"No," Lilli says. "I just kept asking till someone knew where it was."

They start toward the house, but a drunk oil hand stumbles out of Chili-Noodles and almost crashes into Lilli before Gerhard catches him. The drunk shoves back at him and walks away cursing. Lilli watches placidly, as if Fullerton is just what she pictured.

When they get to the house she looks at it that same

way, the small rooms, tin washtub, and coffee can of fat. On the sitting-room wall there are orange crate labels from Anna's job. She brings home the most evocative ones—KLONDIKE, REMBRANDT, MARCO POLO. On other evenings, when Gerhard looks up from a book at them, they're like ten-second vacations.

"These pictures help, but it's a hard room," Lilli says. "That's why this is a rental. Have you thought about buying? I'd think you could get something so reasonably out here. That's how you start having value."

She begins a discourse on the advantages and methods of buying a house—what banks are looking for in a borrower, the five warning signs of a sinking foundation, the truth about escrow. At first Gerhard thinks it's just a young person's mania for her first job, but after a while he sees it for the tactical move it is. *I love everything you tried to take me away from,* Lilli's saying. *I love selling the land under people's feet, and the houses they have to work too hard to get. Without me, where would the banks be?*

They sit down to dinner, Anna's best casserole. After her second bite Lilli says, "Are you in touch with anyone?"

"Anyone—?" Anna says.

"From Sunland."

"Oh," Anna says. "No, we haven't been."

"I'm surprised," Lilli says. "And you have nothing in your house from there."

"We left quickly," Gerhard says.

"I hear from Tilda," Lilli says. "She and Patrice are in Munich. Richard can send your letters on. It's not hard."

Gerhard pauses. "I suppose we think more about what we're doing now," he says.

"I do too," Lilli says. "But I still think about it every day. I have to."

"Why?" Anna says.

"Because I have to remember how to act. What things

are polite to talk about. And when people ask how you are, it doesn't mean you tell them all about your dreams and how you're digesting. You say 'Fine,' and you don't get mad that it's only the surface. You realize it's saving everyone three hours a day."

"I see," Gerhard says.

"But mostly it's that you can't tell people very much about yourself or where you've been. It's enough trouble being from another country. You don't want to say you're from another world. Do you tell them?"

"Not—" Anna says. "No."

"And so—what was it for?" Lilli says.

It's quiet for a moment. "Did you like it there?" Gerhard says.

"Yes," Lilli says. "To a point."

"Then it was for that."

"It was for *me*?" She gives her first smile of the evening but it's an incredulous one, as if someone's tried to sell her some bad escrow.

"That's not what I said," Gerhard says. Anna's face is nothing but nerves.

Children are welcome but we're unable to terrorize them, Gerhard thinks.

I'd like to see you try.

"And Benji's in New York?" Lilli says.

"Yes," Anna says. "He was going on to Berlin but that's not certain now."

"Please tell him hello from me. Do you know where Rose is?"

"No."

It's quiet for a moment, and then Anna says, "You know, I'm playing music with people again. For dancing. I don't know if I'd have the nerve for that, if we hadn't been there."

"That's good," Lilli says. "Is it jazz?" Anna shakes her

head. "In Los Angeles jazz is all they play now."

"You should come hear her some time," Gerhard says. "Saturday nights."

"I don't know when I'll have a Saturday night off," Lilli says. "I'm always getting ready for Sunday." She looks at her wristwatch. "I should get to the streetcar."

They walk her into town. Gerhard hopes Anna's not too hurt. She is, it seems, but relieved that Lilli's all right.

"That wasn't so bad," he says as the streetcar pulls away.

"She won't come again," Anna says.

"Yes she will. She won't live here, but she'll visit. She lives where it suits her."

As this railway siding of a town suits us, he thinks. Work, rest and people, just like Richard said, but the people for us turn out to be the kind we started out with, whose idea of starting the world over is called the weekend.

He holds Anna till she falls asleep. At dawn he gets up, eats an orange she brought from work, makes coffee and their lunches, brings in the newspaper and reads:

WOMAN LEADER OF BERLIN 'REDS' REPORTED SLAIN
Rosa Luxemburg Shot, Karl Liebknecht Drowned, Amid Renewed Riots

He falls into a chair and puts his face in his hands. It sounds like the army but it could be the police. You never change, he thinks, and you're the same everywhere. Of course you come in here and break our little peace, of course you kill someone whose words are a shield and a blanket all at once:

An entire old world still needs overthrowing and an entirely new one needs constructing. But we will do it, young friends, won't we? We will do it! Just as it says in the song:

We surely lack nothing, my wife, my child,
Except all that which prospers through us,
To be as free as the birds:
Only the time!

The sun's up. Gerhard's hands move by themselves, closing the paper, putting Anna's sandwich and orange on top of it, wiping tears from his face. When he gets outside he nearly runs, desperate to be at work, crushing rock and lining ditches, the men telling the plots of Western movies.

Thirty-Seven

Lilli gets off the streetcar from Fullerton so tired she can barely walk home. The night streets are beautiful, though, with electric signs softened by halos of damp air, and music coming from restaurants that stay open late. I was sharp with them, she thinks, but whose idea was it to raise me in the land of endless honesty? And after all that, not one keepsake of Sunland in their house. Not that I have any either, but I don't want them.

She crosses the apartment house courtyard, waters her hydrangea, goes inside, and almost falls asleep before Dawn knocks on her door. Dawn lives two units over and thinks Lilli's apartment has the most original decor she's ever seen. Really it's just lack of money. In place of art, Lilli pins up pictures from calendars, or advertisements that promise *THE SECRET WAY TO RICHES* and *LET US MAKE YOU FAT.* The painted lampshades come from junk stores. She'd have liked a few of Mother's orange crate labels but she wasn't about to ask.

"Is this new since I was here?" Dawn says, pointing at a bust of Cicero. "I love your imagination. I wish I could send the motorists to see *this.*"

Dawn comes from Minnesota and works at the Automobile Club. Lilli's been to see her there, smiling behind a counter in a tight sweater and kerchief, marking up maps to show people where the paved roads and toilet stops are. She's told Lilli she can barely believe she gets paid to be glamorous.

"Some of us are going to a picture Friday night," she says. "Why don't you come?"

"Fridays are hard," Lilli says.

"Do come, though. They're nice people and it's the Million Dollar Theater. How long since you've been to a movie?"

"A year?"

"Oh *no*," Dawn says. "They're getting better every month. You won't believe how real they are now."

Really it's been five years. The year before they left Germany, Lilli saw a short one called *The Grasshopper and the Ant*. Benji said it was just puppets, but she dreamed about it for a month. "All right," she says.

Friday night she rushes home from work, changes clothes and goes to the Million Dollar Theater, a spectacle that tries to look Mexican, Egyptian and Roman all at once. Through the windows she sees a lobby fancier than the Hotel Adlon's, all marble and chandeliers. A poster ringed with lights says:

NEXT WEEK! Pauline Frederick, The Queen of Emotionalism, in ASHES OF EMBERS from Paramount Pictures! This new play gives Miss Frederick's genius tremendous scope. She has a dual role, in the climax of which she chokes herself (as her double) into insensibility—a magnificent technical and dramatic achievement.

There's a photograph from the movie, a man and woman in fancy clothes looking upset. There's no chance they're puppets.

Lilli finds Dawn and her friends near the back of the

ticket line. Donald's a surveyor's assistant, his girlfriend Ruthanne works at Western Title Search, and Molly's in men's shirts at Bullock's. They all dress for ambition, the way Dawn does. Lilli wishes she'd worn her Sunday selling dress.

"Hello, James," Dawn says, as another friend walks up to meet them. He's tall and grinning, with a brush of blond hair and a strong build. His clothes are as plain as Lilli's, twill trousers, a canvas shirt open at the neck, and a tweed coat. If it wasn't for his shiny shoes he could be a farmer.

"This is Lilli," Dawn says.

He shakes her hand as he gets in line with them. "A pleasure. James Lever."

"Did you see Bill Brennan?" Molly asks him.

"I sure did. Bomber Brennan to you." He turns to Lilli. "I sell sporting goods, wholesale mostly. The Bomber's trainer ordered Indian clubs. I delivered them myself. He's training in Chula Vista."

"We used to go down there," Ruthanne says. "We'd make a pit for clams."

"Sure," James says. "Dawn told me a great route. Beautiful trees, and those rocks that stack up in layers? Then bang, you're over the ocean." He shakes his head in pleasure. "Brennan's fantastic, the shape he's in. He's got sparring, weightlifting and malted milk. We swam together. We swung the clubs. It's fine to see someone like that." He holds a cupped hand out from his own arm muscle. "He's going to get killed up there but he'll look good doing it."

"How do you know?" Donald says.

"He's a sacrifice," James says. "How they used to sacrifice people to the gods? That's all it is. They're just warming Dempsey up for Tom Riley." He turns to Lilli. "That's not my normal day, going down there. On my normal day I sell men's supporters to Holy Names."

"James!" Dawn says.

"It's Holy Names," James says, spreading his hands in innocence. "Our supporters are a sacrament. You can't fault me." He turns to Lilli. "Are you Catholic? I didn't mean anything."

"No," Lilli says, and wonders if there's a joke she'd still blush at.

"Do you play something? Tennis?" She shakes her head. "Everyone should have a sport," he says. "An hour a day. It gets the poisons out. I could show you."

They start talking about the actor in the movie they're seeing, Charlie Chaplin. Lilli's heard his name but that's all.

"I read an interview with him in *Photoplay,*" Dawn says. "He said, 'There's nothing interesting about me. I have no fads, no automobiles, and I'm not really funny.'" Everyone laughs, as if his saying that is the funniest thing of all. James offers to buy Lilli's ticket but she already has her money out.

Inside, the auditorium walls are crammed with Pans, gargoyles and ladies with cats' heads. An usher gives them programs and points them to their seats with a riding crop. James sits next to Lilli and says, "What line are you in?"

"I show model homes," she says. "At Rosewood Glen."

"You're smart," he says. "That's the future out there. Schools, church and shopping as far as the eye can see."

The chandeliers dim and a platform rises in front of the stage, bringing an orchestra of forty musicians into view. The conductor walks on and the audience claps.

Lilli holds her breath. If this is this movie, Dawn is right. The people are so real it's frightening.

Then a cellist drops her sheet music and the conductor waits for her to pick it up. When they make a mistake in a movie, they do it over till it's perfect. Benji told her that. She hopes no one saw her look startled.

After the music there's a movie about things in the

news, more real than any movie she's seen, but there's no trouble telling it from life. Then the Charlie Chaplin movie, *A Night in the Show*, comes on. Lilli laughs along with everyone else, but she thinks she knows what Chaplin means when he says he's not really funny. The whole movie's about the rude things people would like to do but know they'd be put away for, in jail if not a sanatorium.

Chaplin plays two different men who go to a theater, a rich one and a poor one. The rich one lights matches on people's heads, smacks the orchestra conductor, and puts snakes in a tuba. The poor one pours beer on the rich one, throws ice cream at the singers, and drenches everyone with the fire hose. They wreck the show, but the audience in the movie likes it better than if it went right. The audience around Lilli likes it even more.

Charlie Chaplin's everything the Sunland people wish they were, she thinks. He's against the regular world and having manners, and he wants the poor people to beat the rich ones, but instead of scrabbling around in the dirt by Driscoll, he's famous. People don't want to be taught a lesson with songs about slavery. If you say what you mean with seltzer, they put your picture in *Photoplay*.

When the lights come up James grins at her, his face red from laughing. "Don't you *love* him?" he says.

ೞ

After the show, he waits for her streetcar with her and asks where she's from. "Germany," she says, "but we moved to Illinois when I was little. What about you?"

"From here," James says.

"All your life?"

He nods. "It's a rare condition. I could show you around some time. Can I phone you?"

"I don't have one."

"At work?"

"All right."

She gives him the number. Three days later he calls and says, "Do you still want to learn tennis?"

"Oh," she says, imagining tripping over herself and breaking her arm. For certain she doesn't have the clothes.

She says yes anyway, puts on a long yellow dress and meets him at the Mount Washington Railway, a one-car train that goes up a hill near downtown. He's in serge pants, an open shirt, and a corduroy coat with the collar turned up. He's probably got tennis clothes at home, Lilli thinks. He's being nice.

"The fare's a dime," he says, handing her one the way her father did that first day here. "They're trying to sell properties up there."

The train goes ratcheting up the mountain. James asks where her family lived in Illinois. "East St. Louis, on a farm," she says. "I helped out with the mules."

"Why'd you move out here?"

"The ocean," she says, though she hasn't seen it since their ship from Panama.

The city spreads out underneath them, asphalt roofs, business towers, raw lots like Rosewood Glen and a ridge of hills through the middle of town. When they step off at the top, there's a pink hotel surrounded by flowers.

James leads her around the back, to two tennis courts with a sign saying GUESTS ONLY. A man and lady in spotless white outfits are playing on one of them. For a minute Lilli's sure the lady is the Queen of Emotionalism from the movie poster, but then decides she's being foolish.

On the other court a man in older tennis clothes is hitting balls over the net by himself. "Harvey," James says to him.

"James," Harvey says. "Here for a lesson?"

"No, I'm past hope. I'm handing it off to Lilli here."

"Hello, Lilli."

Harvey drags his basket of balls outside the lines. James thanks him and hands Lilli a racket. "Take a swing," he says. "Here."

He puts a hand on her shoulder, another on her arm, and shows her the motion. She feels his touch in her stomach. When he lets go she tries swinging the racket by herself, liking the weight in her hand and the breeze it makes. "There you are," he says. "Let's try it out."

He goes to the other side of the net and hits a ball to her. She misses it by a foot. He hits another one and she does even worse.

"I'm sorry," she says. "I must not have the knack for it."

"Don't worry," he says, and walks up to the net. "Look at me. I've got conformation but I'm missing speed, agility, and willpower. Once you know that, you just enjoy yourself. Do you know what percentage we sell to professionals? Six percent. Do you know what the future is? Amateurs. Factories, machines, leisure time, confusion of purpose—amateurs. All set?"

She nods. He hits another ball to her. This time she hits it back. It goes over his head and high into the sky before it falls out of sight.

"Did you see that?" James says.

"How's the backhand?" Harvey says.

James comes around the net and reaches for her upper arm. "May I?"

She feels herself blush but says, "All right."

"Make a muscle," he says, and feels her arm. "Cripes. What have you been doing?"

"Nothing," Lilli says. "Well, carrying trees, I guess. To put them in, at work."

"Trees," James says. "Can Harvey see?"

"All right."

Harvey puts his hand there too. "You'll want to get that registered," he says.

"Try just tapping it," James says.

It takes a few tries, but she does. In a while they get into a rhythm, letting the ball bounce on the clay and stepping up to hit it. She keeps a silent count of how long their volleys go—ten hits, then fifteen.

They keep on after Harvey and the couple are gone, then go out on the hotel's observation deck to see the ocean. James points toward it and says, "There's that ball you hit. It's doing barrel rolls, see? People are cheering." Then he looks around in earnest, his eyes like a bird's, as if he knows the cliffs and inlets by heart. They ride the train down under sunset clouds, sitting close this time.

ᔆ

The next week he picks her up at work and says, "I'm taking you someplace out of the ordinary. I don't think they have this in Illinois."

They drive to a restaurant near the University of Southern California. The sign says HELIOTROPE NATURE CAFÉ, with pictures like the ones on Rose's banners—goddesses, goat-men and people in ancient clothes, all walking toward a golden sun.

Inside the floor is red and the walls are orange. Plants move in the breeze outside the back window, like an aquarium. Most of the rough wooden tables are taken. Half the customers look as healthy as Rolf, the others like they'll be dead in a week, and some of each kind have still-pool eyes like Herman and Dara's. In the corner a man with long hair plays a piano, the music sort of classical but drifting.

A man in a purple shirt leads them to a table. He looks like Jules, with that same theatrical manner. Lilli reads the menu: Watercress-Sorrel Surprise, Mint-Mung Ambrosia, Kale. "It's so strange," she says.

"They're nice people, though," James says. "It takes all kinds," but what Lilli means is that it's strange seeing people like these outside of Sunland.

Their waitress glides over looking like Patrice—the same long hair and dreaming smile, even the silk clothes. When the food comes it's just what Lilli remembers, grains and beans gritting against each other, mushrooms swimming in whey custard.

The waitress comes back. "Do you like it?" she says.

"Yes," Lilli says. "May I ask you something? Are there other places like this? In Los Angeles, I mean."

The waitress smiles wider. "Yes," she says. "For the food, four cafés I can think of. For the *understanding*—there's a bookstore, an art gallery, a hiking club…"

"What is the understanding?" Lilli says.

The waitress thinks. "Hope," she says. "People are waking up, do you know? They're coming to their senses. There can't be another war like that. People have to come back to the earth now."

The man in the purple shirt comes up behind her. "Have you been to Ojai?" he says. Lilli shakes her head. "That's a whole town," the man says. "That's a vortex."

"But really everywhere," the waitress says. "More all the time."

Lilli thanks them and they walk away. You can think that, she thinks, but the truth is you'll never have more than a few little districts, scattered around cities or next to colleges, like this one. The rest of us can only carry so many of you around.

A week later, though, James takes her to a restaurant in the Chinese neighborhood off Alvarado, with ducks and chickens hanging in the window. He orders fried rice and three kinds of meat. They're about to start eating when Lilli says, "Do they make bok choy here?"

The waiter hears her, smiles, and brings a plate of it

laid out like a wheel, green spokes and a rim of gleaming bulbs. Lilli eats one. It gets at her where the Heliotrope Café didn't.

This is stupid, she thinks. I have money and a job now. I could come back here tomorrow if I wanted, or never. But she keeps seeing that night in the yard with the lanterns, Tilda with her seeds, Jules with his newspapers, Jorgen listening to the two-stringed violin. When she looks at the bok choy plate it's clouded by tears and empty.

"Oh," she says. "I've eaten it all."

"No, I got one," James says. "You have to watch me every minute. Are you all right?"

"Yes." She puts her hand on his. "Would you take me home?"

☘

They drive there without talking, but when he pulls to the curb she asks if he'd like to come in. "I guess so," he says. "Dawn's always talking about it. I should see for myself."

He fusses over her apartment almost as much as Dawn does. "You're one surprise after another," he says. When he turns around from looking at a doorway framed in postcards, she takes him in her arms, tilts her head up and kisses him.

"Oh, say," he says. They kiss again and Lilli feels her heart beat, but when she unbuttons the top of her blouse and tries to take his hand inside it he says, "No, wait. No."

She lets go of him. He points at her blouse and turns his head away.

Lilli buttons it. "I can't get married now," he says. "There's no way I could."

"No, I—"

"You know I like you," he says, "but I'm just getting started in business. I'm just getting my feet under me."

She wants to tell him it's not how it seems, that she's

never done it, she's just seen other people do it, but even after being raised at Sunland she knows better than to say that. She says she's sorry instead.

"It's all right," he says. "I should go. I'll phone you."

When he leaves she lies on her bed and cries. Now I'm the Queen of Emotionalism, she thinks. But no, if I was her or Rose or Diana I'd be irresistible, and I've just been resisted and mortified all at once. It was fine hearing Richard explain life, but those explanations only worked where no one was just getting their feet under them, where the last thing they wanted was to touch the ground.

James doesn't phone, and after a week Dawn comes by to say he's asked her out but she wanted to talk to Lilli first. Lilli says it's fine and starts looking for a new apartment. When she finds one, she starts to put the postcards and funny advertisements in her suitcase but stops. I was wrong to think I didn't have any keepsakes here, she thinks. This whole room is a keepsake. It's Rose's house. I just didn't see it. She puts the decorations in a box and leaves them at the curb.

It's hard sleeping in her new place, and she spends a lot of time walking. One Saturday on Flower Street she hears people singing. The tune's familiar but it takes her a block to place it. It's one of Roland's songs. Why would people sing that here?

She gets closer and sees the building it's coming from, a big auditorium with banners saying <u>CHRIST SPIRIT REVIVAL TODAY - LOVE IS IN THIS BUILDING</u>. Most of the people going inside look poor but they're dressed up in that poor way, everything starched and spotless.

Lilli crosses the street and walks up to the building. A man in a blue suit, with a white carnation in one lapel and a red one in the other, is shaking people's hands as they come to the door.

"Hello!" he says to Lilli, taking her hand as if he's known her forever. "Blessed and beloved! Oh, we've been waiting for you! Just waiting for you to arrive!"

She can hear what the people inside are singing now:

I am climbing Jacob's ladder
Through the stars I make my way
I am meeting my redeemer
Meet him on that glory day.

When Roland sang it, it went:

I am running from the sheriff
With his deputies and dogs,
I can hear them close behind me
In the washes and the bogs

They will catch up with me sometime
But I'm still a day ahead,
And I'll spend ten years in prison
Just for one night in your bed.

"Won't you come in and see?" the man with the carnations says, holding the door open. "The beautiful robes on the choir? The miracle healings?" Lilli has tears in her eyes, and the man likes that. "The *answers*," he says, just loud enough for her to hear.

"Thank you," Lilli says. She lets go of his hand and walks away, down Eighth Street to Hamburger's Department Store.

The phonographs are on the third floor. She buys one with a built-in loudspeaker, takes it home, winds it up, slides the complimentary record out of its sleeve and starts it playing. The song is called "Ja-da, Ja-da, Jing Jing Jing, For Children's Chorus and Xylophone." It seems like such a miracle to hear all those people in her apartment that the song is halfway through before she realizes it's maddening. She takes the needle off and watches the record spin, a span of light on each side of the label like moonlight on water.

The next day, at a music store in Hollywood, she finds a record of "The Memphis Blues." The clerk plays her some jazz, "Aunt Hagar's Blues" and "Avalon," and she buys those too. In Glendale she finds the song about the flood.

She asks at one shop if they have any blues songs, like the ones Bernard knew. The man says you couldn't give him a blues record, that every tune is the same and it's just coloreds bragging about crime and worse. She doesn't go back there. The week she finishes her real estate classes she goes to Hamburger's and buys a Brahms violin concerto, six records in a pasteboard album.

One day in March she tries a new record store on the west side. They don't have anything she wants but it's a nice day, and she keeps walking north past her streetcar stop. In a while the houses run out and the street turns to a dirt road, then a trail leading up into mountains. She keeps going, takes her jacket off, and wipes the sweat from her face with her handkerchief.

An old man and lady come down the trail in canvas clothes, wide hats and walking sticks. The lady smiles and says hello.

"Hello," Lilli says, her throat dry. "Do you know where we are?"

"About two miles from the top," the man says. "You should have a canteen if you're going up." He takes his off and holds it out to her.

"No, I—how will I give it back to you?" Lilli says.

"That's all right," he says. "We've got hers. You keep that for your walks."

Lilli starts to say no but thanks him instead. Now she feels like she has to go all the way up, even though her shoes are wrong for it.

For a while it looks like the dull places west of Sunland, all gullies and scree, but farther up there are hillsides full of wildflowers and outcrops glinting with minerals. The view from the top is so wide it hurts her eyes, all those miniature beaches and buildings blinking in the sun.

After a while she starts down, seeing hawks, rabbits, and a man painting a portrait of a woodpecker. When she comes to a creek she walks halfway across it on rocks, sits down on one and takes her shoes off. Both heels are blistered. At first she's annoyed, but then she puts her feet in the water and studies the blue veins in her skin and her toe hairs waving in the current.

That's not bad, she thinks. If I'd known there was a section like this I would have come sooner. I should find out if there are others. I should buy a radio sometime too, for Benji's sake. For now I'd better put my shoes on and get down before dark. Not yet, but soon.

Thirty-Eight

His first morning in New York, Benji asks the hotel clerk where the public library is. The man sends him to a new branch at Forty-Second Street. There are two stone lions outside, as if to say, "We don't shush you at our library, we eat you alive"—another point in New York's favor.

Inside he finds the *Hawkins Electrical Guide*, takes the five books on either side of it to the reading room, and starts to study. He comes back every day and stays till closing, working his way through those books and two years of *Wireless Age* magazine. In the second week he cashes his steamship ticket to pay the hotel and cuts back on food.

After three weeks he goes back to the Woolworth Building and walks around the block twice for nerve before he goes in. When he looks at the lobby frieze on a starving stomach, Mr. Woolworth appears to offer him a dime and snatch it back, laughing.

He takes the high-speed elevator, pressing his palms against the back wall to stay upright. On the twenty-seventh floor he walks into the Marconi Wireless Telegraph Company of America's reception room, a long rectangle with cheap carpet and a few men waiting on sofas. The receptionist sits at a desk between two artificial plants. There's no wall behind her, just a partition a few feet short of the ceiling. Sounds pour over the top of it, voices and chattering telegraph keys. She says, "Yes?" but Benji pauses before answering. He's dizzy again, this time from being one partition away from that much signal.

"I came to ask about work," he says.

"Are you a telegraph operator?"

"An engineer."

"Applications are Thursdays," she says.

When he comes back three days later there are ten men on the sofas filling out applications. The receptionist gives him one. He stares for five minutes at the line asking for his degrees and experience, then thinks of the watch repairman on the ship and writes *I can fix any apparatus you have*.

He waits five hours. The other men go inside and come out. The telegraph operators change shifts. The sounds over the partition get quieter.

Finally it's just Benji and the receptionist. She takes a call on her intercom and says, "You can go in now. See Mister Morris."

Behind the partition it's one big room with a bare floor, sash windows and tin lampshades. The telegraph operators work on one side, tapping out code under clocks showing the time in cities around the world. On the other side, men work at benches covered with meters, dials, Audion tubes and circuit boards.

A man in his thirties, with a pipe and a belly, waves Benji over. "I'm Morris," he says. "I had to see for myself. 'Any apparatus you have.'"

"I think it's true, sir," Benji says.

"Something I wonder sometimes," Morris says. "Say you're transmitting and you've got a condenser in series with your aerial. How much does that take off your wavelength?"

"Wouldn't that depend on the capacity of the condenser?" Benji says.

"You could be right," Morris says. "How about this apparatus? Can you fix this?"

He points at a wooden box on his workbench, with dials and meters on the front, a mass of disconnected wires inside, and a telegraph headset attached to it. Benji pulls a wire aside to look. "It's a signal amplifier," he says. "Like the ones Edwin Armstrong built."

"Actually it's one he did build," Morris says. "Recently." Benji drops the wire and pulls his hand back. "Don't let that impress you, though. Can you wire it?"

I shouldn't be surprised, Benji thinks. Look where we're standing. "Yes," he says.

It takes him half an hour, with Morris watching the whole time. The books he's read take him halfway, then logic, then hunger. When he makes the last connection, his fingers white on the screwdriver, Morse code pours out of the headset.

"Assistance and errands to start with," Morris says. "Coiling wire, tipping instruments, going for sandwiches."

To start with, the man said. It's all Benji can do not to grab his arm.

☙

A few months later they start letting him wire, just as the Marconi Company changes its name to the Radio Corporation of America and joins with Westinghouse to sell people radios for their houses. The first time Benji hears music on a tube-amplified set, in 1920, the leap in quality from crystal makes him stand at attention.

"Yes, they're ducky," Morris says, "but no one's buying the damn things. That's why we're going to Pittsburgh in November."

"What's in Pittsburgh?" Benji says.

"A commercial broadcast. The presidential election. Anyone with a radio will know who wins before the newspapers go to press."

"And you're going there?"

"You are too. You're the potentiometer man. Play some handball. Get that wrist built up."

That night Benji writes to Mother and Father: *Plans for Berlin set aside. Whatever might happen to me in the future, I'm writing you today from exactly where I want to be.*

He and Morris drive through sleeting rain to Pittsburgh three days before the broadcast. In the radio shack on the roof of the Westinghouse building, they meet two other engineers and a man named Leo Rosenberg, who's going to read the election returns on the air. On the night of the broadcast Benji's job is to watch one meter and adjust one dial for six hours. He tries to shut out Leo's voice till he realizes that listening to him makes it easier to concentrate, not harder.

"O.K.," Leo tells the listeners, "that's sixteen million votes so far for Harding, and nine million for the Democrat Cox. Now, in a minute or two we'll be getting to the state results, but first there's something we'd like you to do. If you're hearing this broadcast, do us a favor, drop a card in the mail and let us know. That's KDKA, Westinghouse, East Pittsburgh, Pennsylvania. O.K. then, let's take a look here..."

At five in the morning they finish the broadcast and go back to their hotel. Benji sleeps for three hours before Morris knocks on his door. "We're going downtown," he says.

The five of them drive to Smithfield Street, park across from a home furnishings store, and wait. In half an hour a man comes out carrying a wooden box with dials on the front, glass tubes on top, and a headset.

"That was us, sir," Morris says. "We sold you that." Twenty minutes later there's another one. Everyone cheers except Leo, who's fallen back to sleep.

Benji's still getting over his surprise from last night. He thought an election announcer would sound official, like a government spokesman, but Leo wasn't that way at all. He said "O.K." and "Do us a favor," and cleared his throat right into the microphone.

It's not lectures and plays at the touch of a dial we're selling, Benji thinks. It's company. Take the loneliest place you can think of, that Kansas prairie I saw from the train. No, even lonelier: my apartment. There's an iron bed and flowered wallpaper, an occasional voice from the street, but mostly silence. Add in some thoughts of Rose, then Jorgen, and there are nights that last twenty hours. But soon there'll be someone like Leo, the friend you never knew you had but now can't do without. We should go back to our hotel and phone in to RCA. We should tell them to start making those new sets now and never stop.

1921

Thirty-Nine

Lilli shows two or three houses every Sunday, strikes contracts that make banks and buyers think they're beating each other, and becomes a Top Fifteen producer three months in a row. When she hears about the ridge road being built across the city, she decides to have a look. It's not her territory but it could be.

She has a car now, a Packard she bought lightly used. One slow Sunday she fills the canteen the old man gave her, drives to the end of the canyon road, and walks up the mountain. At the top there are steam shovels, backhoes and a new dirt roadway. A sign says EDWIN P. MULHOLLAND SCENIC HIGHWAY - YOUR TAX DOLLARS AT WORK.

Lilli walks east, sizing up the open lots and existing density. Half a mile along, in a clearing by the road, a dozen people are sitting on rocks and stumps. They're all different ages, in walking clothes like the old hiking couple's, with clipboards, books and binoculars.

A bird lands in a tree. One of the people says, "White-breasted nuthatch." Someone else says, "Check," and they mark it on their lists.

A lady in jodhpurs smiles at Lilli and nods at an empty stump. She sits down. After a while someone says, "Hairy woodpecker."

Between birds, the people drink from Thermos bottles and watch the sky. Lilli keeps meaning to get back to walking but stays, listening to the names of the birds and the quiet between them. It's funny, she thinks, but if someone made a phonograph record of just that I'd buy it. When the people stand up and say their goodbyes, she's still there.

A man walks up to her and says, "I don't think I remember a better day. For this time of year, I mean. Spring's a different story." He's about her age, tall and thin in a windbreaker jacket. "Is this your first time with us?"

"Yes," Lilli says. "Really I came up to see about the road."

"Oh, yes." He makes a face. "It's a shame. They're going to start paving it soon. Everyone's upset about it."

"Everyone?" Lilli says. "Don't you think some people are pleased?"

The man pauses. "You're right. I shouldn't be so categorical. The birdwatchers are upset. I can speak to that, anyway."

"The ones who can walk here, yes," Lilli says. "What about the ones who aren't fit enough to do that? Maybe they'd like to see some birds too."

"That's true," he says.

She doesn't know why she's arguing with a stranger, but it bothers her that he's so put out about a road being paved. She was like that about the one going past Sunland, but she was fourteen at the time. You can't be that tender forever.

"May I walk down with you?" he says.

"All right," she says. "I was going to see where it crosses the canyon roads. I'm in real estate."

"Ah," he says, as if that explains everything. He leads her onto a path lined with sticker bushes. That'll make a nice afternoon, she thinks, getting those out of my clothes.

"What do you do?" she says.

"I'm a teacher. Eighth and ninth grades, in Hollywood."

"I learned those at home," Lilli says. "All I missed was lunch and recess."

"Were you working?"

She nods. "With mules."

"Where was your farm?"

She's about to say Missouri but stops and says, "Outside Driscoll," the most truth she's told anyone. "It was a crazy place, if you want to know. My parents took us there. They didn't believe in money or machines. It made no sense. It probably doesn't make sense hearing about it, either."

"Oh, I don't know," he says. "I'm from Minnesota, but I've been in Los Angeles a while."

"I sell as many houses as people with college," she says.

"I'm sure you do."

She pauses. "I don't generally tell people all that."

"I'm flattered you told me, then," he says. "I hope it's not because you won't see me again." That's pretty bold for someone from Minnesota, Lilli thinks. Or Hollywood, for that matter.

They cross the stream on the rocks. "My name's Edward, by the way," he says. "Do your parents still live out there?"

Lilli shakes her head. "In Fullerton. They're so ordinary now, you'd never know."

"Do you see them?"

"Only once. I said I'd go back to hear my mother play, but I haven't."

"Play?"

"She plays music for dancing."

"Is it jazz?"

"No. I asked her that too."

He smiles. "Maybe it's that ancient-modern business.

People jumping around in Greek ecstasy."

Lilli shakes her head. "Not where they live."

"How do you know?" Edward says.

Forty

The oranges roll toward Anna all day on a belt, already sized, washed and stamped. She wraps them in tissue and puts them in crates. By afternoon the word CAL-CREST becomes a secret message, then a road sign, then a senseless row of symbols, and finally a hallucination, hanging in the air for an hour after work.

When she walks into the Grange on Saturday night Laszlo's there, practicing his double bass. She puts her case on a bench, opens it and takes out her violin. There are three photographs pinned to the case lining. One is Lilli in Panama, pretending to hold a steam shovel as if it's a bug. The next is a re-creation of that pose in the woods at Sunland when she was nearly a teenager, with a real grasshopper on her hand. The third is one of the photos of the band that they sold in the Welcome Building, the one where Anna looks wild, her hair and scarf blurred and her face lost in the music. If she moved like that here, they'd call a minister.

She practices with Laszlo till Bob arrives and lets people in. It's a good turnout, enough for four squares. Bob's voice moves them along like a train conductor's:

Allemande left with the old left hand,
Right to your partner and a right and left grand—

—"allemande" meaning "the German step," though Anna doubts they changed it for the war.

She watches Laszlo's hands for the first two choruses. When she looks up, Lilli and a young man are at the back of the room, talking to Gerhard. Anna manages to keep playing but repeats the same three notes till Bob turns and looks at her.

They start the next song. The young man takes Lilli into a square and shows her the steps. She looks up at Anna once, just long enough for their eyes to meet.

When the dancing's over Anna goes down to talk to them. The young man's name is Edward. He's thin and serious-looking, but he danced like the farm boys.

"That was fine fiddling," he says. "I haven't heard that music since I got to California. I didn't know if I would again."

Gerhard asks if they want to stay the night. "Thank you," Edward says, "but she's showing three houses to-morrow."

"Just two," Lilli says. "But he has birdwatching."

"In the city?" Anna says.

"Oh, you'd be surprised," Edward says. "You should come some time."

Lilli hesitates a second but nods agreement. "We should start back," she says.

Anna shakes Edward's hand and hugs Lilli. Be casual, she thinks, just a little hug, the way she does. If you crush her to your chest it'll be another two years before you see her again.

She and Gerhard help put the chairs away and then walk home, saying hello to people on the way. The last three blocks, when they're alone, he puts his arm around her and tells her how good she sounded.

"Thank you," she says.

"I told you she'd be back," he says.

They turn onto their street. Some nights the wind smells like oil, the earth's embarrassment. Tonight it's oranges, not the ones you pack all day but the two you steal home for breakfast.

1925

Forty-One

Anna comes home from work and finds a package in brown paper, postmarked New Mexico. Inside are a book and a letter written in looping India ink, with drawings of barrel cactus and curious lizards, all made of ovals.

If pressed, he admits that our own life here is more than comfortable. The students flock around him the way he likes, and I paint in light that does half the work for me. I've had one show here, of work I'd kept private in the past. Everyone insists it went well. Our creations mean as little to the world as ever. We still make them.

Do you hear from anyone? I can give you gossip if you like. Our greatest concern, of course, was for Astrid, Linda and Trudy. They've opened a bakery in upstate New York, where Hasidic Jews and Russian Orthodox Christians dot the landscape. There was a free love community there that was going to be Jesus's earthly kingdom but became a silverware company instead. People who grew up there come to the bakery sometimes. Astrid says Trudy and Linda can pick them out every time.

Manfred and Rolf were invited to leave the canyon by the county agent not long after they settled there. Rolf is in Goleta, building houses. Manfred went back to Berlin, went to his publisher's offices, put a sandy notebook down on someone's desk and said, "Late. I know." That became the book you see here, <u>Poems from a Canyon</u>.

There's a drawing of a saguaro cactus with a long, person-like shadow, and then:

Anna, I realize as I write this that I was waiting to get in touch till things might be less raw from that time, or till our eyes adjusted and we saw the light we had there as well as the dark. I hope that's the case for you. I love you all, but you my correspondent first and always.

Please be well,
Rose

Anna writes back that night:

Dear Rose,

Of course I'm happy to hear from you. I've often wondered

how you are. Thank you for Manfred's book, which completes my collection of his works so far.

Yes, we are all fine. Gerhard is the foreman of an irrigation crew here in Fullerton, where I work in a packing shed and play music for square dancing. When I see that on paper it sounds like the most ordinary life in creation, but it's a California sort of ordinary and suits us well.

Gerhard's practically an American now, down to the baseball and ice cream in the park. Lilli lives in Los Angeles, where she sells real estate, and is married to a young man named Edward, of whom we're very fond. Benji lives in New York, working for the National Broadcasting Company. He's had a few sweethearts, sometimes more than one at once, but hasn't found anyone to be serious with.

One day a crate came from him, a radio set of our own. Gerhard got it working and we heard the people Benji had written us about, the Happiness Boys, the A and P Gypsies, and so on. A few weeks later, turning the dial from one broadcast to another, I heard something that took my breath away: Roland, singing his song about the "friendly town." It was only there for a minute, till the wind shifted up where the radio waves are and blew it away.

I said to myself that it could use a violin, but not mine. But later that day I heard a tune in my head, an unfamiliar one because I was making it up right then. It was like the jazz music I've heard but gentler, with a feeling like when I'd walk through the mist on my way to bake in the mornings. I found some music paper and wrote it down.

No one's heard it but Gerhard. When I played it for him he was quiet for a minute, then said, "How do you do that—all of you? Where do you get it from?"—as if, with four minutes of music, I'd become one of the mysterious people who do that. That's love, I thought, but it got me to write three more. Maybe no one else will hear them, or maybe they will.

Two years ago, at Christmas, we had Benji and Lilli here

together for the first time. They were nervous with each other at first, but then fell into talking about New York and Los Angeles, the burdens of their success, the car traffic and subway trains, the scarcity of time to catch their breath.

At first I thought this was small talk, but I was mistaken. These are their true topics now, their most treasured. When they visited again last year they went straight back to it. Lilli's husband Edward listened for a while, then came into the kitchen to talk to me. He loves her dearly, but the speed of his pulse is closer to ours.

I hope we'll see each other someday, and that in the meanwhile we can keep writing. Please give our love to Richard. I'm glad to know about the two of you, both for its own sake and because, just once, I was able to see something before you did.

Love,
Anna

1934

Forty-Two

When Lilli first saw the news about the stock market going down she thought it would be good for real estate, because people always need a place to sleep. She was right for a while, but within a year her buyers were losing their jobs and backing out of deals. One day downtown she saw a long line of people and thought it must be for a show or a sale, but it was for soup and bread. The next time she went there, people were coming out of an all-night movie theater at eight in the morning with blankets under their arms.

Now people are coming to Los Angeles from Oklahoma and Texas with nothing, even though the police try to keep them out. The low end of the canyon road is lined with old cars, clotheslines and cook fires. Edward's school has some new students, and he takes a little household money to buy them milk and sandwiches. "If they're too hungry they stop coming," he says. "Then I lose a customer."

William's five. Lilli tries to keep enough business coming in so they don't have to move him away from his friends. She doesn't like most of the business she's getting, though, helping people sell their family homes at bad prices. She wishes they wouldn't thank her but they always do.

One day William brings a friend home from school. Ned's clothes are worn and his shoes flap, but he runs around playing with William for two hours, up and down stairs and in the little yard. He stays for supper and eats three helpings. When Lilli and Edward are washing dishes, the boys come in and William asks if they can drive Ned home.

"It's by the General's Hospital," Ned says.

"I know where that is," Edward tells William. "I'll take him and you can stay with Mother."

Ned says to William, "No, you come too."

Edward starts to say something but Lilli says, "We'll all go."

They drive into Boyle Heights at dusk and park where the road ends. "It's in the bungalows," William says, pointing up the hill.

To get there they walk through an encampment with houses made of canvas, cardboard, branches and tin. One has a front wall made of Bon Ami boxes and a chimney of welded coffee cans. People are everywhere, cooking, washing, fighting, talking, and trying to get an old car started. Some smile at them and others turn away.

They walk up to the bungalows, tiny cabins circling a single kitchen and bathrooms. When they get to Ned's cabin, a woman comes to the doorway and holds him to her side.

"Hello," she says. "I'm Hazel." She's around thirty, thin and short, in an old flowered dress. "I hope he wasn't trouble to you." Her voice has those damp-sounding vowels everyone knows are Oklahoman now.

"None at all," Edward says. "These two ran all over. I think they rescued some stagecoaches."

"It was trains," William says. "We saved them."

"Trains, then," Edward says. He introduces himself and Lilli.

This is when Hazel would ask them in, but the cabin behind her is too small. Lilli sees a few things over her shoulder, a bed on the floor, a bag of corn meal and a flaking world atlas.

"We haven't been here long," Hazel says. "We're not settled in as such."

"That takes a while," Lilli says. "I know it did me."

A dog runs up to them, barking and baring its teeth. Lilli pulls William back. Hazel holds Ned closer, shouting "No!" at the dog and "Doris!" at a cabin nearby. A girl comes out to take the dog away.

"I'm sorry," Hazel says.

"No, it's fine," Lilli says. You should have a foyer, she thinks, a stupid thought except that every home deserves one.

"I'd better get him to sleep," Hazel says. "What do you say, Ned?"

"Thank you," Ned says.

"You come over any time," Lilli says.

Ned and William say goodnight to each other in the solemn way little boys do. Halfway home, William in the back seat says, "Why do they live there?"

It's quiet for a second. Lilli thought he was asleep.

"Things are mixed up right now," she says. "They won't always be."

"When?"

"We'll have to see."

Three days later Lilli gets a letter from Tilda, with a Zurich postmark and no return address. She tears it open at the mailbox. Her last two letters to Tilda in Germany came back unopened and there's been nothing for three months.

Dear Lilli,

I hope I haven't worried you, but it was unsafe writing from Munich. We're in Switzerland now, though it's not clear how long we can stay.

In Germany they began arresting people like Patrice and me almost the day Chancellor Hitler was appointed. He has formed a Federal Bureau to Combat Abortion and Homosexuality. One has to admit the genius of that. I doubt very much the Chancellor and his friends lose sleep over abortion or homosexuality, but they know there are people who do. At any rate, several friends of ours were taken and none have come back.

We feel stupid for having come back from California to Munich, but it was a friendly city once. Now you never know how people will act or which old friend will cut you dead, please pardon the expression.

Josef has joined the Party. He's at Freiburg University, officially a lecturer in music but really a professor of rattling on about natural living and firing Jews from the faculty.

Jules's collages were declared degenerate by the government last year. He said the authorities had made the common mistake of confusing the artist with the work, then left with Suzanne for London.

Everything with us is if if if. Someone has taken all the money we had and promised us Paraguayan passports, which we can use to get visas for Brazil. We can go there on a cargo ship from Italy, if all this happens before we're sent back to Munich.

We're scared and so tired but we persist in being hopeful. The light and snow here are beautiful. Patrice sends love. I'll write again when we land safely. When, not if if if.

Love always,
Tilda

Lilli cries for a minute, then writes a letter asking for help with their case and makes eight copies of it in long-hand. *Dear President of the United States Roosevelt, To the Ed-*

itor of the Los Angeles Times, Dear Mr. Will Rogers, and one for Benji because he might know someone to send it on to. Edward suggests the Department of State so that's five, and three in case they have more ideas. There must be thousands of them crossing through the mail now, but Lilli sends hers anyway. If America can take a girl raised at Sunland and give her a profession and a family, why can't it save Tilda and Patrice?

A week later she gets a letter from Richard, forwarded by Mother. He says he still holds the deed to Sunland but that no one's lived there for years. He wants to sell it and send checks to everyone he can locate, and asks Lilli to put it on the market for him.

"It's a pain," she tells Edward. "It can't be worth anything now."

"You could let someone else do it," he says.

"Someone else might cheat him. He'd have no idea. Then I'd be taking money away from Tilda and everyone."

"You could do it yourself."

"I will. But screw him for putting me in this position."

"You didn't hear that, William."

Lilli writes to Richard that she'll do it and puts the listing out. A few weeks later she gets a letter from the U.S. Army. They're starting a recovery agency, the Civilian Conservation Corps, to plant trees and put young men back to work. They want the land for barracks and a tree farm. The offer's low but the description of their goals is lyrical, as if they've put out-of-work poets on the payroll.

She gets the price up a little and considers it settled till another letter comes from Richard. He's satisfied with the terms but wants one more condition: that he, Rose, Lilli, and her parents give the land over in person.

"For God's sake," Lilli says to Edward. "I don't want to see Rose. Why do they have to be so close to everyone?"

"She was nice to you, wasn't she?" Edward says.

"To a point."

"You made up with your brother."

"I don't blame Father or Benji so much. If I was a man I'd probably have been the same way."

"Now I have to meet her," Edward says.

"You're funny," Lilli says. "I'm not mad at her. It's just taken me so long to sort it out."

"Oh, me too," Edward says. "And we were just Methodist."

They drive there on a Saturday afternoon. Driscoll's been built up since she saw it last, then beaten down like everywhere else. When they get to Sunland the gate is open and there's a new parking area, with a few Army cars and trucks in it. William's asleep but wakes up to walk up the hill with them.

The buildings, in weeds and disrepair, look futuristic and dated all at once, like the ruins of a world exposition. "Do you see what I mean," Lilli says, "how crazy these are?"

"I don't know," Edward says. "If they were in Venice Beach you'd have people waving money at you."

They hear voices and turn to see Rose, Mother and Father walking up. William jumps into Father's arms and lets Mother stroke his hair.

When Rose sees Lilli she stops walking, smiles and says, "*Oh.*" She's still beautiful, in a dark blue dress with a little black in it.

She opens her arms, and after a second Lilli goes to them. I wonder if we could be friends, she thinks. If I was showing a house and they lived on the block, I'd probably use them as a sales point. "They're the most *interesting* people," I'd say. "She's a painter, a force of nature really, and he's a thinker, *very* unusual—"

Rose lets go of her and stands back for a look. "This is William," Lilli says.

"Hello, William," Rose says. William smiles up at her, already beguiled, but Rose is looking at Lilli again. "Your *hair*," she says, and turns to Edward. "The ladies used to wait in line to braid it. I'm Rose."

"I guessed. I'm Edward."

"A great pleasure."

Richard comes up the hill with two men in Army uniforms, introduces himself to Edward and shakes hands. He's wearing the same gray trousers and white shirt as always, and a bolo tie with a turquoise slide.

"I'm Captain Danzig," one of the army men says. "This is Lieutenant Frank." He shakes his head. "Whatever is the story of these buildings?"

"Rose designed them," Father says.

"Oh," Danzig says. "Very nice."

They walk around the land for an hour, with Father pointing out the old irrigation lines and the army men telling them about the Conservation Corps. "It's perfect," Richard says. "When the money's gone, there's nature. And the government leads the way. The *army* leads."

"Well," Captain Danzig says.

"May I send you some people?" Richard says. "I have students who should be doing nothing but this."

"There's a procedure," Lieutenant Frank says.

Richard turns toward Lilli and her family. "We'll hold Tilda and Patrice's shares till we get their address," he says. "They'll get Josef's share too."

"Is he missing?" Father says.

"No, but we can always hope."

Rose takes Lilli's hand. "You'll write?"

Lilli looks at her. I wouldn't really talk about them that way to a prospect, she thinks. It's just something I'm afraid I'd do. She looks down the path and sees her young self, with bare feet and flower chains. She was so filled with shit, as the Americans say, but no, she knew something, too. You can't send her away altogether.

"Yes," she says.

The others walk down to their cars but Lilli stands still. "Are we sleeping here?" William says.

"No," Lilli says. "Just staying another minute."

The cars drive away as a green truck comes in, full of pine saplings. The land always looked good at this hour, orange light on the mountains and a few dark-bottomed clouds on the inland side. William's restless but Lilli tells him to wait and listen to the breeze, that it's a special one here, that if you listen to it long enough there's music.

About The Author

Charlie Haas's writing has appeared in *The New Yorker, The Threepenny Review, Esquire, New West,* and many other magazines. His screen writing credits include *Over the Edge, Tex, Gremlins 2,* and *Matinee.* His novel *The Enthusiast* (HarperPerennial) was a *San Francisco Chronicle* Notable Book of the Year.

Afterword

It has never been possible, has it, truly, just to come out and announce the current fantasy, not even in days gone by, when it seemed so simple.
Tom Wolfe, *The Electric Kool-Aid Acid Test*

What possessed me? For once I know the answer.

Several years ago, I ran across some photographs that looked as if they were taken in 1965: young people with clothes out of folklore and hair down to here, hanging out in California canyons, dancing, playing guitars, and holding fresh fruit up in the sunshine. But the captions dated the pictures fifty years earlier than I expected.

I did some reading and learned that, around the turn of the twentieth century, there was an informal movement in Germany that combined elements of Expressionist art, anarchism, free love, nature- and sun-worship, and antipathy to the city and technology. The adherents of this movement were often called *naturmenschen*, and one of their main gathering places was Monte Verità in Ascona, Switzerland. The central figures there included Otto Gross, a brilliant and eccentric early psychoanalyst who worked with Freud and Jung but broke with them over what he saw as their patriarchal bias. Gusto Gräser, an itinerant advocate of sincerity and simplicity, spent time there as well.

The historian Martin Burgess Green left us several excellent books about this group, including *Mountain of Truth: The Counterculture Begins, Ascona, 1900–1920;* and the biographies *Otto Gross* and *The von Richtofen Sisters: The Triumphant and the Tragic Modes of Love.*

A number of artists, writers, dancers and theater people were influenced or intrigued by the *naturmenschen.* Hermann Hesse, Franz Kafka, Franz Werfel, Frank Wedekind and D.H. Lawrence are a few of those who incorporated their ideas (or veiled portraits of Otto Gross) in their work.

Starting in the late 1800s, some Germans who took up the ideas of Ascona came to California, settling in Los Angeles, the canyons east of town, Ojai, San Diego, and San Francisco. Gordon Kennedy's book *Children of the Sun: A Pictorial Anthology From Germany to California 1883–1949* is a useful guide to that migration and its influence. William Pester, who came to California from Germany in the 1910s, attracted American-born followers such as Gypsy Boots, a health-food advocate and L.A. fixture in the '50s and '60s, and eden ahbez, whose song "Nature Boy" was inspired by Pester and became a hit for Nat King Cole.

No characters in *The Current Fantasy* are meant to represent real people specifically. Richard Weiss owes as much to Ken Kesey as to Otto Gross, and Jorgen is not a portrait of Gusto Gräser, though there are elements there. The Lanz family, Rose, and most of the other characters are wholly fictional.

The Expressionist art and poetry in the book come closer to real-life examples. Manfred's apocalyptic poem that Benji translates is a pastiche of Jakob van Hoddis's "World End," which, like Manfred's poem, became a hit-record-like success when it was published in 1911. Rose's paintings that she shows Benji recall those of George Grosz and Ludwig Meidner. Jules's collages are based on Kurt Schwitters'.

The rise of the Nazis was a test that many German artists failed. Rudolf Laban and Mary Wigman, the most famous dancers at Ascona, choreographed works for the regime. On the other hand, Kurt Schwitters, like Jules, saw his work featured in the Nazis' 1937 "Degenerate Art" exhibit and left the country. (Grosz and Meidner were also included in that exhibit.)

The Sunlanders' songs and Sunday concerts forecast bohemian outcroppings that came long after them. More broadly, their impulse to go someplace cheaper and quieter with friendly company has recurred through the years, triumphing over experience and giving at least temporary relief from our hectic world.

Oakland, California
2024

Acknowledgments

Thanks to Rebecca Coffey, Raul Ramos y Sanchez, and the rest of my extended family at Beck and Branch Publishers for their wise notes and support, and for their work on putting this book out into the world.

And to Alan Rifkin, who featured the book (then called *Sunland*) on his excellent fiction podcast The Last We Fake.
https://thelastwefake.buzzsprout.com

Thanks to Tim Rogers at the University of Redlands for an illuminating interview about San Bernardino County agriculture, and to Jess Lin for a violinist's insights into the Brahms concerto.

For helpful notes on the manuscript in its many stages: Bob Roe, B.K. Moran, Wendy Lesser, Louis B. Jones, John Thorndike, Greil Marcus, Don Wallace, Darcy Vebber, Jane Vandenburgh, Lisa Brenneis, Alan Rifkin, Tim Hunter, Dean Chamberlain, Tracy Johnston, Richard Rizzo, Loretta Ayeroff, Jon Carroll and Steve Radlauer.